RUN MAN RUN

CHESTER HIMES

Run Man Run

Carroll & Graf Publishers, Inc.
New York

Originally published by G. P. Putnam's Sons, Inc., New York

First Carroll & Graf edition 1995

Carroll & Graf Publishers, Inc.
260 Fifth Avenue
New York, NY 10001

Library of Congress Cataloging-in-Publication Data

Himes, Chester B., 1909–
    Run man run / Chester Himes. — 1st Carroll & Graf ed.
        p.   cm.
    ISBN 0-7867-0209-5
    I. Title.
  PS3515.I713R86   1995
  813'.54—dc20   95-10408
                                                  CIP

Manufactured in the United States of America

10 9 8 7 6 5 4 3 2 1

RUN MAN RUN

1

Here it was the twenty-eighth of December and he still wasn't sober. In fact, he was drunker than ever.

An ice-cold, razor-edged wind whistled down Fifth Avenue, billowing his trench coat open and shaving his ribs. But it didn't occur to him to button his coat. He was too drunk to give a damn.

He staggered north toward 37th Street, in the teeth of the wind, cursing a blue streak. His lean hawk-shaped face had turned blood-red in the icy wind. His pale blue eyes looked buck wild. He made a terrifying picture, cursing the empty air.

When he came to 37th Street he sensed that something had changed since he'd passed before. How long before he couldn't remember. He glanced at his watch to see if the time would give him a clue. The time was 4:38 A.M. No wonder the street was deserted, he thought. Every one with any sense was home in bed, snuggled up to some fine hot woman.

He realized the lights had been turned off in the Schmidt and Schindler luncheonette on the corner where the porters had been working when he had passed before, whenever that was. He distinctly remembered the ceiling lights being on for the porters to work. And now they were off.

He was instantly suspicious. He tried the plate-glass doors set diagonally in the corner. But they were locked. He pressed his face against the plate-glass window at front. Light from the Lord & Taylor Christmas tree was reflected by the stainless-steel equipment and plastic counters. His searching gaze probed among the shining coffee urns, steam soup urns, grills, toasters, milk and fruit juice cisterns, refrigerated storage cabinets and along the linoleum floor on both sides of the counter. But there was no sign of life.

7

He hammered on the door and shook the knob. "Open this goddamned door!" he shouted.

No one appeared.

He lurched around the corner toward the service entrance on 37th Street.

He saw the Negro at the same time the Negro saw him. The Negro was wearing a tan cotton canvas duster overtop a blue cotton uniform, white work gloves and a dark felt hat. He held something in his hand.

He knew immediately that the Negro was a porter. But sight of a Negro made him think that his car had been stolen instead of lost. He couldn't have said why, but he was suddenly sure of it.

He stuck his right hand inside of his trench coat and staggered forward.

The Negro's reaction was just as sudden but different. Upon seeing the drunken white man staggering in his direction, he thought automatically, Here comes trouble. Every time I get ready to put out the garbage, some white mother-raper comes by here drunk and looking for trouble.

He was alone. The other porter, Jimmy, who was helping him with the garbage, was down in the basement stacking the cans onto the lift. And the third porter, Fat Sam, would be in the refrigerator in the pantry getting some chickens to fry for their breakfast. From there, even with the blower turned off, he wouldn't be able to hear a call for help. And he doubted if Jimmy could hear him down in the basement. And here was this white mother-raper already making gun motions, like an Alabama sheriff. By the time he could get any help he could be stone cold dead.

He looped the heavy wire cable attached to the metal switch box once around his wrist, fashioning a weapon to defend himself. If this mother-raper draws a gun on me, I'm gonna whip his head 'till it ropes like okra, he thought.

But another look at the white man changed his thoughts. This makes the third time a white mother-raper has drawed a gun on me down here, his second thoughts ran. I'm gonna quit this job, if I live and nothin' don't happen, and get me a job in a store where there's lots of other people working, as sure as my name is Luke Williams.

Because this white man looked dangerous. Not like those other white drunks who were just chicken-shit meddlers. This white man looked mean. He looked like he'd shoot a colored man just for the fun. A snapbrim hat hung precariously on the back of his head and his yellow hair flagged low over his forehead. Even from a distance Luke could see that this face was flushed and his eyes had an unfocused maniacal look.

The white man staggered to a stop at point-blank range and stood weaving back and forth on widespread legs. He kept his hand inside of his coat. He didn't speak. He just stared at Luke through unfocused eyes. Whiskey fumes spewed from his half-open mouth.

Luke began to sweat, despite the fact he wore only a cotton duster. Working twenty years on the night shift had taught him anything could happen to a colored man downtown at night.

"Look, man, I don't want no trouble," he said in a placating voice.

"Don't move!" the white man blurted thickly. "If you move you're dead."

"I ain't gonna move," Luke said.

"What's that you're holding in your hand?"

"It's just a switch for the elevator," Luke said nervously.

The white man drew a revolver slowly from beneath his coat and aimed it at Luke's stomach. It was a regulation .38-caliber police special.

Luke's voice went desperate. "I just came out here to bring the elevator up with the garbage. This is just the safety switch."

The white man glanced briefly at the folded iron doors on which he was standing. Luke made a slight motion, pointing to the female plug in the wall. The white man looked up in time to catch the motion.

"Don't move!" he repeated dangerously.

Luke froze, afraid to bat an eye.

"Drop it!" the white man ordered.

Gooseflesh rippled down Luke's spine. With infinite caution he detached the cable from his wrist and dropped the switch to the iron doors. The metallic clang shattered his nerves.

"I ought to gut-shoot you, you thieving son of a bitch," the white man said in a threatening voice.

Luke had seen a night porter shot by a stickup man. He had been shot three times in the stomach. He recalled how the porter had grabbed his guts with both hands and doubled over as though attacked by sudden cramps. Sweat leaked into the corner of his eyes. He felt his own knees buckle and his legs begin to tremble, as though he had already been shot.

"I ain't got no money, I swear, mister." His voice began to whine with pleading. "There ain't none in the store neither. When they close this place at nine they take—"

"Shut up, you son of a bitch," the white man cut him off. "You know what I'm talking about. You came out here an hour ago, using that switch as a blind, and watched out while your buddy stole my car."

"Stole your car!" Luke exclaimed in amazement. "Nawsuh, mister, you got me wrong."

"Where is the garbage then?"

Luke realized suddenly the man was serious. He became extremely careful with his words. "My buddy is down in the basement stacking the cans on the elevator. When he's got it loaded he'll rap for me to bring it up. I plugs in the cable and pushes the switch. That way can't nobody get hurt."

"You're lying, you were out here before."

"Nawsuh, mister, I swear 'fore God. This is the first time I've been outside all night. I ain't even seen your car."

"I know all about you night porters," the white man said nastily. "You're nothing but a bunch of finger men and lookouts for those uptown Harlem thieves."

"Look, mister, please, why don't you call the police and report your car stolen," Luke pleaded. "They'll tell you that we porters here are all honest."

The white man dug into his left pants pocket and brought out the velvet-lined leather folder containing his detective badge.

"Take a good look," he said. "I'm the police."

"Oh no," Luke moaned hopelessly. "Look, boss, maybe you parked your car on 35th or 39th Street. They both run the same way as this street. It's easy to make a mistake."

"I know where I parked my car—right across from here. And you know what happened to it," the detective charged.

"Boss, listen, maybe Fat Sam knows something about it," Luke said desperately. "Fat Sam is the mopping porter." He figured Fat Sam could handle a drunk cop better than himself. Fat Sam had a soft line of Uncle Tom jive and white folks who were distrustful of a lean Negro like himself were always convinced of Fat Sam's honesty. "He was mopping the floor on the side and he might have seen something." Anyway, once the cop got inside and Fat Sam got some hot coffee into him, maybe he'd come to his senses.

"Where's this Fat Sam?" the detective asked suspiciously.

"He's in the icebox," Luke said. "You go in through the door here and it's on the other side of the pantry. The door might be closed—the icebox door that is—but he'll be inside."

The detective gave him a hard look. He knew the Harlem expression. "By way of Fat Sam," meant by way of the undertaker, but the Negro looked too scared to pull a gag. So all he said was, "He'd better know something."

2

The pantry had white enamel walls and a red brick floor. All available space was occupied by the latest of equipment needed for a big fast turnover in short orders, but it was so expertly arranged there were ample passages from the outside and the basement and into the lunchroom.

Racks of glassware and dishes, stacked eight feet high, sat on roller coasters. Fitted tin trays, empty now to be returned, on which cooked items came fresh each morning from the factory, were stacked six feet high. Heavy metal trays filled with freshly polished silver were stacked beside the silver polishing machine. Everything was spic and span and in readiness for the rapid service which would begin at breakfast.

An atmosphere of sterilized order prevailed, such as in

a hospital. It was so typical of all New York stores and offices after the night's cleaning the detective experienced a definite feeling of doubt as he silently crossed the red brick floor to the refrigerator.

He paused momentarily beneath the red light above the closed door that indicated there was someone inside. The feeling was so strong that he was making a mistake he debated whether to turn around and leave. But he decided to scare the Negroes anyway. It'd be good for them. If they were innocent it'd help keep them that way. He pulled open the door.

The fat black man in a blue denim porter's uniform, holding an armful of frying chickens, gave such a start a chicken flew from his arms as though it were alive. His eyes popped. Then he recovered himself and said testily, "Jesus Christ, white folks, don't scare me like that."

"What'd you jump for?" the detective asked accusingly.

"Force of habit," Fat Sam confessed, grinning sheepishly. "I always jumps when somebody slips up on me while I'm handling chickens."

"You're a goddamned liar," the detective accused. "You jumped because you're guilty."

Fat Sam drew himself up and got on his dignity. "Guilty of what? Who the hell are you to come in here accusing me of something?"

"You were mopping the floor along the 37th Street side," the detective charged. "You could see everything happening on the street."

"What the hell you got to do with it?" Fat Sam asked while picking up the fallen chicken. "I could see everything happening inside too. I could see all over. Are you one of the firm's spies?"

Slowly and deliberately, the detective flashed his badge, watching Sam's face for a sign of guilt.

But Fat Sam looked unimpressed. "Oh, so you're one of them. What's that got to do with me? You think I'm stealing from the company?"

"There was a car stolen from across the street while you were working on that side," the detective said in a browbeating voice.

Fat Sam laughed derisively. "So you think I stole a car?

And hid it here in this icebox, I suppose?" He looked at the detective pityingly. "Come on in and look, Master Holmes. You won't find nothing in here but us perishables —meat, milk, juices, eggs, lettuce and tomatoes, soup stock, leftovers, and me—all perishables. No automobiles, Master Holmes. You been looking too long through your magnifying glass. That ain't no automobile you see, that's a cockroach. Haw-haw-haw."

For a moment the detective looked as though he had swallowed some castor oil. "You're so funny you'd get the stiffs laughing in the morgue," he said sourly.

"Hell, what's funnier than you looking in here for an automobile?" Fat Sam said.

"I'll tell you how you did it," the detective said in a blurred, uncertain voice. "You came back here from out front and used that telephone by the street door. Your buddy was working and he didn't notice." By now the detective had got his eyes focused on Fat Sam's face and they looked dangerous. "You telephoned up to Harlem to a car thief and told him to come down and lift it. That's right, ain't it, wise guy?"

Fat Sam was astonished into speechlessness. The cracker's even got it all figured out, he was thinking.

"What was his name?" the detective asked suddenly.

And suddenly Fat Sam realized the man was serious. He felt cold sweat break out on his skull beneath his short kinky hair.

"I don't know any car thief in Harlem or anywhere else," he said solemnly.

"You stood out there toward the front of the counter, faking with your mop, where you could watch both Fifth Avenue and 37th Street at the same time and give a signal if you saw a police car come in sight," the detective hammered as though trying to get a confession.

Covertly Fat Sam studied his face. Bright red spots burned on the high cheekbones and the lick of hair hung down like a curled horn. He couldn't make out whether the white man's eyes were blue or gray; they had a reddish tinge and glowed like live coals. The thought came to him that white folks could believe anything, no matter how foolish or impossible, where a Negro was concerned.

In a careful voice he said, "Take it easy, chief. Let me fix you a good hot cup of coffee. You drink some hot coffee and give this problem some study. Then you won't believe the first thing pops in your mind, 'cause you'll see that I couldn't 'a had anything to do with stealing a car."

"The hell you didn't," the detective accused bluntly and illogically.

He and Fat Sam were about the same height, a little over six feet, and his stare bored into Fat Sam with a diabolical malevolence.

"As God be my secret judge—" Fat Sam began eloquently but the detective cut him off.

"Don't hand me that Uncle Tom shit. I'll bet you're a preacher."

Fat Sam was touched to the quick. "What if I have been a preacher?" he challenged hotly. "You think I've been a porter all my life?"

"A chicken-stealing preacher like you is just the type to be a lookout for car thieves," the detective said brutally.

"Just because I've been a preacher don't mean I stole any chickens, or cars either," Fat Sam replied belligerently.

"What's that you got in your hands?" the detective asked pointedly.

"Chickens," Fat Sam admitted. "But I ain't stealing these chickens," he denied. "I'm just taking them. There's a difference between stealing and taking. We're allowed to take anything we want to eat. I'm taking these out to fry them on the grill. Okay?"

The detective reached beneath his coat and drew his service revolver. With slow deliberation he aimed it at Fat Sam's stomach.

"You'd better tell me who the car thief is or you'll never eat fried chicken again," he threatened.

Fat Sam felt his intestines cramp. "Listen, chief, as God be my secret judge, I'm as innocent as a baby," he said in the gentle tone one uses on a vicious dog. "You've been drinking kind of heavy and naturally you're upset because someone lifted a car on your beat. But it happens all the time. You're going about it like it's your own personal problem."

"It is personal," the detective said flatly. "It's my car."

"Oh no," Fat Sam cried. He tried to stem his laughter but couldn't. "Haw-haw-haw!" His mouth stretched open, showing all his teeth, and his fat belly rocked. "Haw-haw-haw! Here you is, a detective like Sherlock Holmes, pride of the New York City police force, and you've gone and got so full of holiday cheer you've let some punk steal your car. Haw-haw-haw! So you set out and light on the first colored man you see. Haw-haw-haw! Find the nigger and you've got the thief. Haw-haw-haw! Now, chief, that crap's gone out of style with the flapper girl. It's time to slow down, chief. You'll find yourself the last of the rednecks. Haw-haw-haw!"

Fat Sam's laughter had authority. It touched the white man on the raw. He stared at Fat Sam's big yellow teeth and broke out with frustrated rage. Instead of scaring these Negroes they were laughing at him.

"And when I find who stole my car he's going out of style too," he threatened. "Out of style and out of sight and out of life. And if you had anything to do with it you're going to wish you'd never been born."

Fat Sam wanted to tell the detective that he wasn't frightened by his threats, but it didn't look like the time to tell this white man anything. The detective had gone off again as though in a maniacal trance and his shoulders rose as though he were heaving.

"Control yourself, chief," Fat Sam urged desperately. "You're gonna find your car. It ain't like you lost your life."

Slowly the detective returned the service revolver to its holster. Fat Sam breathed with relief; but the relief was short-lived for the detective drew another revolver from his trench coat pocket. Fat Sam felt his throat tighten; it got too small to swallow. Hot sweat broke out beneath the cold sweat on his body, giving him the itch. But he was afraid to scratch. He watched the detective through white-walled eyes.

"Take a good look," the detective said, waving the pistol in front of him.

It was a .32-caliber revolver with a silencer attached. To Fat Sam it looked as big as a frontier Colt.

"This pistol was taken off a dead gangster," the detective went on in his strange unemotional voice. "The serial number has been filed off. The ballistic record is in the dead file. This pistol doesn't exist. I can kill you and the son of a bitch who helped you steal my car and go down the street and buy a drink. No one can ever prove who did it because the weapon will never be found. The weapon doesn't exist. Got it, Sambo?"

A chicken slipped from Fat Sam's trembling hands. His shiny black skin began turning ashy.

"What're you thinking about, chief?" he asked in a terrified whisper.

"You wait, you'll see. First I'm going to knock the bastard down." He went into a frenzy of rage and began jumping about, demonstrating just how he would do it. "Then I'm going to kick out his teeth. I'm going to break his jaw and kick out his eyes" . . . Fat Sam watched the antics of the raving madman in fascinated terror . . . "then I'm going to kick him in the nuts until he's spayed like a dog." He was talking through gritted teeth as he jumped about. A tiny froth of saliva had collected in each corner of his mouth.

Fat Sam had never seen a white man go insane like this. He had never realized that the thought of Negroes could send a white man out his head. He wouldn't have believed it. He had thought it was all put on. And now this sight of violence unleashed because of race terrified him as though he had come face to face with the devil, whom he'd never believed in either.

"Then I'm going to shoot the son of a bitch in his belly until his guts run out," the detective raged on in a deadly voice.

Three sounds followed one behind another like a cold motor coughing.

Fat Sam's eyes widened slowly in ultimate surprise. "You shot me," he said in an incredulous voice.

The chickens slipped one by one from his nerveless fingers.

The detective looked down in shock at the gun in his hand. A thin wisp of smoke curled from the muzzle and the smell of cordite grew strong in the small cold room.

"Jesus Christ!" he exclaimed in a horrified whisper.

Fat Sam grabbed the handle of the tray to support himself. He could feel the sticky mess pouring from his guts. "God in heaven!" he whispered.

He fell forward, pulling the tray from the rack along with him. Thick, cold, three-day-old turkey gravy poured over his kinky head as he landed, curled up like a fetus, between a five-gallon can of whipping cream and three wooden crates of iceberg lettuce.

"Have mercy, Jesus," he moaned in a voice that could scarcely be heard. "Call an ambulance, chief, you done shot me for nothing."

"Too late now," the detective said in a voice gone stone cold sober.

"Ain't too late," Fat Sam begged in a fading whisper. "Give me a chance."

"It was an accident," the detective said. "But no one will believe it."

"I'll believe it," Fat Sam said as though it were his last chance, but his voice didn't have any sound.

The detective raised the pistol again, took aim at Fat Sam's gravy-coated head, and pulled the trigger.

As the gun coughed, Fat Sam's body gave a slight convulsion and relaxed.

The detective bent over and vomited on the floor.

3

The sound of a laboring truck caught the detective's attention. He experienced a shock of fear. A shudder ran through his body and he suddenly felt the cold. He listened intently in an effort to identify the vehicle. When convinced it was not a police van he felt a vague relief, even though he knew it was only his sense of guilt that conjured up such an idea.

It sounded like the motor of a hydraulic lift. He thought of the lift from the basement, but that would be electric and could scarcely be heard from his position.

For an instant he experienced a sense of someone standing behind him, watching his movements, and was overcome with a wild, raw panic. He wheeled toward the open door, pointing the cocked revolver, prepared to shoot on sight.

Then he realized the sound came from a garbage truck outside. There was no other sound like it. Breath flowed from his stiff lips in a soft hissing sound.

He pocketed the revolver and stepped quickly into the pantry. There was no one in sight. He quickly crossed to the street door and locked it on the inside. He didn't stagger but his legs felt wobbly. Sweat trickled into his eyes and his head felt burning hot. Drops of sweat formed in his armpits despite the chill of his body and trickled down his ribs.

Seeing the mop sink on that side of the refrigerator, adjoining the silver polishing machine, he took off his hat, ran cold water over his face and head and dried himself on a cleaning cloth spread over the side of the sink.

He felt less panicky.

Of all the rotten luck, he thought.

He returned to the refrigerator to close the door. He saw his own filth on the wooden floor and smelled the putrid whiskey stink and lingering cordite fumes. His stomach ballooned into his mouth and he had to bite down a return of nausea.

His gaze lit on the gravy-crowned body of Fat Sam. His thoughts became fuddled again. He felt only pity for the man he'd killed.

Poor bastard, he thought. Dead in the gravy he loved so well.

He turned out the refrigerator light from the switch panel beside the door and pulled the door shut softly, like closing the lid of a coffin.

Fat Sam went by way of Fat Sam, he thought.

He was breathing heavily, but he couldn't control it. He felt spent. A couple of glasses of milk was what he needed, he thought. He didn't know there was milk in the containers in the lunchroom. He thought it was kept in the refrigerator and he could not open the door again.

Suddenly his stomach fell from hunger. He had to eat something or he would be sick again, he knew. He went over and foraged in the food trays stacked along the

outside wall. He found half of a cold broiled chicken and
ate a leg ravenously. It made him think of Fat Sam with
his arms filled with the chickens he had intended to fry.
He thought of him as he had seen him living, a big black
man with popping eyes who might have been jolly. A man
you could have sat down with and eaten fried chicken and
talked about life. A man who would have known a lot
about women. Maybe a funny man. Women always love a
funny man, he thought.

The realization of what he'd done exploded inside of
him like a dynamite blast. He hadn't intended to shoot
him but the hole in his head made it murder. He might
have gotten away with it if he hadn't shot him in the
head. That and the illegal gun. He knew he couldn't talk
his way out of that.

He was scared more than he'd ever been in all his life.
Scared of the law he'd sworn to uphold. Scared of the
court where he would be tried. Scared of the pure and
simple process of justice. . . . But he was no longer
panic-stricken. It was the Negro who was dead. He was
still alive. There was no reason why he couldn't keep alive
if he didn't go haywire. There were no witnesses. And the
gun didn't exist.

His nerves drew taut and his mind got sharp and
cunning. The only thing to do now is to clean it up, he
thought. Wipe the slate clean.

He went out into the lunchroom where he could watch
the loading of the garbage truck. On that side were two
great plate-glass windows with long cushioned seats beneath, where clients could wait for a place at the counter.
But he didn't sit down. He stood far back in the shadow
where he could see without being seen.

The truck was backed at an angle to the curb and two
porters were rolling the big galvanized garbage cans from
the lift. He recognized Luke but the other porter he hadn't
seen.

The motor of the truck was running noisily. It gave
him a sense of reassurance. Noise wouldn't disturb the
people in this neighborhood, no matter what happened.

The driver stood on the pavement behind the truck and
took the cans as they were passed to him and dumped

them over the loading lip of the intake compartment. When it was filled he worked a lever that brought down the big steel plate that pressed out the water and packed the garbage into the body of the truck. He worked the truck alone.

He was a big, rangy, slow-motioned man of about sixty. He had a lined brown face and kinky gray hair that showed beneath a greasy cap. The easy manner in which he handled the heavy cans gave the impression of great strength.

Automatically the detective counted the cans; there were fifteen in all. They have a hell of a lot of garbage for a place of this size, he thought.

When they had finished with the cans, wooden crates containing empty tin cans were loaded in the same manner. But when it came to the cardboard cartons, the driver flattened them out and stored them into a separate compartment.

He must sell them to some paper mill, the detective thought. Every mother's son has got himself some kind of racket to go along with the job.

He could see that the three men were talking and laughing as they worked, although he couldn't hear what they said. He looked at the second porter for some time. He was a younger man than the others and he looked different, more educated; he seemed to listen mostly although he laughed with the two others.

When they'd finished loading, Luke gave the driver a carton of leftover sandwiches. It was the policy of the firm to throw day-old sandwiches into the garbage, but the porters saved them for the garbage man. The detective had no way of knowing this, and he thought they were selling them. He smiled indulgently.

The driver climbed into his seat, waved a hand and drove off. The detective was relieved; for a moment he had feared the porters might invite him inside for coffee. It was better they hadn't.

He had forgotten Fat Sam other than as a motive and a vague sense of guilt. Most of the scare had left him. He now felt sad. There was something sad about killing a man in the midst of so much food, he thought. Maybe *ironical* was the word.

He watched the two porters load the empty cans back onto the lift. Their breath made geysers of steam in the cold air. He saw the young porter get into the lift with the empties and Luke pick up the switch box and push the DOWN button. As the elevator descended, the young porter's head disappeared with the garbage cans and the heavy steel doors closed slowly above him on the steel arch at the top of the lift. A moment after the doors had become level with the sidewalk, Luke removed his finger from the button and pulled the cable from the plug.

The detective hastened back into the pantry and unlocked the street door. Then he stood to one side so he could block Luke's retreat once he had entered. His right hand was stuck into his trench coat pocket.

Luke caught a glimpse of the detective standing beside the door when he opened it. He stopped stock-still, suddenly apprehensive. The detective's strange expression gave him a shock. He had been telling Jimmy and the garbage man about the drunken detective losing his car. But he hadn't expected to find him standing beside the doorway in such a threatening attitude; he'd expected to see him talking amicably to Fat Sam and having coffee and sandwiches.

"Er-er, didn't Fat Sam know anything about your car, chief?" he asked hesitantly, standing before the open door dangling the cable foolishly. He was afraid to enter.

"No, he didn't, George," the detective said strangely. "I guess I made a mistake."

Luke did a double take. The detective's face was blue-white with huge red splotches, but he looked sober enough. Sam's got him sobered up, Luke thought with relief. Grinning widely, he stepped inside and hung the cable on a hook beside the door.

"It happens," he said philosophically. "My name's Luke though, not George."

The detective drew his hand from his pocket and wiped it hard down over his face. "Yeah, Luke, it happens," he agreed. "Even the best of detectives can make mistakes sometimes."

Luke threw him another quick searching look. He was startled by the difference in the man's expression. He don't

look like the same man, he thought. He looks sad. Fat Sam
must have been quoting the Bible to him.

"I'm supposed to be one of the best of detectives and how
I made that mistake I don't know," the detective said slowly.
He sounded tired.

"Ain't nothing to worry about," Luke said encouragingly.
"I knew just as soon as you got a little coffee inside of you to
combat all that good bourbon you've been drinking you'd
remember where you parked your car."

"It's not my car I'm thinking about, it's my coming in
here meddling with you colored men," the detective confessed. "You were only doing your work and attending to
your business."

Luke's eyes popped. Sam must have really given him the
works, to get a city dick talking like a convert at a revival
meeting, he thought.

"Aw, forget it, chief," he said. "We're used to that kind
of thing. White folks get to drinking and the first thing they
think about is colored folks stealing something from them.
You're from the South, ain't you?"

"That's the hell of it," the detective said. "I was born and
raised in Jackson Heights on Long Island and I've never
lived outside of New York City in my life. I never had
nothing against colored people. I don't know what made
me think like that—suspecting you porters. I guess I must
have just picked it up."

Luke batted his eyes. He didn't know just what to say.
The man made him uncomfortable. He didn't want to agree
that being a Negro made him automatically suspect. But he
didn't want to rile the man, now that he had quieted down.

"Well, anyway, you're gentleman enough to admit you
were wrong, which the average white man in your case
wouldn't do," he said diplomatically. But he felt uneasy,
nevertheless; he wasn't accustomed to white people admit-
ting they were wrong. "Takes a man to admit up that he's
wrong," he added compulsively, annoyed with himself because he felt he had to support this mother-raper. He wanted
to pass but the detective stood in such a way he couldn't get
by. "Excuse me," he said finally. "I want to see how Fat
Sam is coming along."

But the detective wouldn't let him pass.

"Listen, Luke, I want to tell you what happened to me tonight," he said. "I owe it to you boys." He sighed. "I was working my beat, Times Square, when I saw a rumble taking place in the Broadway Automat. A drunk claimed he'd been rolled by some floozie he'd picked up. I caught her as she was turning into 47th Street and he made a positive identification. I should have taken her in but she was a good-looking whore and it was a good chance to score. So I propositioned her if she'd kick back his money and take me on, I'd let her go. I'd already been guzzling the booze or I wouldn't have done it."

He ran his hand down over his face again and Luke stared at him in growing horror. Something about this white detective's confession filled him with a sense of dread. Perhaps it was the way this white man referred to a white woman, talking to a Negro. It wasn't natural for a white man to talk like that to a colored man. But he gave a sickly grin and tried not to show what he was feeling.

Unnoticing, the detective talked on. "We stopped in several bars on the way. Then I got the bright idea to park my car on a side street where it wouldn't be spotted by the lieutenant. I went up to her pad with her and killed another half bottle. Then I had a blackout. The next thing I knew I was outside on Fifth Avenue and I couldn't find my car. I didn't even know what street I'd parked it on. I started to go back and ask her where I'd parked it, but I couldn't find the house. I couldn't remember what the entrance looked like, or even what street it was on. It could have been on any of these side streets from 39th to 35th. I couldn't even remember the whore's name. Then when I looked into my wallet I found she'd clipped me for my last hundred and twenty bucks."

Luke whistled in amazement, as was expected. But he wished to hell the detective hadn't told him all that. He didn't know why, but it put a burden on him, a sort of unspoken responsibility, for what he didn't know. But he kept the note of agreement in his voice and said, "No wonder you felt mad with the world. I wondered what was troubling you. I suspect I'd felt the same way. But I swear, ain't none of us had anything to do with stealing your car—if it was stolen."

"I know that now," the detective admitted.

Luke tried again to get past him, but he seemed extremely reluctant to let him go.

"Wait, Luke, listen—you know one thing? I've blown my career, destroyed it, just like that," he said, snapping his fingers.

"Aw, it ain't that bad," Luke said reassuringly. He felt he just had to reassure this white man who had suspected him, as if it were an obligation; he couldn't let him down. "You just feel bad because you made a mistake and you've got a hangover. Everything looks worse than it really is when you got a hangover."

"No, it's finished," the detective stated. "I'll keep on being a cop but I won't feel the same. I won't have any pride left. Listen, Luke, I'm thirty-two years old and a bachelor. A woman chaser."

"Hell, chief, all young policemen are women chasers," Luke said. "Ain't nothing strange in that. It's natural, being around so many women and getting it for free."

"Matt Walker's the name," the detective said suddenly, sticking out his hand. "Just call me Matt, Luke."

Luke stared at the outstretched hand. Suddenly he realized he was supposed to shake it. He shook it as though with enthusiasm. "Matt," he said experimently.

"That's right—Matt," Walker said. "But I don't mean what you're thinking, Luke. About the women, I mean. It's not women that's my downfall. Listen, I graduated from New York City College. I was a guard on the basketball team and had a chance to turn pro. But I had to go into service for two years and when I came out I was rusty. So I joined the force. I spent five years in uniform, the last three driving a patrol car. Meanwhile I was going to the school for detectives and I graduated with honors. I'm a marksman with a pistol. I've been in plainclothes for two years, on the Times Square beat, the really big time."

Suddenly Luke lost all sympathy. These people, he thought. These mother-raping people with all their chances.

"What you need is some of Fat Sam's fried chicken," he said with forced enthusiasm.

"Fried chicken," Walker echoed strangely.

He acts like a sick man, Luke thought. Like a man on his deathbed. But he kept on with his bogus jubilance and said,

"Yes sir, fried chicken is good for what ails you. It ought to be ready now, and I'm sure there'll be plenty for you too. That is if you don't mind eating downstairs with us. We wouldn't have any objection to your eating at the counter, but the firm don't allow us to feed anybody in here. And sometimes the super sits in his car across the street and watches us through the windows to see what we're doing."

That information gave Walker a turn but he only said, "I'm not really hungry, Luke."

"It won't be any trouble," Luke insisted. He finally got up the nerve to push past the detective. "I'll tell Fat Sam," he said as he crossed the pantry toward the lunchroom door.

"I wouldn't bother him about it," Walker said curiously.

But Luke didn't pay him any attention. He opened the door into the lunchroom and called, "Fat Sam! Hey, Fat Sam!"

But the lunchroom was dark and deserted. Fat Sam was not at the grill frying chicken. Luke turned and looked at Walker in surprise. "He must have finished and taken it downstairs," he said lamely, but he was thinking it was strange the detective hadn't mentioned it.

"He's in the icebox," Walker said.

Luke glanced at the switch panel beside the refrigerator door. The lights were off.

"What's he doing in there with the lights off?" he asked suspiciously. "He can't see."

The detective's face contorted in a crooked grimace that was meant for a smile. "Take a look," he said.

A sixth sense warned Luke against opening the door. He glanced covertly at the detective, thinking there was something very strange about the way he looked and talked. It gave him the creeps.

"Go ahead," the detective said.

Luke was suddenly overcome by a terrifying premonition. But there was nothing he could do about it. He was like a bird charmed by a snake. As though controlled by the white man's thoughts, he switched on the lights.

"Open the door," the detective said.

Luke wanted to refuse. He wanted to tell the white man to open the door himself. But one glance into the detective's opaque, hypnotic eyes and his will flowed away like water.

With infinite dread he slowly opened the door and looked inside with dazed eyes. He saw Fat Sam's body crouched down between the crates of lettuce and a can of whipping cream.

"He's hurt!" he exclaimed, moving quickly to Fat Sam's assistance. He slipped in the vomit which he hadn't noticed and looked down. "He was sick," he said. "He must have fallen." Kneeling down beside Fat Sam, he took hold of an arm and asked, "Sam, are you hurt? Are you—" He saw the blood oozing from the gravy that covered the back of Fat Sam's head and his voice stuck in his throat. Finally his voice came out in a whisper, "He's been shot."

He knew the detective was standing behind him, watching him. He knew the detective had shot Fat Sam in the back of his head, that was why he'd been acting so strangely. He wanted to turn around and accuse the detective. But he couldn't move his head.

"You don't believe I could have killed him accidentally, do you?" the detective asked from behind his back.

Luke looked again at the bullet wound in the back of Sam's head and knew it couldn't have been an accident.

But he said, "Sure," in a weak, sick voice, then tried again to make it sound more convincing, "Sure." That didn't sound convincing enough and he added in a louder tone, "You were just pointing your pistol at him like you was doing with me outside and it just went off accidentally. Yes sir, anybody could see that right away."

"No, you don't believe it," the detective said regretfully. "Nobody would believe it. A colored man shot with a hot gun by a drunken white cop. Who's going to believe it was an accident? Nobody."

"Me, boss, I believes you," Luke said in a voice that sounded like a prayer.

"Nobody," Walker contradicted. "Neither the judge nor the jury nor the public nor anybody. You can see it for yourself—me standing in court saying it was an accident—and nobody on God's green earth believing it. Maybe if this was Mississippi they'd let me off even if they didn't believe it. But this is New York State, and here they'll fry me."

"No they won't, boss," Luke said in that prayerlike voice. "I'll tell 'em it was an accident. I'll tell 'em I saw it. I'll say

Fat Sam jumped on you and all you did was shoot him in self-defense. I'll say he had a carving knife . . ." His voice petered out in futility. "But I swear before God that I believe you," he whispered.

"It's a dirty shame," the detective said.

Slowly, as though it were manipulated by invisible strings, Luke's head pivoted until he faced the doorway. But tears filled his eyes, blurring the vision of the detective standing there with the pistol pointing at him. He couldn't tell there was a silencer attached to the pistol because all he could see of it was the round hole of the muzzle.

He knew it would come out of that little round hole and there wasn't anything he could do to stop it.

It caught him directly between the eyes.

4

"I looked over Jordan and what did I see
Comin' for to carry me home . . ."

Jimmy sang the verse of the sweet old spiritual in a low bass voice as he washed the garbage cans and stacked them against the wall beside the lift. He took the cans from the lift and held them upside down over the washing machine which spurted jets of boiling water up inside of them, washing and sterilizing at the same time.

The garbage cans, empty milk cans, cleaning utensils and empty tins were kept in a basement room beneath the 37th Street sidewalk.

As a rule Luke helped with this chore while Fat Sam cooked their breakfast. But he knew that Luke was detained by the drunken cop. He didn't have any complaint. Luke was the boss, more or less, by reason of being the longest employed.

Anyway, it wasn't a hard job for Jimmy. The cans were heavy, but he handled them with the tireless ease of a man who didn't know his strength.

His size was deceptive also. He was six feet tall and weighed one hundred and eighty-two pounds, but he looked much smaller. He had the big-boned, broad-shouldered, flat-chested, muscular build of the southern farmhand accustomed to heavy plowing, coupled with the sleepy-type, sepia-colored good looks that Joe Louis had at the age of twenty-four. His eyes were alert and intelligent.

As always when he worked with his hands, his mind was crowded with numerous thoughts. He was thinking with amusement about all the modern labor-saving equipment used by the Schmidt and Schindler chain such as the garbage can washers; in some stores they even had refrigerated garbage rooms to keep the garbage from stinking—like all those deodorants for the working class. And yet they couldn't get along without the old "muscle grease" supplied by the likes of him.

And he was also thinking about the company's custom of calling the *automats* "stores," and the central kitchen the "factory." There were more than a hundred stores throughout New York City but only three or four *luncheonettes* with counters served by waitresses like this one.

While in the back of his mind was a knot of irritation imposed by the drunken cop. He was hungry but reluctant to go upstairs and see what was holding up Luke and Fat Sam. He didn't want to get embroiled in some stupid argument with a drunken white man. Fat Sam and Luke could take it, but he was too quick-tempered. Lots of folks attributed his temper to the fact that he was young. But it wasn't that, he thought. He just wanted to be treated like a man, was all.

He smiled as he recalled some of the run-ins he'd had with various superintendents. Once he'd accused the company of withholding too much tax from overtime pay, and in the course of the argument he and two of the top superintendents had begun shouting at each other. Finally one of the supers had said, "You argue too much, I can't do anything for you." And he had shouted in reply, "Then what the goddamn hell are you talking to me for?"

The only reason they hadn't fired him was because they couldn't get anyone else who could do his work. It was his job to polish all the stainless steel in the lunchroom, and one had to have a sort of genius for that kind of work to keep it from streaking. It tickled him to think how much abuse American bosses took from the workers in order to get the work done. Evolution of the profit system, he thought. Years ago the boss kicked the worker in the pants and threatened to fire him if he didn't toe the line. Nowadays with the unions and federal relations boards and specialized work, the boss kept his goddamn mouth shut.

He was laughing to himself as he finished sweeping the floor, took up the trash and put away the broom.

Cop or no cop, he was going up and get his breakfast, he resolved. As hungry as he was he could eat two fried chickens by himself. And because he'd been made to wait so long he'd also have a bowl of cereal with heavy cream, a pint of fresh orange juice, six pieces of buttered toast, some whipped potatoes and fresh green peas, a lettuce and tomato salad, a package of vanilla ice cream with a can of sliced peaches in heavy syrup for dessert. He'd make the company pay for the white son of a bitch meddling them. Anyway, the superintendents were always pointing out they were privileged to eat all they wanted. And he always did. Although it'd be cheaper for the company to double his pay than feed him, he was thinking as he left the garbage room and went into the other part of the basement.

He stopped in the storeroom where the seasonings, condiments, canned goods and soaps were kept and hung up his tan canvas duster which he shared with the day porters, then went next door into the men's locker room and put his cap and gloves in his locker.

Next door was the waitresses' locker room, but they didn't come to work until seven o'clock and he'd only seen a few of them at night when they were going off work as he was coming on.

The main hall held the steam-heated soup kettles, a bread-slicing machine, a meat slicer and a big old-fashioned refrigerator packed with a variety of sliced cold meats.

He stuffed three slices of boiled ham into his mouth and went to the end of the hall, past the engineer's control room, and ascended the stairs.

There was a landing halfway up where the staircase made a right-angle turn. He was looking up as he made the turn. That was when he saw the detective for the first time.

Walker had just closed the refrigerator door after having

shot Luke between the eyes and had started down to the basement to finish off the third porter. But the murder of Luke had shaken him and he had halted for a moment to get himself together and reload. He was standing at the head of the stairs with his left side toward Jimmy and the revolver with the silencer attached dangling loosely from his right hand.

"Went out like a light," he was muttering to himself when he sensed Jimmy's presence and jerked about to face him.

The first thought that struck Jimmy's mind when he saw Walker's flushed, taut, skeletonized face was, My God, the Phantom of the Opera! Seen from below, Walker looked inhuman and nine feet tall. His trench coat hung open like a ragged opera cape and blond hair flagged down over red-tinted eyes that looked completely insane.

The son of a bitch is crazy drunk, Jimmy thought. Fat Sam hasn't been able to handle him.

His guts tightened into a knot but he didn't stop. He wasn't going to let the son of a bitch think he was afraid of him.

Walker's teeth bared like a vicious dog's and the pistol came up level in his right hand. He didn't speak.

Jimmy ducked from reflex an instant before Walker fired. The bullet burned a crease along Jimmy's left ribs. Rage exploded in his brain as though all his emotions and sensations had gone off in one big blast. For one brief instant his mind became oversensitized, as at the moment of death. He saw Walker's face as though it were magnified a hundred times; saw the tracery of capillaries in the maniacal eyes; saw the sweat drops oozing from skin pores as big as whiskey glasses; saw the blond hair stubble growing from hard white jaws like wheat stalks on a snow-covered field; saw distinctly the outlines of the amalgam fillings in Walker's uneven yellow-stained teeth. The picture was burned on his memory with the acid fire of fury.

It lasted but an instant and his body had never stopped its violent reflex motion.

Charge the mother-raper! one part of his insensate mind urged. *Get his gun and beat his brains to a pulp!*

But the other part of his mind screamed the warning, RUN, MAN, RUN!

His panic-stricken muscles were straining in incredible frenzy like a wild stallion in a fit of stone-blind terror. Before Walker could shoot again he had turned on the staircase, as though performing a grotesque ballet step, and started down.

The second shot creased the back of his neck, burned through his fury like a red-hot iron and lighted a fuze of panic in his enraged brain. He was in an awkward position, his left leg crossed over his right onto the stair below, left arm raised in reflexive defense, right arm groping forward, and his body doubled over in a downward slant like an acrobat beginning a twisting somersault. But his corded muscles moved as fast as a striking snake. His taut legs propelled him in a burst of power across the landing and his right side slammed into the wall, bruising him from shoulder to hip.

"Mother-raper!" he cursed, gasping through gritted teeth, and came off the wall turning, pushing with his right leg and right arm and right hip simultaneously, spinning like a whirling dervish, moving so fast he was around the corner and out of range before Walker's third shot dug a hole in the white plaster wall where a fraction of an instant before, the shadow of his head had been.

He went down the bottom stairs in a somersault. It was started and he couldn't stop it, like doing an exercise in gym, so he took it, catching the third stair with the palms of both hands and making the circle, landing on his feet in a squatting position on the concrete floor of the front hall in the basement, his body still in the act of propulsion.

Walker charged down the top stairs, teetering as though half blind. He missed the last stair before the landing, slammed sidewise into the wall and fell to his hands and knees.

"Wait a minute, you black son of a bitch!" he screamed unthinkingly.

Jimmy heard him and came up from his squatting position with a mighty push.

The minds of both were sealed, each in its compelling urge, one to kill and one to live, so that neither registered the humor in Walker calling to Jimmy to wait and get himself killed.

Jimmy turned the corner into the garbage room, thinking vaguely of escaping through the lift, leaning to one side for greater leverage. His rubber-soled shoes slipped on a greasy spot on the concrete floor and he crashed against the door-jamb in passing, bruising his left leg from ankle to hip. He was out of range before Walker could take aim again but he could hear him coming down the stairs in a shower of footsteps. Then he realized he couldn't get the heavy lift doors raised without the lift being in motion.

He had turned out the lights in there on leaving and the idea came to him to trap Walker in the dark. But light shone in from the hall through the open door and he'd have to double back and shut it. He skidded to a stop and whirled about but he had gone too far. Walker was already entering the doorway, running in a careful manner, holding the pistol forward ready to snap a shot.

Jimmy had lost precious seconds by his last maneuver and was caught like a sitting duck. There was no place to hide, no time to dodge, nothing to grab and throw. The galvanized two-gallon bucket containing the rags, sponge and soap which he used to clean the stainless steel sat on the floor to his right. From sheer instinctive reflex, the blind unthinking compulsion of a man to defend his life, he kicked the bucket as though he were kicking a field goal, drove it in a straight incline toward the leveled gun.

Walker fired an instant later and the bullet went through the galvanized bucket in midair and caught Jimmy in the chest, above the heart. The bucket had lessened its force so that it didn't go deep enough to kill, but it hit him like a fist, catching him off balance from the kick, and knocked him down.

The bucket struck Walker in the chest and knocked him down at the same time.

Jimmy turned over quickly on all fours and started running again before getting to his feet. He could feel himself bleeding in the chest. He didn't know how badly he was hit but he knew he had to hurry. He knew the bucket had knocked Walker down and he knew he had to escape before Walker had time to get to his feet again and take aim.

Out of the corner of one eye he noticed the stack of fresh-ly cleaned garbage cans. Spinning about in the same running motion he snatched two cans from on top and threw them back toward Walker just as he was clambering to his feet. The cans knocked his feet out from underneath him again and Jimmy kept turning in a circle and threw two more. The cans rocketing on the concrete floor made noise enough to wake the dead and Jimmy couldn't tell whether Walker was shooting again or not. It was terrifying in the half-dark room with the ear-shattering noise where he wouldn't have been able to hear the silenced shots.

But Walker hadn't had a chance to shoot again. He was fighting off the cans with his arms and elbows, his face livid with rage. "Get away, goddammit!" he shouted, mouthing unintelligible curses, as though the cans had life and could hear him.

Then he saw Jimmy heading for another door at the end of the room but it was a risky shot in the almost-dark with the garbage cans still banging about. There was only one more shell left in the pistol with the silencer and he couldn't take the time to reload. He stumbled after the fleeing Negro, knocking his shins against the frisky cans, cursing in a blue streak.

Jimmy hit the frail wooden door with his right shoulder without waiting to see whether it was unlocked or not. The rusted lock broke and the door banged open against the wall of a narrow, pitch-dark corridor beneath the adjoining building on 37th Street.

He knew the corridor led into other corridors that connected all the basements of the buildings in that block. Somewhere there must be a janitor awake, or a building superintendent, ran his desperate thoughts. Above in the high stone buildings there must be some living people, charwomen or night porters, watchmen with guns, some human eyes to witness his plight and tell his story. But there seemed only himself and the mad cop with the silenced gun in a world of black dark horror.

He ran through the dark in a blind line, trusting to luck, sobbing unknowingly, feeling the blood flowing down his chest and collecting in a warm sticky band above his belt.

Walker ran after him, ricocheting from one wall to the other, cursing steadily and relentlessly. He had to fight down the compelling urge to draw his service revolver and spray the dark with .38-caliber slugs.

Jimmy ran full tilt into a wall, striking his forehead against the calcimined bricks. He slumped to the floor, stunned but not unconscious.

Walker heard him groan and stopped, peering into the dark for the gleam of eyes. He'd always heard that a Negro's eyes shone in the dark like an animal's and he held the pistol ready to fire at anything that gleamed. He could hear the Negro moving but he couldn't see a thing.

Jimmy climbed slowly to his feet. His body felt as though he'd been beaten with a length of heavy iron chain and only the will to live started him running again.

Suddenly he was running off into space. The corridor had made a right turn and dropped three steps. He landed on his knees and the palms of his hands, scraping off the skin on the rough concrete floor. The sharp sudden pain acted as a stimulant; it got him up and going again.

But the pause in the dark had rendered Walker's thoughts rational again. He groped into his inside coat pocket and found a fountain pen torch. The tiny beam showed him the turn in the corridor and the descending steps. But by then Jimmy had turned another corner and was out of sight.

For a moment Walker considered reloading the pistol. He had felt the loose empties in his pocket when searching for the torch and thought some of them to be good. But he couldn't risk taking the time, what with this maze of corridors and the Negro was already out of sight.

Jimmy was running now with his left hand dragging the wall and his right held straight out in front. He turned two corners in the dark and came out suddenly in a short lighted corridor. He'd lost sound of the pursuing footsteps. He felt a surge of hope. He saw a closed door to his right, opened it and looked in. There was an unmade bed, cigarette-scarred dressing table, dirty clothes hanging over chairs, an empty pint whiskey bottle and glass atop an oilcloth-covered table. But no occupant. He supposed it was the room of a janitor's helper.

As he closed the door to leave he heard footsteps somewhere behind him.

"Help!" he yelled, plunging ahead. "Help! Somebody help!"

No one answered.

He turned at the far end of the corridor as Walker turned into the corridor at the near end, and went into another corridor. A glance to the left showed a long expanse of brightly lit whitewashed walls and a clean concrete floor. He turned right. Before him was a heavy oak door. He could hear the footsteps plainly. There wasn't time to turn back to the corner and grapple with the mad killer. If the door wouldn't open he was dead.

"Hey!" he heard a voice call. "Hey!"

He didn't look around. All it meant to him was death. Son of a bitch calling, Hey, let me kill you. His stomach was tied in a knot as small as a pea and nausea came up into his mouth like week-old vomit.

He reached out his hand for the doorknob.

This is where Mrs. Johnson's young black son loses sight on the world, he thought with a flash of that bitter self-corroding irony which white people call "Negro humor."

He turned the knob. It turned. He pushed the door and it opened.

"Hey! Hey there!" he heard the voice again.

Hey yourself, he thought.

Light shone briefly through the open door on what looked like rows of electric sewing machines, spinning in a slow circular movement about a large square room. He felt so lightheaded it seemed as though he were floating after them. When he turned to close the door he fell heavily against it. His stomach drew in from the effort to keep erect and he felt the warm sticky blood flow down his leg. He thought he was urinating on himself.

In a daze he groped for the lock without realizing what he was doing. It was a Yale lock and he pushed down the button releasing the catch and the bolt snapped shut.

He didn't hear the voice calling, "Hey! Who the hell's that hollering?" Nor the sound of shuffling footsteps down the corridor, approaching the door. He didn't hear the man try the knob and shake the door and shout in an irritated, half-drunken voice, "Open that door and come out of there, whoever in the hell you are. I gotta finish cleaning up."

He was unconscious before he hit the floor.

5

At 5:22 A.M. the window washer appeared. He was a slight, dark-haired, incommunicative man of Italian extraction. He wore a leather jacket over a blue pullover, army surplus pants, shearling-lined boots and a logger's cap with ear-muffs. He carried his pail, brush, sponge, chamois and squeegees with him, but had handles stored in each of the places he served.

He entered through the back door on 37th Street. Without announcing his presence, he stood on the edge of the sink and took down two sections of a telescoped handle from the top of the refrigerator, then filled his pail with clear cold water from the tap.

He started on the inside of the front windows, first removing the vase of gladiolas from the polished oak window ledge. Attaching the soft wash brush to the long handle, he washed the top of the windows, using a minimum of water so that not a drop splashed on the stainless-steel window frames. Then with half the handle he did the middle section, and washed the bottom by hand. In the same manner he used the squeegee in quick downward strokes, catching the dirty water at the bottom of the pane in the sponge with a quick flip of the wrist. Lastly he wiped the window frames with a damp chamois and moved on. He never looked back.

He worked rapidly and automatically with sure deft motions. He was proud of his skill and the work absorbed him completely.

The absence of the porters was unusual, but he scarcely noticed it. He supposed they were downstairs eating and hadn't heard him arrive. Anyway, it didn't concern him. He had his work to do and didn't like to waste time jawing with colored philosophers. He'd come to the conclusion that all colored porters were philosophers, deep down. There must be something about the job. With him it was different. He was his own boss. He had his own clients: shoe stores, notion stores, haberdasheries, clothing stores, restaurants, all within walking distance. He cleaned their windows once every working day, inside and out, for which he got a stated weekly fee. From there he would go to the cafeteria at the corner of 36th Street, S & S's nearest competitor, then down across 34th Street. He had to be through with them all by 7:30 at the latest. He didn't have time to discuss the problems of life. Maybe colored porters had more problems of life than himself. Colored porters were great on discussing the problems of life. But the only problem he had was when it got so cold the water froze to the panes before he could squeegee it down. And talking about it couldn't help it. He worked from three to four hours a day and grossed $177 weekly. That wasn't bad, he was thinking.

He was finished on the inside in eight minutes. He stopped at the sink to change water and went outside. His breath made vapor geysers, but he didn't feel the cold.

He had finished the front on Fifth Avenue and had begun on the 37th Street side when the milk truck drove up.

"How goes it, Tony?" the milkman greeted.

"Fine," Tony said without breaking motion.

"Everything's always fine with you," the milkman complained.

"Why not?" Tony said.

The milkman grunted and looked about for the empties. He went to the back door and stuck his head inside and called, "Hey, Luke . . . Sam . . . hey fellows."

No one answered.

Turning back to Tony, he asked, "Where the hell's everybody?"

Tony shrugged. "I haven't seen them."

The milkman knew where the empties were kept. It wouldn't have taken him but a minute to go down to the basement and get them, but it was the age of specialized work and it wasn't his job to bring them up to the sidewalk.

Expressing his disapproval by the preciseness of his actions, he unloaded three five-gallon cans of milk with pump lids, a five-gallon can of coffee cream and a three-gallon can of heavy cream with plain lids, and lined them against the wall beside the elevator doors.

He got into his truck, started the motor and drove off. Tony didn't look around. When he'd finished he emptied his pail, squeezed out the sponge and chamois, put the handle back on top of the refrigerator and went down the street to the next job.

He was still washing the inside of the windows of the 36th Street cafeteria when the S & S factory truck came down 37th Street from Madison Avenue, and he didn't see it. The driver circled out from the curb and backed in at an angle before the pantry door. He climbed down, slapping his gloved hands together, opened the pantry door and bellowed, "All right, lovers, the chow's here!"

No one answered. He didn't expect an answer. Unloading the truck was a sore point for the night porters. They were due off at six o'clock, but he seldom arrived before ten minutes to six and most times later. Usually they were dressed and ready to go home, waiting impatiently with the canvas jumpers worn over their street clothes. He turned back to the truck, expecting them to appear behind him, silent and evil.

The factory trucks were especially constructed with red lacquered, airtight wooden bodies, bearing the S & S crest in gold letters, not unlike the mail trucks of England.

The driver pulled down the tailgate which became an elevator platform, and opened the double doors. The platform was lowered hydraulically to the street by a lever inside the body. He stepped onto it and ascended to the floor of the truck, went inside and began checking the items for delivery to that store.

Still no porters appeared.

Hell, he didn't give a damn, he told himself. It wasn't his job to unload it.

He had four trays of chicken pies, three of baked macaroni, three of baked beans and frankfurters—those were the casserole items. There were two stacks of trays of cakes and pastries, and another smaller stack containing five trays of raw hamburger patties and two trays of raw minute steaks. In addition there were two large enclosed aluminum racks of pies, two five-gallon cans of soup stock, two five-gallon cans of concentrated hot chocolate, a box of S & S bacon, a carton of S & S coffee, a package of cold boiled ham, two packages of sandwich cheese, two aluminum baskets of sandwich bread, a basket of rolls and a crate of oranges. They'd have to get whatever else they needed from the second and third deliveries during the day.

He pushed the racks onto the platform at the back and peered around for the porters.

Where the hell are those boys? he thought with growing irritation. That goddamn little fat manager ought to be here too by now.

He looked at his watch. Six minutes to six.

He heard someone whistling in high shrill notes the rhythm of "Rock Around the Clock" and poked his head around the side of the truck. Well, here come two rocks, anyway, he thought.

Two colored day porters approached from the direction of the 35th Street exit of the Independent Subway's 6th Avenue line, which came down from Harlem.

One was clad in a light tan camel's hair overcoat, dark brown narrow brim hat with a gay feather in the band, and a silk foulard muffler with a deep maroon background. His young brown face looked excessively good-humored for so early an hour on a cold miserable morning. His companion, who was older, wore a blue Chesterfield overcoat with a velvet collar, black bowler hat, and a white silk knitted muffler. Both wore black shoes, dark trousers, and suede gloves to match their coats.

They'd been recounting their amorous adventures of the night past and unaccountably the young man had broken into rhythm. The older man looked at him indulgently.

"Come on, sports, let's move this chow," the truck driver greeted them as they came up.

"Where're the night porters?" the older porter asked. "That's their job."

"They've already left," the driver said. "And this stuff can't wait."

The older porter pulled back his sleeve and looked at his watch. "It ain't six o'clock yet, just three minutes to six," he protested.

The young man consulted his watch. "I got five minutes to six."

"You better take that thing back to the Jew," the older porter said.

The driver looked at his watch again. He had four and one half minutes to six but he said, "I got six o'clock on the head, and I just set mine by Western Union."

At that moment a short fat apparition rounded the corner, head bowed into the wind. He was bundled up so completely in a dark tweed ulster, dark plaid muffler and a black slouch hat that only the steamy lenses of his horn-rimmed glasses were visible.

"Here's the boss now," the young porter said. "What time you got, boss?"

"What's going on here, boss man?" the driver asked in a condescending voice. "I can't get my wagon unloaded." The truck drivers felt more important than the store managers and liked to rub it in.

The manager eased off his glasses and took in the situation. "Where's Luke?" he demanded.

"They gone home," the older porter said.

"Goddamn son of a bitch to hell!" the manager said.

"Who you mean by that?" the porter challenged.

The manager stormed into the pantry without replying. He was late and weary and irritated almost beyond control. His wife had kept him up until two o'clock playing bridge and he'd lost nine dollars, then she'd had cramps all the rest of the night from something she'd eaten and he'd been nursing her with hot-water bottles until he'd had to leave for work.

"Bastard son of a bitch to all hell and gone," he raved to himself as he hung his hat and coat on the hooks inside the door. Then controlling himself, he opened the door wide and hooked it open and said in a placating voice, as though choking on every word, "Come on, boys, let's get the food inside."

The porters didn't argue. Without stopping to change their clothes, they took down the grappling hooks and dragged the stacks of empty trays outside for loading when the truck was unloaded, then carried out the four-wheeled dollies to bring in the stacks of food from the factory.

"That man just don't come to work evil some mornings,"

the young porter said of the manager. "He comes to work evil every morning. His wife must beat him."

"It's this job what's beating him," the older porter said.

The manager had come out to give a hand just in time to hear what they said about him. He turned around and went back inside.

Grinning broadly, the driver lowered the loaded platform to the level of the sidewalk.

"That ain't no way to talk about your boss," he said.

"Hell, he ain't going to be here long," the older porter said.

They talked as they worked. Grappling the handles of the bottom tray, they drew the stacks onto the dollies with accustomed skill and wheeled them inside and down the inclined floor, stacking them about the staircase railing and along the wall. They looked like comic opera figures performing these chores in their good clothes.

"Where you guys get the money to buy such fine clothes?" the driver asked enviously.

"You're like all the white laborers I've ever seen," the older porter replied. "You think we've got to be doing something illegal just 'cause we dress decently."

The driver shut up. He didn't like to be called a laborer and that wasn't what he meant.

Another two expensively dressed porters appeared and pitched in without being ordered. They stacked the cans of soup stock and spinach alongside the refrigerator and the pie racks in the corner. All of them made derisive comments about the food selected for the day's menu.

It was the manager's duty to make up the menus, but he chose to ignore their remarks as he checked the deliveries. He went about with his list, poking into trays, uncovering cans, examining the pastries and pies. The only comment he had to offer was, "Goddamn son of a bitch!"

The white sandwich man and one of the white short-order cooks arrived together, looking like tramps in their worn overcoats and weather-beaten hats, although they earned much more than the porters. After them, a few minutes late, the other help straggled in.

One of the porters went down to the basement and

brought up the lift for the bread baskets. The sandwiches were made in the basement hall.

"Man, you ought to see how they left them garbage cans," he said in a loud voice to everyone. "They look like they been fighting down there."

The manager's ears perked up. "Goddamn sons of bitches!" he said.

Several of the men turned to look at him. He bent over suddenly to peer into the creamed spinach. He didn't have any authority over the night porters. But by God this was carrying it too far, he thought angrily. He'd have something to say to the superintendent about them leaving before time.

Everyone began conjecturing on the reasons the night crew left before time.

"They must have all got drunk," someone offered.

"Maybe they got hold of some chicks."

"It ain't like Luke to walk off the job."

The others agreed.

"Now that Fat Sam might do anything if he's juiced. And that other boy, Jimmy what's-his-name, I don't know nothing about him. But you're right about Luke."

Jimmy was relatively new on the job and he held himself aloof. He never saw any of the others after working hours except by accident and they felt that he was a little uppish. He wasn't well liked. They didn't say anything bad about him; they just didn't say anything good.

Finally most of them went down into the locker room and left the porters to finish the unloading. They were still talking about it as they changed into their starched white working uniforms.

"Fatty's gonna complain to the superintendent, that much's for sure," the colored dishwasher remarked.

They all agreed with him.

Every man had a locker of his own with his own personal lock. Judging from the size of the locks, they didn't trust one another.

The sandwich man finished changing his clothes and began slicing the cheese. The dishwasher went upstairs and turned on the steam in the dishwashing machine. It was too soon to start the dishwashing machine and the manager rushed in from the pantry and shouted, "Goddamn son of a bitch!"

The dishwasher gave him such a black evil look he scurried back into the pantry.

By then the porters had finished unloading. At the instant the manager came in from the lunchroom where the dishwashing machine was located, the young porter in the tan coat playfully scooted a heavy iron dolly across the floor. The steel edge caught the manager on the anklebone and he turned pea green with pain.

Grabbing his injured foot in both his hands he hopped about on the other foot and raved in earnest, "Goddamn son of a bitch to hell of a bitch bitching son of a bitching hell of a bitching black bastards!"

All of the colored porters gave him threatening looks but he continued to rave, "Goddamn son of a bitching bitch of a bitching—"

The cereal cook had just gone into the refrigerator to check the orange juice on hand before juicing the crate of oranges. He came dashing out as though he'd suddenly gone crazy and ran into the manager, knocking him down.

"They's daid!" he screamed in a high keening voice. "They's daid! Both of 'em! They's in there daid!"

"Who in the goddamn son of a bitching hell is dead?" the manager screamed back, rolling about on the floor with his bruised ankle clutched in both hands.

The help came running from all directions to see the cause of the commotion.

"W-w-w-who's daid?" the gray-faced cook screamed, his eyes bucking whitely with indignation. "Both of 'em's daid, thass who! Luke and Fat Sam both! They's shot in the haid and both of 'em is in there stone cold daid!"

For a moment the tableau held, mouths open, eyes stretched, breath held.

Then the manager got up, standing on one leg like a crane, and said quietly, "I'll call the police," and hopped one-legged toward the telephone.

6

When detective Walker saw the janitor's helper approaching down the brightly lit corridor his first thought was, Now I've got to kill another one.

He had almost caught up with the Negro porter. He had had him cornered, ready for the kill. And now this drunken imbecile had to appear on the scene.

Walker watched the janitor's helper as he staggered down the corridor to the dead-end room where the porter had taken refuge. He stood back of the corner, peering with one eye. He had him limned in the bright light against the painted tin sign at the far end of the corridor which read APEX DRESSES with an arrow pointing toward the closed oak door.

The janitor's helper would have seen him if he had been more observant but his attention was focused on the door. No doubt a broken-down alcoholic, a wino, Walker thought; he looked like one in his filthy rags and run-over shoes. A dirty bastard, repulsive to the sight. Dirtying up the world. Walker's thoughts began justifying the murder before he had committed it. Probably the bastard had just been on the job for a couple of weeks. In another week he'd be fired for drunkenness. He'd be back on Skid Row in the Bowery, drinking the squeezings of canned heat and bay rum, sitting with other crum-bums around a bonfire in the gutter made from packing crates, a burden to the city. The kind of bastard who'd be better off dead; the world would be a better place without him. Furthermore, it would confuse the issue. The murders of the three Negro porters could be attributed to a single motive, but that of a white janitor's helper in another building at the same time would look like the actions of a maniac. No one would ever think of him as a maniac.

He backed out of sight to reload. But he found only empties in his pocket. . . . He stood there tallying up the bullets he had used. He always loaded a six-shooter with five bullets, resting the hammer on the empty chamber; and he always carried five spares. So he'd shot the first one—that was Fat Sam—three times, and then a fourth . . . The sound of the janitor's helper hammering on the locked door distracted him. The goddamned imbecile, he thought. Why the hell doesn't he unlock it? He must have a key, or at least he could get hold of one. . . . Fat Sam four times . . . He felt like shouting, Cut out that racket so I can think! . . . And then the second one just once. Right between the eyes. That one had been Luke. And this last one, he'd shot at him three times on the stairway and once in the basement. He must have hit him one of those times at least; he never had missed a target with four shots in a row. But he needed two bullets to finish it—one for this white scum and one for the Negro. And he didn't have but one.

The janitor's helper gave up and turned back down the corridor to call the superintendent. Walker listened to his shuffling footsteps. Suddenly he had the bright idea of beating him to death. That would solve the problem. He reversed the pistol in his hand and gripped it by the silencer. One quick rap on his temple and he'd never know what hit him.

He was stopped by another voice calling from somewhere above, "What the hell's going on down there, Joe?" The voice held an unmistakable note of authority.

"There's a burglar in the Apex sewing room," the helper replied.

Walker glanced around the corner at the ceiling of the corridor and noticed a ventilator duct. Beside it, painted on the whitewashed ceiling, a green arrow pierced the green-lettered word, EXIT.

"You keep out of the way, I'll call the police," the authoritative voice directed.

Walker realized his position if he was caught. For an instant he contemplated turning back toward the S & S luncheonette. Then he had the brightest idea of all.

The janitor's helper had turned the far corner and Walker heard the sound of an elevator door opening and closing. He ran silently in the direction indicated by the green exit arrow until he came to another. He passed the elevator door. The green arrows took him through a maze of corridors until he came to a sheet-iron double door with a bar handle opening onto a utility passageway to the sidewalk.

When he came out to the street it took him a few seconds to get orientated, then he realized he was on 36th Street between Fifth and Madison avenues. The building he had just left fronted on Fifth Avenue.

He found the entrance adjoining the 36th Street cafeteria. It was a commercial building occupied by small manufacturers of toys and dresses. There was a directory flanking the doorway listing the nameplates of the occupants. He found Apex Dresses at the bottom of the list. He looked inside through the heavy glass-paneled door.

A charwoman was scrubbing the tiled floor of the entrance hall. He tried the door and found it locked. The murder pistol hung heavy in his right coat pocket. There was no point in trying to get rid of it. He had to use it again, for one thing. And it was safer in his pocket. No one was going to search him.

He knocked on the locked door. The charwoman looked up stupidly. He beckoned. She shook her head and went on working. He knocked again and showed her his badge through the glass panel. She clambered slowly to her feet and came grudgingly to the door.

"What do you want?" she asked in a harsh voice.

"Open up, I'm the police," he shouted.

"I ain't got the key."

"Go get the superintendent. He phoned for the police."

She looked at him suspiciously and turned and shambled toward an inside door. She was met by the janitor's helper, who came forward swinging a heavy ring of keys.

The detective saw them exchanging words. The janitor's helper looked at him suspiciously. Then he came forward slowly and shouted through the locked door, "Let's see your badge."

Walker held his badge close to the glass panel. The janitor's helper bent close to peer at it. He looked up at Walker and finally unlocked the door.

"You're taking mighty goddamn long to get this door open," Walker said. "The superintendent phoned for the police."

"You got here mighty fast," the janitor's helper said suspiciously. "He just got through phoning."

"I know when he phoned," Walker said.

The janitor's helper blinked, trying to assimilate that information. He was saved from replying by the superintendent, who came hurrying forward.

"There's a burglar down there in one of the sewing rooms," the superintendent said. Then on second thought he asked, "You're from the police, aren't you?"

Again Walker flashed his badge.

"All right, this way," the superintendent said, ushering him toward the elevator.

The janitor's helper followed. The charwoman made as if to follow too, but the superintendent said, "You get back to work."

They rode down two floors and in a moment Walker found himself back in the dead-end corridor which led to the sewing room.

"Give me the key," he ordered.

The superintendent took a ring of keys and selected one. "Be careful, officer, he might be armed," he cautioned.

"You two stand back," Walker said, drawing his .38-caliber service revolver.

He went forward with drawn pistol, unlocked the door and gave it a quick hard push. It opened a few inches and was stopped by a soft, heavy obstruction. Walker put his shoulder to it and pushed it inward.

The unconscious body of the porter lay in a pool of blood. Walker leaned over quickly, picked up the limp left arm and fingered the pulse. He found the pulsebeat strong and regular.

The goddamned son of a bitch is still alive, he thought angrily, and drew back his foot to kick him over the heart. Three or four swift kicks ought to finish him and no one would ever know how he got the bruises. But he was arrested by a voice at his elbow.

"My God, he's wounded!" the superintendent exclaimed.

"Either that or dead," Walker said. "He looks more like he's dead. You'd better phone the precinct station and tell them to send an ambulance."

"Joe, you phone," the superintendent ordered his helper, who was peering from the doorway. "I'll stay here and help the officer."

"You'd better phone yourself," Walker said. "And take Joe with you, he'll just be in the way."

"No, let him do it," the superintendent said. "Go ahead, Joe."

He looked down at the unconscious figure and exclaimed spontaneously, "Hell, this is a porter from the Schmidt and Schindler lunch counter." His voice held a note of surprise. "He isn't a burglar. But what the hell's he doing in here shot?" He bent down and felt the pulse. "God's fire, he's alive still."

Walker could scarcely contain his displeasure. "All right, let's get him straightened out and see if we can stop the bleeding," he grated, clutching the body beneath the armpits and dragging it brutally across the floor.

"Jesus Christ!" the superintendent protested. "What the hell you trying to do? You don't want to kill him, do you?"

Without replying, Walker ripped open the porter's uniform. Buttons scattered over the floor. The chest wound had opened again and was bleeding profusely.

Walker looked about the room, as though searching for something. It held only rows of big operator's sewing machines and the special-made operator's chairs.

"Just don't stand there!" he shouted at the superintendent. "Go get some water."

The superintendent was a small elderly man with a thin ascetic face and graying hair. His cheeks glowed with two red spots of anger.

"Let him alone," he said in a tight, furious voice. "Wait for the ambulance. What kind of officer are you? You ought to know enough not to minister to a wounded man. For the way you're treating this man, I could have you suspended."

Walker stood up and looked at the superintendent with an opaque gaze. He would have killed the superintendent instantly if he could have thought of a suitable explanation. Even if he'd had enough bullets for the illegal gun he would have killed him on the spot, finished the porter and shot the helper dead the moment he returned. But then he'd have to kill the charwoman too. That could have been managed also, he thought, but he didn't have the bullets.

"It was best to lay him on his back," he said in a slow, careful voice. "And I advise you to let me take the responsibility. You're going to have a lot of explaining to do yourself."

"Nonsense," the superintendent snapped.

Walker knelt quickly beside the body and began searching the pockets. The porters wore only thin underwear beneath their cotton uniforms, for it was hot all night in the steam-heated restaurant, and they carried everything they needed in their uniform pockets.

In addition to handkerchiefs, scraps of soap and a dustcloth, a ring of keys and two small screws, Walker found only a green Schmidt and Schindler worker's identification card, giving Jimmy's name, employment number and home address. He transferred the card to his own pocket and would have taken the keys too, but the superintendent looked on disapprovingly. He heard people approaching outside and started to straighten up.

At that moment Jimmy opened his eyes. At sight of Walker bending over him, his eyes stretched wide in terror. Instinctively he reached up and clutched Walker's arm, trying to pull him down so he could grapple with him. He was frightened for his life.

Walker jerked his arm loose from Jimmy's hand, the quick, savage motion lifting Jimmy from the floor and throwing him aside so that when he fell back, his head struck the floor. Saliva drooled from the corners of his mouth.

"Take it easy, boy," the superintendent said, drawing near. "He's a detective, he's going to protect you now."

The new face swam into Jimmy's dazed vision. Relief overcame him at the thought of being saved, but the killer was still there, standing over him. "He shot me," he said in a blurred voice. He felt himself growing faint, sinking down into unconsciousness again. He had to tell the other man before he went out. "He's the one who shot me."

The superintendent didn't understand. He bent over to hear better. "Who did you say shot you, boy?" he asked.

Jimmy's face tightened from the effort to speak. "You got to believe me, mister, he's the one who shot me. He did it himself." He saw the disbelief on the man's face and became desperate. "Search him," he whispered. "He's got the pistol in his pocket." Then he lost consciousness.

The superintendent looked at Walker with slowly growing horror.

"He's delirious," Walker said sadly.

Two patrol car cops came into the room ahead of the janitor's helper. Walker exhibited his badge.

"This man's been shot," he said authoritatively, taking command of the situation. "The ambulance has been called for. One of you stay here and the other come with me. Maybe the gunman's still on the premises."

"I'll stay," one of the cops volunteered. "Where shall I tell them to take him?"

"Better send him to the Bellevue psychiatric ward," Walker said. The cop's eyebrows went up. "He's off his nut," Walker explained. "He was conscious for a minute and talking crazy."

"He accused the detective of shooting him," the superintendent said.

The cops were startled. Their suddenly blank indrawn stares went from the superintendent to the detective and back again.

"That's what I mean," Walker said.

"He claimed that the detective still has the pistol," the superintendent persisted stubbornly.

With a quick, angry gesture Walker drew his service revolver and thrust it into the first cop's hand. "Does that look like I've shot anyone?"

The cop turned the revolver over and handed it back. "This gun hasn't been fired," he said flatly.

The superintendent walked away.

"All right, come on," Walker said harshly to the cop who'd accompany him. "Let's get to work and try to find out who did shoot him."

They went through the corridors with drawn revolvers. Walker led the way. He went in a roundabout way back to the passage where he had chased the porter. When they came to the unlighted corridors, he let the cop lead the way with his torch. They found the basement room where the Schmidt and Schindler garbage cans were stored. It was full of cops.

"What's happened here?" Walker asked.

"Double murder," a harness cop replied. "Two colored porters shot dead in the icebox."

The cop accompanying Walker whistled softly. "Jesus Christ!" he exclaimed.

"Who's in charge?" Walker asked.

"A sergeant from homicide now," the harness cop replied. "But the big brass ain't far behind."

Walker ran upstairs and found the homicide sergeant trying to establish order in the back room.

"You're looking for the third porter," he greeted.

The sergeant eyed him with hostility. He resented precinct detectives butting in. "Who are you?" he asked.

Walker showed his badge. All right, he wasn't a precinct detective, the sergeant noted. So what? It didn't diminish his hostility.

"You know Brock?" Walker said.

"Yeah," the sergeant admitted grudgingly.

"He's my brother-in-law," Walker said.

Brock was another sergeant in homicide. His name worked like a card of admission. "That so?" the sergeant said. "Yeah, we're looking for him," he admitted.

"I found him shot in the basement of the building next door."

"Yeah? Dead?"

"Not yet. I had him sent to Bellevue."

"Good. Now we got an eyewitness. None of these jokers here want to admit knowing anything about it."

"He won't be much help," Walker said. "He's off his nut."

The sergeant grunted. "It's a nutty business."

Walker moved over to the refrigerator and opened the door and fiddled with the light switches, planting his fingerprints all around.

"Watch out! You're leaving fingerprints," the sergeant warned.

Walker snatched his hand away. "I doubt if they'll figure with all these people around."

"They sure won't if you keep smearing yours over all the others," the sergeant said. Then suddenly he grinned. "Don't mind me, just be careful is all."

Walker grinned back.

7

Now it was 11 A.M.

Big hard flakes of snow drifted from a low gray sky, diminishing visibility. Traffic crawled through the streets. But nothing had changed. In all the places in the city where crimes had not been committed during the night, business went on as usual.

The circus performed by the police and the citizens was just about over. This circus had been staged a thousand, a hundred thousand, a million or more times. It scarcely changed and almost never solved anything.

For a fleeting moment Sergeant Brock of homicide wondered why they did it, what did they expect to accomplish, whom did they expect to fool? The moment of doubt passed as quickly as it had come and he was a cop again, sworn to uphold the law and assigned to solve murders.

He was assisting Lieutenant Baker of the homicide department in the preliminary investigation which was the circus of his mind. There was a big silent young man from the D.A.'s office following them around and sitting in on all questioning, as was his duty. His sharp brown eyes behind rimless spectacles saw all but he said nothing. Lieutenant Baker conducted all the interrogations.

He had begun with the day porters, questioning them separately, seeking a shape to the life the murdered men had lived. It came out that Luke was a home man with a wife and eleven children and if he had a vice no one knew of it. Fat Sam was just the opposite. He lived with a big sloppy woman who looked quite like him and they spent most of their time boozing around bars and having street scenes. None admitted knowing anything about Jimmy.

The white men had been questioned next. As with one mind they all declared they didn't know the night porters; they were not acquainted with them. Of course they had seen them around but none admitted to ever seeing one of them off duty.

The waitresses were all white and they didn't know anything about anything. Although when they were asking about Jimmy, Sergeant Brock distinctly heard a little blond waitress say, "He's cute." But when he looked at her she was looking away and didn't appear interested.

While the lieutenant was questioning the help who were being detained in the locker rooms, the assistant medical examiner arrived and pronounced the bodies of Luke Williams and Samuel Jenkins "dead on arrival." He filled in two tags with vital statistics provided by their S&S identity cards and when the bodies had been photographed, tagged the toes and had them taken to the morgue.

By then the place was swarming with Schmidt and Schindler superintendents, upsetting the fingerprint crew and setting Lieutenant Baker's teeth on edge with their gratuitous advice. Finally Lieutenant Baker herded them into the women's locker room—they refused to go into the men's—with the suggestion, "All right, gentlemen, stay here and have an orgy while we go on with our work." There was a lot of giggling but the lieutenant firmly shut the door and posted a guard.

The police had a few minutes of respite. The fingerprint men dusted all the surfaces in the pantry, lunchroom and basement and all the doorknobs and collected so many different prints they were appalled. That necessitated fingerprinting all of the help, including the superintendents.

While they were thus engaged, the three interrogators— Lieutenant Baker, Sergeant Brock and the assistant D.A.— went into the building next door where the wounded porter had been found, and questioned the superintendent and his helper, Joe. The superintendent told them of being informed of a burglar by his helper, of calling the precinct station, of the detective arriving almost immediately following his phone call. He had taken the detective to the basement and they had found the wounded porter in the Apex Company sewing room, lying unconscious in a pool of blood. He had recognized the S&S uniform the porter had been wearing and had realized instantly he wasn't a burglar. He had had to caution the detective about handling the wounded man so roughly. And then when the porter had regained consciousness, he had accused the detective of being the man who had shot him.

Both detectives assumed that blank, indrawn look of all police when a brother officer is accused of a crime. But they did not attempt to discredit the superintendent's statement. The assistant D.A. asked the superintendent to come to his office later and make a formal statement, which the superintendent agreed to do.

The helper's story was practically the same. He had heard someone in the basement and on investigation he had found the door to the sewing room locked. No, it was not usually locked at that time, he still had to mop the floor. No, there was nothing to steal but the sewing machines and they were bolted to the tables. He would have taken a look, he declared, but the super had told him to leave it alone while he called the police. He had been suspicious when the detective had arrived so quickly after the super had telephoned; the super had just finished telephoning and he was just coming from his office when the detective was hammering on the front door. No, he hadn't noticed anything strange about the detective other than he looked drunk, but that wasn't strange for a detective at that hour in the morning. No, he hadn't heard the porter accuse the detective of shooting him, he hadn't been there, he had gone to let in the patrol car cops and when he got back the porter looked unconscious just like he had left him.

The assistant D.A. told him he'd better come down to his office and make a formal statement too.

"At the same time with the super?" he asked.

"No," both the assistant D.A. and the superintendent said in unison.

On second thought the assistant D.A. asked him if he had heard any shooting previous to his discovery of someone in the sewing room. No, he hadn't heard anything that sounded like shooting. The superintendent remembered that the porter had said the detective still carried the gun, but on examination by the patrol car police the detective's pistol proved to have been unfired. No, they hadn't heard the porter make the accusation, he had told them about it.

"Well, that finishes us here," Lieutenant Baker said.

When they returned to the Schmidt and Schindler luncheonette they found a number of newspaper reporters collected in the cold on 37th Street, clamoring for the details of the murders. But first the lieutenant telephoned homicide and asked to have detective Walker report to him. Then he telephoned Bellevue and ordered Jimmy transferred to the hospital ward of the county jail downtown. He was informed that the porter was still unconscious from loss of blood and that it would be dangerous to transfer him at the time.

"All right, as soon as you can," he said.

Finally he went outside and issued a statement to the press to the effect that the murders were a mystery and they had discovered no leads but expected to uncover some when the investigation moved into Harlem.

He ordered the help released from the locker rooms and rounded up his crew and left.

Authority was returned to the Schmidt and Schindler superintendents. Orders were issued thick and fast. The women were set to cleaning the already spotless counters. The men were put to cleaning the inside of the refrigerator where the porters had been murdered. All the shelves and containers were emptied and every scrap of food was put into the garbage. Then all the empty shelves and containers which were not discarded were scoured and rinsed with boiling water. The wooden, ribbed floor where the bodies had lain were scraped, scrubbed and washed down with scalding water spurting from a plastic hose. It was as though they were trying to wash away the deed itself.

Two police cars were stationed in the street to keep away the curious and the morbid and the regular sightseers who collect at the scene of a murder.

By eleven A.M. the murder had been expertized, efficiently, unemotionally, thoroughly, and as far as was discernible the slight pinprick on the skin of the city had closed and congealed.

Lieutenant Baker had intended for the assistant D.A. to assist him in the interrogation of detective Walker and for Sergeant Brock to go up to Harlem and question the victims' relatives. But it didn't work out that way.

Brock asked to sit in on the questioning of Walker, who was his wife's brother. The lieutenant hadn't known this; he was embarrassed. But he consented for Brock to sit in.

"Just keep quiet is all," the assistant D.A. demanded.

Then Walker wasn't there. The lieutenant telephoned his house and when no one answered, telephoned the bureau of the special detail out of which Walker worked. But no one had seen or heard from him. So the lieutenant had broadcast a reader for him to be picked up. Then they sat down to wait.

"It's incredible to think a detective shot those men," the assistant D.A. said. "What possible motive could he have?"

The lieutenant sucked at his pipe and said nothing. The assistant D.A. looked pointedly at Brock. He seemed to be seeking confirmation of his own conclusion. Brock realized he was on a spot. But he refused to be drawn into prejudgment.

"Let's wait and hear what he has to say," he said.

Almost imperceptibly, the lieutenant nodded approval.

"I think they were killed by someone from Harlem," the assistant D.A. said. "Although that's just between us. Legally my mind is open."

Brock examined a blank spot on the wall.

Finally the lieutenant admitted, "It's a possibility we're going to look into."

"Maybe they belonged to some terrorist group and were executed for some reason or other, perhaps for refusing to bomb the luncheonette."

Both detectives looked at him.

"It does sound foolish," he admitted. "But this is a foolish business."

"It is that," the lieutenant agreed wholeheartedly.

They were saved from further discussion by the arrival of detective Walker.

Walker wore the same clothes he had worn all night. His face was redder and his eyes were red-rimmed. He gave Brock an accusing look but nodded dutifully, then turned toward the lieutenant and asked, "You want to talk here?"

A uniformed cop who had entered with Walker placed a chair for him facing the lieutenant's desk.

"Sit down, Walker," the lieutenant said.

A stenographer came in with a notebook and stylo and

took a seat at the end of the desk. The assistant D.A. sat flanking the lieutenant on the other side. Brock sat apart.

"Tell us all you remember about last night," the lieutenant ordered Walker. "And don't leave anything out."

"Only the commissioner has the right to cross-examine me," Walker said but he was pleasant enough.

"In most instances," the lieutenant agreed. "But in this instance you have been accused of homicide and that's in our province."

Walker smiled. "Right, Lieutenant, I have no objections."

He leaned back in his chair and closed his eyes and began to speak. "As you know, my tour of duty is from eight to four in the Times Square district. I deal chiefly with prostitutes and pickpockets but occasionally there are shootings and robberies in the district—"

"You're on a special assignment?" the assistant D.A. asked.

Walker looked at him and smiled. He appeared rather boyish. "Not exactly," he replied. "It was formerly called the vice squad. Now we're just ordinary detectives, based in the central police station."

He paused to see if the assistant D.A. was satisfied and the lieutenant said, "Go on."

"Last night, shortly before going off duty, I took a final check on the Broadway Automat to see if there were any wanteds inside or any prostitutes working. There wasn't anybody in there but bums—"

"How could you tell?" the assistant D.A. asked.

Walker looked at him again but this time he didn't smile. "Bums look like bums," he said flatly. "What else you expect them to look like?"

"Go on," the lieutenant said shortly.

"When I came out I saw a prostitute running toward me— that was south—from 47th Street." He looked at the assistant D.A. defiantly and said, "I knew she was a prostitute because she looked like a prostitute."

The lieutenant gave an almost imperceptible nod.

"A big man in a dark overcoat without any hat was chasing her. I cut in front of her and seized her, then I moved to seize the man. But I saw he had an open knife in his hand and I let go the woman to stop him. He tried to get around me to get at the woman and I had to sap him to subdue him."

"You struck him with your pistol?" the assistant D.A. asked. Everyone looked at him, all of them wondering what he was trying to get at.

"I sapped him with my sap," Walker said shortly. "He fell to the ground and when I looked around for the prostitute she was running around the end of the old Times building headed down Broadway toward 42nd Street. I knew I'd never catch her on foot and I couldn't leave the man lying in the street so I ran around the corner on 46th Street and got my car and stopped to put the man in the back and then went after her."

"Did you have an official car?" the lieutenant asked.

"It was my own personal car," Walker said.

"What kind of car?"

"A Buick Riviera."

"That's a lot of car for a detective first grade," the lieutenant remarked.

"It's my money," Walker flared.

"He's a bachelor," Brock intervened.

"Go on," the lieutenant said mildly.

"I didn't see her in either direction on 42nd Street so I drove on down Broadway to 34th Street without seeing a single living soul. I turned in Herald Square and came back up Sixth Avenue to 42nd Street again—"

"What was happening to your prisoner?" the lieutenant interrupted.

"He was still out—"

"It didn't worry you?"

"I didn't stop to think. I wanted to find that whore—"

"Why the urgency? What was the charge?"

"Oh, I forgot to tell you. He said she had robbed him."

The lieutenant nodded.

"I turned over to Fifth Avenue, still without seeing a soul, and again I drove down to 34th Street—"

"Hadn't it occurred to you she might have gone into a house by then?" the assistant D.A. asked.

"She could have," Walker admitted. "But I wasn't thinking." Again all three officials looked at him sharply. "I just wanted to catch that thieving whore." The bright red spots stood out on Walker's cheeks and his eyes began looking wild.

The lieutenant and the assistant D.A. regarded him curiously, but Brock looked away in embarrassment.

The next instant Walker had gotten himself under control and by way of explanation for his outburst said, "I don't like the hookers; it seems unjust for a prostitute to steal a sucker's money when he intends to pay her."

The homicide men were not impressed by his opinion, and the assistant D.A. didn't quite understand. But they all passed it.

"Anyway, I turned again on 34th Street over to Madison," Walker continued. "I was going north on Madison when I saw this woman coming south from the direction of 42nd Street. She must have seen my car at the same time for she ran around the corner on 36th Street heading toward Fifth Avenue. It's an eastbound street—36th—and I couldn't drive into it—"

"Why not?" the lieutenant asked. "There was no traffic about and you were on police business."

"I wasn't thinking," Walker said. "I just parked on Madison at the corner and got out and ran after her. I had to cross Madison and just as I turned into 36th Street she ran up the steps of a house way down the block and disappeared. When I got there the entrance was locked. I tried to find some way into the back entrance but all those houses are adjoining—"

"Did you take the number of the house?" the lieutenant asked.

"No, but I—"

"Where is the house in relation to the building on the corner where the porter was found wounded?"

"I think it's the second house—"

"You *think*?"

"It was the second house," Walker flared.

For a moment no one spoke, then the lieutenant said mildly, "Go on."

Walker seemed to be getting his thoughts together. Finally he said, "That was when I saw the Negro."

A pregnant silence followed. All three regarded him with steady speculation.

"What Negro?" the lieutenant asked softly.

Walker shrugged. "I don't know. I heard someone behind me and there was a Negro coming toward me—"

"Which direction had you been facing?"

"Madison. The Negro came from toward Fifth—"

"From the direction of the building on the corner?"

"Yes. My first thought was that he was a prowler—"

"Why?" the lieutenant asked.

"Why what?" Walker was genuinely puzzled.

"What made you think he was a prowler?"

"Oh, that. Hell, why else would a Negro be in that neighborhood?"

"There are Negro janitors and porters and some might even live there."

"This one was a porter."

Again there was a pregnant silence. But no one broke it.

"When I moved to apprehend him," Walker continued, "he said if I was a policeman I was just the man he was looking for. He said there was a burglar hiding in the basement of the corner building. It was then I noticed he was wearing a Schmidt and Schindler porter's uniform—"

"You hadn't noticed before?"

"There hadn't been any before. I had just seen the Negro." Walker seemed to wait for another question.

But all the lieutenant said was," Go on, you had just seen that the Negro was wearing a uniform."

Walker gave him a searching look, but he was well under control. "I asked him for some identification and he produced a Schmidt and Schindler worker's identity card," he continued. "He said the burglar had first been discovered in the Schmidt and Schindler luncheonette on 37th Street and had escaped through the basement—"

"What did this Negro look like?" the lieutenant asked.

"Look like? Like a Negro, what was he supposed to look like?"

"Was he tall, short, fat, slim?" the lieutenant questioned patiently. "Black, yellow, brown? Young, old, middle-aged?"

"I didn't notice, he just looked like a Negro. I didn't study him. If I was going to catch this burglar I didn't have much time—"

"That's not much to go on," the lieutenant said mildly.

"Well, I remember seeing the name *Wilson* on his identity card—"

"Have a reader put out for a Negro Schmidt and Schindler porter named Wilson," the lieutenant directed the stenographer, who sat scribbling at the end of his desk. The stenographer started to get up, but the lieutenant said, "Not now. Just make a note of it. Or a Negro named Wilson masquerading as a porter."

"Yes sir."

"Go on," he said to Walker.

"I went with the Negro to the entrance of the building on Fifth Avenue. There was a charwoman scrubbing the front hall floor. I knocked. She was so stupid it took me some time to get across to her that I was a detective. She went for the superintendent and when I looked around, the Negro had disappeared."

"You didn't look for him?"

"No, I figured he had gone back to the Schmidt and Schindler luncheonette. And then the janitor's helper in the building came staggering to the door with the keys and acting all suspicious because the superintendent had just telephoned for the police and I had arrived too soon."

"You told him that the Schmidt and Schindler porter had brought you?"

"I told him nothing. He was just a stupid wino and it would have probably taken him all night to figure it out."

The lieutenant gave an almost imperceptible nod. Walker glanced at him suspiciously.

"You told the superintendent about your informant?"

"He didn't ask. I just followed him down to the basement where they thought the burglar was hiding."

"Instead, you found another Negro Schmidt and Schindler porter," the lieutenant supplied. "This one was wounded."

"That's right."

"And he accused you to your face of shooting him?"

"That's right."

"How do you account for that?" the assistant D.A. asked.

Walker looked at him. Slowly he spread his hands. His breath came out in a sigh. "I don't know," he confessed. "It'll take a psychiatrist to figure it out. That's why I had him sent to Bellevue." He paused in thought for a moment. "The way I figure it, I was the first person he saw on regaining consciousness and he thought I was the one who

had shot him. Or maybe he didn't even think about it,
maybe the image of the one who had shot him was still in
his mind—he went out seeing it and came to imagining he
was seeing the same one—his mind didn't allow for the
time gap. Or maybe he was just having hallucinations. Maybe he never saw the one who shot him—"

"He was shot from in front," the lieutenant said.

"Anyway, I couldn't have shot him unless I was two people. At the time he was shot I had a prisoner in my car and
I was chasing this whore who I'm sure knows me—by sight
anyway."

"We'll find the prostitute all right," the lieutenant said.
"But you haven't told us what you did with the man."

"I haven't got to it."

"All right, go ahead."

"Just a minute," the assistant D.A. said. "You think then
that the wounded porter was delirious?"

"Definitely. The man who shot him was probably a Negro
too."

"Then the Negro porter you met on the street—the informant—might very likely be the murderer himself?" the
lieutenant suggested.

"Very likely," Walker said. "At least I think so now."

"But it didn't occur to you at the time?"

"I wasn't thinking and I didn't know about the murders
until afterwards."

"Did you look at the bodies?"

"I was going to, but the sergeant in command stopped
me."

"Ump!" the lieutenant grunted. "Well now, let's get on
to your prisoner."

"I had gone next door to the Schmidt and Schindler
luncheonette and had found the men from homicide there,
and that was how I learned about the murders. The sergeant
cautioned me about leaving fingerprints—"

"Yes, they found your prints all over."

"That's what he said, I was leaving them all over. Then
suddenly I remembered my car and prisoner—"

"What made you remember them all of a sudden?"

"How the hell do I know? I just remembered them, that
was all. I went down 37th Street to Madison and when I

looked for my car across the street at the corner of 36th Street it was gone and the prisoner was gone. I felt like I was going crazy and having hallucinations myself. I'd lost the whore, I'd been accused of shooting a strange Negro, I'd lost my prisoner and my car—"

"You'd also lost the Negro porter who had informed you of the burglary," the lieutenant reminded him.

"Yes, him too. I called in and reported my car stolen— you can check for yourself—"

"I believe you."

"I didn't mention the prisoner because I hadn't taken his name. Then I went back to the lunchroom to tell about the Negro I'd met on the street, or maybe find him if he was there. But all of you were interrogating the superintendent in the other building and the homicide men wouldn't let me enter—"

"Why didn't you come around to the other building and ask for us?"

"I didn't think."

The lieutenant gave him a long, critical look. "For a first-grade detective you don't seem to have your thoughts very well organized," he said.

Suddenly Walker wilted, he cupped his burning face in his hands. "It's been a rough night," he confessed.

He's been drinking heavily, the lieutenant thought, and Sergeant Brock, his brother-in-law, thought, He's blind drunk, but he doesn't show it.

"All right," the lieutenant said, not unkindly, "some time today take a look at the colored workers in the restaurant and try to spot your man, and if you don't see him there take a look at the bodies of the two murdered porters in the morgue and see if either of them is the one."

Walker composed himself and straightened up. "May I go now?"

"Take a seat out in the hall until the stenographer transcribes his copy. Then you can come in and read it and sign it and I'll witness it. Okay?"

"Then go and get some sleep," Brock said.

He and the lieutenant looked across at one another as Walker left the room.

9

It was 3 P.M. and it had stopped snowing but fog was closing in. The upper stories of the midtown skyscrapers had disappeared as though being slowly swallowed by the cephalopodan sky. The brightly lighted storefronts were scattered oases in the gloom, faintly luminous, and car lights of the congested traffic made a slowly spinning pageantry, vaguely seen. Pedestrians walked with care.

New York City.

Already the snow removers were out on Fifth Avenue and gloved and overcoated laborers were shoveling piles of snow from the sidewalks into waiting trucks.

As Brock drove slowly in the stream of northbound traffic he had a fleeting image of a city in the stomach of a cloud. It was a clean and peaceful and orderly city being slowly consumed.

But when he came into Harlem at 110th Street and turned west on 113th Street the image suddenly changed, and now it was the image of a city already consumed with only bits of brick and mortar left to remind one that there had ever been a city.

Brock wasn't given to imagination and he felt as though his mind was playing tricks on him. He realized, of course, his mind was making a block to keep him from thinking about Walker. But he was too old and tough a cop to feel that he had to think about Walker now. There would be plenty of time after all the facts were in to begin thinking about Walker. Now was the time to try to find a motive.

Meanwhile as he drove down the slum street he was assailed with a feeling of disgust. At least they could clean the goddamned streets, he thought as his car skidded from side to side over weeks' accumulation of snow.

The crosstown streets in Harlem which did not serve through traffic or bus lines were seldom cleaned of snow all winter, and piles of frozen garbage now covered with a mantel of snow lay along the curbs.

Brock firmly closed his mind.

Already news of the murders had spread in Harlem and the few Negroes he saw on the street eyed him with hostility. He didn't let it worry him. He could take care of himself. Physically, he was a tremendous man built like a telephone booth and about the same size. He had a cube-shaped head with a weather-reddened face and small, colorless eyes that remained cold and inscrutable. He wore a look of joviality which did not show in his eyes at all.

The building in which Luke Williams had lived was a scabby tenement near Eighth Avenue, with the outside walls flaking away and a number of broken panes in evidence replaced with yellowing newspaper. Before entering he locked his car securely and cased the street.

The dark damp hallway was unlighted and the stink of urine and salted pork bones being cooked in too old cabbage hit him in the face. He hesitated an instant at the bottom of the stairs and debated whether he should draw his pistol. A black man could stand unseen in the dark and cut his head off.

Then he put the thought from his mind as ridiculous and started up the stairs. What was happening to him? he asked himself. This was the best policed, the richest, the most civilized city in the world, and here he was, a police detective sergeant of the Homicide Bureau, experiencing trepidation on entering this residence of supposedly law-abiding, respectable people—at least it had the approval of the city. He'd better get his thoughts straightened out, he told himself, and get his subconscious rid of Walker. It affected his whole point of view.

He stopped before the door of the third-floor-front apartment and knocked. The door was cracked on a chain and a dark-skinned woman with streaks of gray in her straightened hair peered at him. Suddenly her eyes filled with repugnance.

"I suppose you're from the police," she said in a flat, resigned voice. "After he was killed."

The last was like a curse. He fumbled for the leather folder holding his badge and tried to keep the guilty feeling from his voice, "Yes. Sergeant Brock. And you're Mrs. Williams. May I come in? I have to ask you a few questions about your husband."

Silently she unchained the door and opened it. He quickly
noticed she was a big woman, big-boned, with distinct
African features. She looked very strong. There was more
bitterness in her expression than grief.

She wore a black cardigan over a long, blue woolen dress
and the backs of her hands were almost the same color as
her sweater.

Then his quick glance surveyed the room. In the center
was a large oval table holding an ashtray and table lamp
and surrounded by a number of straight-backed chairs in
various stages of repair. To one side stood a potbellied
coal stove on a tin plate flanked by a worn, grease-slicked
armchair. Luke's chair, he supposed. On the other a double
bed covered with a maroon cotton chenille spread was
pushed into the corner.

The black faces of many wide-eyed children peering
around the frame of an inside door looked like a stack
of disembodied heads. Their mother went over and closed
the door in their faces, still without speaking, and then came
back and turned on the table lamp.

"Sit you down, sir," she bade the detective, and seated
herself on the edge of the bed.

Brock sat on a straight-backed chair and put his hat on
the table and took out his notebook and stylo. He looked
at her. The whites of her brown eyes were clear with no
hint that she had been crying. She sat erect with her hands
in her lap. She seemed bitterly resigned as though she had
transferred the burden of her grief and worry to someone
else.

There was no need of any preparatory talk. She had
heard of Luke's murder on the one o'clock news broadcast and she had telephoned his sister and asked her to go
down to the morgue and identify the body. She had gone
to the PS and brought the younger children home and that's
as far as she had got. She supposed someone from the
company would come up to see her later. And she hadn't
heard anything from the three older ones. Her eldest, a
nineteen-year-old girl, worked as a sales girl in the 72nd
Street Automat and she would be at work. She must have
heard about it, but she hadn't telephoned. She didn't have a
telephone herself, and had to use Mrs. Soames' next door.

Her eighteen-year-old son was in the army at a camp in Augusta, Georgia, and she didn't know whether he had heard or not. But he would be coming home to help her soon as he heard. And her seventeen-year-old son—she didn't know where he was, just somewhere in Harlem. He and his father had never got along and she didn't know what he would do; she had heard he was living with a woman.

"Can you think of any connection he might have had with the murders?" Brock asked with his stylo poised. "Anything, a chance remark, a seemingly innocent question, anything?"

"Lord, no, he's not a mean boy, just wild. Once he got away from here I doubt if he's ever thought of his father."

"I'll take his name anyway."

"Melvin Douglas."

They had eight younger children and all were living at home and went to school.

"We have four rooms," she said in reply to Brock's look. "It's crowded but we managed."

Their fifteen-year-old son slept in the kitchen and the four girls had one bedroom and the three boys had the other. The youngest still slept in a crib and she and Luke had slept in there in the sitting room, where they all ate, too, when they ate together.

They had come from Marion, Georgia, right after they'd been married, twenty years ago. Luke had come back for her after he'd got his job with Schmidt and Schindler and all their children had been born in Harlem. He had been a good father and a good provider, although she had done day work from time to time, still did, but she'd never had to. He had never done anything really bad in his life, she would swear to it on her mother's grave. Of course she knew he'd been going to see another woman during the past three years, after she had given birth to her eleventh, but that was just male nature.

"Do you know who this woman is?"

"Sure, her name is Beatrice King, she belongs to the same church we do, the Church of God in Christ on 116th Street, but she ain't got nothing to do with this, I'm sure. She's a widow and she's not mean, she just frisky."

He wrote down the name and asked curiously, "Aren't you ever pinched for money? Luke didn't earn enough from his salary to take care of all of you."

" 'Course, after all the children came, naturally we been hard up for money, like all colored people are, but Luke makes—made—more than twice as much as he did when we got married."

The children helped each other. They trusted in the Lord. But she didn't know what they were going to do now.

"Luke had some life insurance?"

"I suppose so. With the company."

The company was their father, only next to God, Brock understood.

Brock was very seldom depressed. A sergeant on homicide couldn't afford to have emotions. But when he left Mrs. Williams and walked down the dark stinking stairs out into the narrow dirty street, he was shaken. He had the feeling that something had gone wrong somewhere. Maybe it had happened just last night or maybe it had happened a long time ago. But somewhere the whole mechanism of the American way of life had slipped a cog, or maybe it was the heart. The heart had missed a beat and had never caught up.

Well, there was nothing he could do about it, he told himself.

He drove north on Eighth Avenue to an address near 144th Street and climbed to the fifth floor. He knocked at the door of what was listed as a kitchenette on the mailbox in the entrance.

A big sloppy light-complexioned woman in a flannel wrapper flung open the door. Her recently straightened hair was in curlers and smelled like a singed pig. Her breath smelled of gin. He looked quickly past her and saw the dirty, unmade bed with two pillows which had large black grease spots where greasy heads had rested.

"Mrs. Jenkins?" he asked.

"No, I'm Gussie, there ain't no Mrs. Jenkins. Why, you from the police?"

Suddenly he felt better, less guilty. He could think of no reason he should feel less guilty on finding a hurt bad colored woman than on finding a hurt good colored woman, but there it was. He felt more at ease. He flashed his badge.

"Lord, what's that man done now?" Gussie asked theatrically. "You got him in jail? He should have been here hours ago."

"He hasn't done anything we know of," Brock said. "But get himself killed."

She flung up her hands automatically, in the gesture of the scandalized, prepared to be scandalized at whatever he had done. It was the traditional attitude. Colored women appear scandalized before the white man at anything bad their men have done. Suddenly she froze, went rigid, in a grotesque posture like a petrified clown. Her light skin paled, her full-blown face sagged with shock. She looked suddenly twenty years older.

"Killed?" Her voice had sunk to a whisper.

"I'm afraid so."

"Whoever'd want to kill Sam? He wouldn't hurt nobody. He wasn't nothing but talk."

"That's what we're trying to find out. May I come in?"

She opened the door wider. " 'Scuse me, I been jarred out of my manners. Was he stabbed?"

He entered the one room and looked about for a place to sit. There was a square wooden table across from the bed, flanked with two overstuffed armchairs, and two straight-backed chairs beside the bed, but all contained articles of clothing and soiled dishes. She removed the clothes from one of the armchairs beside the table and he sat down and put his hat on the table and she sat on the bed facing him. He wondered briefly if there was any reason these women sat on their beds, but quickly dismissed the thought.

"Just tell me in your own words all you knew about Sam Jenkins," he commenced.

All she knew about Fat Sam did not supply him with the slightest motive of why he had been shot. She had met him in a bar where she had been working as barmaid five years before and she'd been living with him ever since. He was a jolly man who liked his liquor and his fun, and that had suited her fine. For the past three years she hadn't been working; he had earned enough to support them both.

Brock got the idea that she did a little hustling on the

side, but he doubted if Fat Sam had known, or whether he would have cared.

She seemed certain that Fat Sam was not mixed up with any racket that would have caused him to be shot; first he was too lazy and secondly he didn't care about possessions. He had hit the numbers several times to her knowledge, once for enough to buy a car, but he had thrown his money away on liquor and good times. He had often told her when he died he didn't want to leave anything behind for someone else to enjoy.

"Did he steal from the company?" he asked just to have something to ask her.

"Not enough for anybody to really mind. He brought home a little food from time to time, ham hocks and the ends of roasts that were going in the garbage anyway. 'Course it was against the rules but if anybody had ever suspected him they'd never said anything."

He got the picture of an amoral, petty-thieving Negro, the usual stereotype. She was the same. He didn't realize this was the reason he felt at ease with her.

When he got up to leave he said, "Well, thank you, Gussie."

"I hope I been some help."

"You've been of great help," he lied. "Would you like to go down to the morgue and identify his body, or does he have some relatives who would want to go?"

"I'll go. If he's got any relatives, I don't know 'em."

Next he drove to the apartment building at the corner of 149th Street and Broadway where Jimmy Johnson, the wounded porter, roomed. He parked before the entrance on 149th Street.

It was a six-story building of light-colored firebrick, in reasonably good repair. One look was enough to tell him that Negroes had not occupied it very long. The front steps and tiled floor of the front hall were clean and the glass panes of the front door were clean and unbroken. But a sprinkling of graffito already marred the light gray walls and a drawing of huge male genitals had been scratched on the elevator door.

It was an automatic elevator, slow, but it worked. He rode up to the fifth floor and knocked at the door of the apartment where Johnson roomed. The door was opened by a middle-aged West Indian who wore a perpetual frown. The West Indian introduced himself as Mr. Desilus and invited Brock to enter, stopping to lock all of the locks on the front door before showing Brock into a parlor that looked out on Broadway.

They were joined immediately by Mrs. Desilus, a very proper dark-skinned woman wearing a black satin dress that reached to her ankles and a glossy black pompadour, and their thirteen-year-old daughter, a bushy-haired girl named Sinette.

Without waiting to learn of Brock's errand, Mr. Desilus assumed the position of a persecuted man. "I'll not have it." he shouted. "We're respectable God-fearing people. I'll have to ask that young fellow to move. We can't have the police coming to our house. What will people think? What effect will it have on our young daughter here?"

Brock was confounded. First, he couldn't understand Mr. Desilus, who spoke with a pronounced accent; secondly, he didn't know where the daughter came into it. He had remained standing as he hadn't been asked to sit down, and now concluding that Mr. Desilus was more concerned about his reputation than the murders or his wounded roomer, he was ready to leave.

"I take it you've heard about the luncheonette murders?" he asked anyway.

Mr. Desilus gave him a pitying look. "We have a radio and a television set. We're not living in the backwoods here."

"Well, I won't bother you again," Brock promised. "But I have to ask you a few questions about your roomer, Johnson."

"I don't know anything about that young fellow, and I don't want to know," he said. " 'Cepting he's always got his head buried in books."

"He goes to college," Sinette said.

"You speak when you're spoken to," her mother reprimanded.

"You better go talk to his girl friend," Mr. Desilus said, washing his hands of the whole business. "She lives on the third floor. She knows more about him than we do; we just gave the poor fellow a place to stay."

Brock stifled a sigh. "Will you give me her name then?"

"I don't know her name," Mr. Desilus said angrily.

Brock looked at him, wondering what he was so angry about.

"Linda Lou Collins," Sinette said, defying her mother. "She's a singer."

"Well, I'll go see Miss Collins," Brock said to Mr. Desilus, "if you'll just let me out."

Mr. Desilus led him to the door and as he was unlocking the many locks he muttered, "I'm going to put that boy out of my house."

Brock counted four locks, one with a bar attached to the floor.

"Don't do that, please, Mr. Desilus, I beg you," he said. "I'd hate to think I was the reason for him losing his room. He's perfectly innocent of any crime, I assure you. No censure will be attached to you in any event. And I'm sure your daughter has nothing to fear."

Sinette wouldn't have liked that last remark.

Mr. Desilus' frown certainly wasn't indicative of sympathy but he grudgingly consented to give the boy another chance, being as they were Christians.

"I thought you would," Brock said and started to add more, but thought it best to leave it at that.

He paused for a moment in the corridor outside the door, attracted by the sound of Mr. Desilus meticulously locking all four locks. Then he took the elevator down to the third floor.

No one answered Miss Collins' door. That was that. He got in his car and drove back to the Homicide Bureau. He had to do some thinking.

10

The turnkey let her into the cell and locked the door behind her.

"Oh, daddy," she cried, half sobbing, her high heels beating a tattoo on the concrete floor as she went swiftly to his cot. "What are they doing to you?"

"Baby!" he exclaimed. "Oh, baby, I wondered when you'd come. It's been all of four days and I'm going crazy."

Her Persian lamb coat smelled of outdoors and damp perfume as she leaned over to kiss him. Her damp resilient lips fused against his dry chapped lips and her fingers dug desperately into his shoulders. Finally she drew back and looked at him. Their gazes locked and each felt the shock of sudden desire.

"Don't talk for a moment," she said. "Just let me look at you."

"You smell so good," he said. "They say the badder the woman the gooder she smell. You must be a bad, bad woman, baby."

The smile started around her mouth and spread quickly all over her face.

"I came and I came," she said, sighing, and sat sidewise on the cot, looking at him as though she couldn't believe he was alive. Her feet scuffled a newspaper which had fallen unnoticed to the floor. Suddenly she giggled. "Sounds naughty, doesn't it?"

He laughed. The morning light slanted through the barred window high up in the east wall, pearling the melted snow-drops on her black felt hat, and suddenly they were somewhere else, enclosed by love. A deep rose glow suffused her caramel-colored skin and her huge brown eyes glowed like liquid light.

"Linda, you sure are a beautiful girl."

"Hug me, hug me, then!"

"You'll have to do all the work," he said ruefully.

Frantically her quick strong fingers explored the outline of his body beneath the covers.

"Jimmy!" she exclaimed in a horrified voice. "Where are your arms?"

He grinned sheepishly. "They've put me in a straitjacket. They don't like me because I accused one of their white detectives of shooting me. They say I'm crazy."

A shadow came over her face. "The dirty bastards," she said but she sounded insincere.

He tried to catch her gaze but she looked away. "You think so too, don't you?"

Instead of replying she jumped to her feet and slipped

out of her coat. Her broad-shouldered, narrow-hipped body with low pointed breasts was dramatized by a turtleneck sweater-dress of tan cashmere. Flinging the coat across the foot of the cot, she leaned over quickly and kissed him again, then sat on the edge of the cot but avoided his gaze.

"So that's why they let me see you without a guard?"

"Because you think I'm crazy too?"

"Don't be silly. The straitjacket."

"Oh, that. No one's been allowed to see me except the district attorney and a bunch of cops."

She turned and smiled at him again, postponing what she'd intended to say. "You're all right now?"

"I'm fine as can be expected, just locked up and can't move is all, like the way they say to keep a woman faithful."

"God, I was frantic when I'd heard you were shot!" she exclaimed, shuddering involuntarily. "I was dead asleep and Sinette kept banging on the door until I answered and she said you were dying in Bellevue. They'd just got it over the radio."

He grinned cynically. "I suppose Mr. Desilus had conniptions worrying about his reputation."

"Sinette was worried about you. Are you sure you're all right?"

"It's just a flesh wound, the one in the chest. I had lost a lot of blood is all. The others were just scratches."

"God, it must have been awful."

"Don't let anybody ever tell you they weren't scared when they were being shot at. You don't know, baby, you don't know."

She shivered.

"Are you cold?"

"Just scared," she confessed.

"Anyway, I'm still alive."

"Let's count our blessings."

"Bullshit," he said. "Just kiss me and you'll feel warmer."

She leaned over again and kissed him.

"Feel warmer?"

She glanced at him through the corners of her eyes and laughed.

"If I could use my arms I'd hug you and that'd make

you warmer still," he said, but it didn't have the intended effect.

Her face clouded again.

"Daddy, why did you do it?"

"Do what?"

She picked up the newspaper that had dropped to the floor and held it spread out before him. The front page carried a banner headline: WOUNDED PORTER FINGERS VICE COP AS LUNCHEONETTE KILLER.

He looked at the headline woodenly. "So the papers finally got it. That'll get the lead out of their pants."

"Now you've made everybody mad," she said accusingly.

"If they're mad, then goddamn them!" he cried angrily. "No one wants to believe my story. I told them the truth: A goddamn drunken crazy cop murders two porters and tries to murder me too and I'm not supposed to talk about it because he's white and it might prejudice the civil rights movement. They've got me locked up as though I'm the crazy one, while the maniac runs free. Let them be mad. If they get mad enough maybe they'll try to get at the truth instead of trying to shut me up."

She looked at him with pity and distress. "They are investigating, daddy, they're doing all they can—"

"So they've been brainwashing you too?"

She was hurt. "Believe me, Jimmy, the district attorney and the commissioner and everyone's on your side."

"I haven't got any side," he raved, squirming beneath the covers as though trying to free himself. "I've got a hole in my front side where that maniac shot me."

"They want to find the killer as badly as you do," she went on, trying to keep calm.

"I told them who the killer was."

"But they don't have any evidence. It's just your word against his. They can't take it to court without more evidence."

"They don't want any evidence."

"He told them another story and they can't prove—"

"I know what he told them," he interrupted rudely. "They read me his statement. He said he was looking for a whore, some whore he'd arrested in Times Square. He claims she got away from him and he was looking for her way down on

36th Street—as if she had wings—when all of a sudden a colored man dressed like a Schmidt and Schindler porter— get that now—another colored Schmidt and Schindler porter appeared out of thin air and told him about a burglar in the basement of the commercial building on the corner. Another Schmidt and Schindler porter—colored porter. He had already murdered two, and had chased me into the basement of that building, and the fourth colored Schmidt and Schindler porter, whom nobody has ever seen before or since, suddenly appears and tells him about a burglar. Do you believe that shit?"

"They know he's lying, Jimmy honey," she said in a soothing voice. "The district attorney told me that—"

"Then why don't they arrest him?"

"They know he's lying but they can't prove he's involved in the murders."

"The hell they can't! The garbage man told them what Luke told him and me about the drunken white detective he'd sent inside to talk to Fat Sam. He ain't got no reason to lie. He doesn't even work for the city; Schmidt and Schindler uses a private garbage-collection company."

"They admit his story is credible," she said. "But he didn't see the detective—he just had Luke's word for it—and Luke is dead."

"What the hell! Do they think there were two drunken white detectives wandering around in the area at that time of morning?"

"I told you, daddy, they believe he was inside the restaurant. They believe that part of your story—"

"Thank them for nothing."

"But they haven't got any proof. Didn't anyone else see him. Both the window washer and the milk truck driver and everybody said they didn't see anyone or hear any shooting."

"They told you an awful goddamn lot. Did they tell you about his fingerprints. They didn't find his fingerprints, I suppose. And what about the garbage cans? What about the bullets that landed in the wall? Ballistics will show what pistol they were fired from."

"They haven't found the pistol; they don't even have any record of the pistol the bullets came from."

"Now goddammit they're going to say there wasn't any pistol, much less a white murderer. I suppose they're going to say the bullets came from an unknown source!"

"And they did find his fingerprints," she went on doggedly. "But he'd been all over the restaurant after you and the—the others were found and he'd left his fingerprints all over everything. I mean when he was in there then."

"Goddamn right! He was alibi-ing for the fingerprints he'd left there when he'd committed the murders—"

"Jimmy darling, listen. They admit your story could be true. They say if it isn't true it shows a vivid and logical imagination. What they think—"

"I know what they think! They think I'm crazy! At least that's what they want everybody else to think."

"No, they don't, honey. I know they don't. I've talked to them—the district attorney and the commissioner and the inspectors and all of them. They don't think you're crazy at all. The district attorney has been in touch with Durham since the first day. He's had your entire past investigated. He's talked with the chief of police and the sheriff and the president of North Carolina College. He knows you graduated with honors. He's talked with your mother and sister in Durham. He knows your sister works in the bank of the North Carolina Mutual Insurance Company—he even knows it's the biggest Negro-owned insurance company in the world. He says there's hardly a white student in Harvard who wouldn't envy your clean record. He even knows that you chose to come to New York and enroll in the law school at Columbia University rather than try to force your way into the white university at Chapel Hill and cause your family a lot of grief and worry. They've even got a statement from your old boss out at the Chesterfield factory—he said he'd take your sworn word against that of all the detectives in New York City. They know all about your studies at Columbia and where you've lived and what you've done since you came to New York. And the Schmidt and Schindler Company is behind you one hundred percent. Don't you think for a minute that anyone believes you're crazy."

"I suppose this isn't a straitjacket they've got me wrapped up in. I suppose I'm just lying here with my arms folded because I don't want to hug you."

"Listen, honey, Jimmy, they want to help you. I know. I'm not easy to fool. You know yourself I never get taken in by what white people say unless I know they're sincere. It isn't that. What they think is that you've got it in for him and are trying to frame him—maybe he did something when he was in the restaurant the first time that made you want to frame him for the murders—"

"They think I committed the murders and shot myself and I'm trying to frame him for it? Is that it?"

"—did something to hurt you in some kind of way," she went on.

"Goddamn right he did! He shot me and tried to kill me."

"I mean what they think is, if he isn't the murderer, then what have you got against him personally?"

"Listen, when he started shooting at me, I didn't even know that he'd already killed Luke and Fat Sam. All I knew he was trying to kill me and I didn't have time to think of anything else. All I accused him of at first was shooting at me."

"They know that too. That's what they can't understand. The superintendent of the other building said that when you came to, the first thing you did was accuse him of shooting you. He said you told him positively that the detective had shot you and that you appeared to him to be in your right senses and know exactly what you were saying. That's what puzzles them."

"Goddamn right! I'm shot by a killer and when I point out the killer who shot me, they're puzzled. What the hell am I supposed to say? That I haven't even been shot? That I was just running through all those basements for my health and then I lay down on the floor and a hole burst open in my chest and the blood started leaking out? Is that what they want me to say?"

"They don't want you to say anything public at this time. All you're doing by talking to the newspapers is making sympathy for him."

"I haven't talked to any newspapers."

"They're saying that maybe you've got a persecution complex."

"Goddamn right! Anytime a Negro accuses a white man of injuring him in any way, the first thing they say is he's got a persecution complex. He's blaming it on the power structure. Bullshit! I suppose it was a persecution complex that got old Luke and Fat Sam shot full of holes."

Sweat had beaded on her upper lip from her effort to reason with him, and her eyes were beginning to look sick.

"Jimmy, daddy, honey, do something for me," she begged. "You know I wouldn't ask you to do anything dishonorable. If I didn't know it was for your own good—"

He saw it coming and tried to head it off. "Linda baby, you believe me, don't you?"

"Of course I believe you, daddy." He saw the doubt in her averted gaze. "Of course I believe you. It isn't that—" He saw the lines of exasperation crease her tight moist brow. "But why would he want to kill all of you? Especially you? You say you hadn't even talked to him, hadn't even seen him. . . ."

He saw the doubt harden into disbelief. He felt crushed inside. Now no one believed him.

"You want me to tell you why he did it?" he asked in a flat, toneless voice.

She looked up quickly with hope in her eyes.

"I don't know why," he said. "He just did it. That's all I know."

The hope went out of her eyes.

"I don't suppose you'll do it, but I wish you would," she said hopelessly. "For your own good, daddy."

"Do what, Linda?"

"Take it back."

He hadn't expected her to ask that. It felt like a sneak punch in the guts. "You mean tell the newspapers what I said about the detective isn't true?"

"You don't have to go that far. You can just give them a statement that you didn't mean it the way they put it. You can say the detective is lying about not being in the restaurant before the murders—"

"But I told you, baby, I haven't talked to any newspapers. They got the story from someone else. No one's been allowed to see me but you."

"But you'll be allowed to see the reporters now."

"If I say the story isn't true?"

She didn't reply immediately.

"Did they ask you to get me to do that?" he pressed her.
"The district attorney and the commissioner and the others?"

"Not exactly. They just explained how it would make it
easier for them to catch the real killer if you don't—didn't
—start off smearing the police department. I mean if you
just wouldn't make a positive accusation—if you would just
leave room for doubt. Even if he shot at you—"

"Even *if* he did?"

"Well, then, he did shoot at you. But you don't know for
an absolute certainty that he murdered Luke and Fat Sam."

"No, not any more than I know that I'm lying here."

"Don't you see, honey, if they let him go, he'll do something to trip himself up—"

"Such as kill me."

"—otherwise they might never get the proof."

He lay looking at her through dull eyes, unable to move.

"Won't you do it, honey?"

"Not as long as I am black."

"We've got to work with them, honey; they're our only
hope, even if they are white—"

"I'm going to keep on saying the son of a bitch shot me
and murdered Luke and Fat Sam until I am dead," he said.

11

Jimmy was dressed and waiting when the lawyer was shown
into his cell.

"I'm Mr. Hanson," said the slim young man, pink-cheeked
and dapper in a Homburg and a Chesterfield overcoat. "I'm
from the legal firm that represents Schmidt and Schindler.
I've arranged for your release."

Shaking hands, Jimmy looked big and country in his duffel
coat and snapbrim hat beside this small neat figure.

"Yes sir, that's what the jailer told me."

Hanson looked curiously about the cell. All this was new
to him: prison cells and violent men. His firm handled only
civil cases. He looked back at the big solemn Negro. They're
a lost people, he thought.

"How do you feel, Jim? Does the wound trouble you still?"

"No sir, I just want to get out of here."

Hanson smiled understandingly. "I can appreciate that."

They left the cell and followed the turnkey through cell blocks of meddlesome prisoners, arriving at the guards' room. Hanson presented some papers to the chief warder which got the barred gates opened.

Outside, Jimmy asked, "What's my status, Mr. Hanson? Am I out on bail, or what?"

"You're free, Jim. No bail, no restrictions. You can go and come as you please. However, you mustn't leave town."

"I'm not thinking of that."

They took an express elevator and rode down in silence, then pushed their way through the crowded corridor toward the westside doorways.

"Are you going home now?" Hanson asked.

"I think I'll stop by the store on my way uptown and let them know I'll be back tonight."

"No, no, don't do that," Hanson advised. "Just report on duty at nine o'clock as usual. But if I were you, I would take several days off, a week or more. Perhaps it would be better if you remained home until your wounds are completely healed. Your pay continues as usual."

"Well, in that case I think I will," Jimmy said gratefully. "I want to catch up on my studies."

"Do that then."

They came out on the broad concrete steps facing the square. Below, taxis were lined along the curb and cars streamed past, worming down the stone canyons beneath an overcast sky. People streamed past them, entering and leaving the court building. It was a busy hour of morning; traffic court was in session.

"If you have any trouble, Jim, resulting from this affair, come directly to me," Hanson suggested, giving Jimmy his card. "Don't discuss it with anyone before talking to me. And I'd further suggest that you don't discuss this affair at all. Okay?"

"Okay," Jimmy said.

While they were shaking hands, Jimmy stiffened. Blood drained from his face, leaving it putty gray. Suddenly in the crowd on the sidewalk below, a face stood out he'd never forget.

Walker was standing to the right of the steps in the stream of pedestrian traffic, his trench coat flaring open in the wind and both hands stuck into his pockets, staring up at Jimmy through opaque blue eyes. This was the way Jimmy had first seen him, impassive, unspeaking, seemingly without thought or emotion; the difference was that then he had been looking down at him with a drawn revolver in his right hand, and an instant later, without one word being spoken, there had been the first silenced shot and the open look at death.

He shuddered involuntarily.

Hanson whirled about, following his terrified gaze, and saw a man standing on the sidewalk. The man looked as dangerous as a man can look.

"Oh, that's Walker, the detective you—" He broke off.

"Yes sir, that's him. I'd remember him in hell."

He looked back at Jimmy's stricken face.

"I wouldn't be frightened of him, if I were you," he said calmly.

"No sir," Jimmy agreed. "I wouldn't if I were you either. He didn't try to kill you."

Hanson frowned. "I can't discuss that. But my advice to you is to ignore him, don't give any attention to what he might say or do; and keep away from him. The police have him under surveillance. They know what they are doing."

"I sure hope so," Jimmy said. "That's all I want to do, I promise you, keep away from him as far as possible. But I'd feel easier if he was locked up."

"That might happen yet," Hanson said. "But in the meantime, don't let him worry you. He has no authority to approach you; he has been suspended during the period of the investigation."

"Well," Jimmy said slowly, "that doesn't help me much."

Hanson appeared embarrassed. He didn't know what to say. It wasn't as if Negroes were like other people. You had to give them special assurances, and he had already given all the assurances he could give.

Jimmy noticed his embarrassment and said, "Well, I guess I'll be going." But he hesitated as though afraid to go alone.

Hanson took out his wallet and extracted a five-dollar bill. "Here, you'd better take a taxi."

Jimmy shook his head. "Thanks just the same, sir, but I'll be all right on the bus. I live at 149th Street and Broadway and the bus stops at 145th Street. Nothing can happen to me in that crowded neighborhood."

Hanson looked at him doubtfully, but said nothing.

Jimmy walked quickly away without looking in Walker's direction.

Hanson watched him cross the park and walk down Centre Street toward Chambers and Broadway where he'd catch the bus. Then he turned and watched Walker to see what he would do.

But Walker gave no sign of further interest in the boy. He kept looking up toward the entrance as though waiting for someone. A moment later another man who looked like another detective rushed from the building and hailed him, "Hey, Matt!" and ran down the steps to join him. They shook hands and talked briefly and then the man took Walker by the arm and they went down the street in the opposite direction taken by the boy.

He's not giving the boy a thought, Hanson concluded and signaled for a taxi.

Jimmy sat beside a gray-haired white woman in the only vacant seat on the bus and tried not to think. What good was thinking? he asked himself. It'd only be a form of self-torture. He couldn't do anything himself and no one believed him anyway.

Across from him a blear-eyed soul brother was talking in a loud voice to another soul brother. "You just got to tell those mothers, man, don't be scared of 'em. . . ." The listening soul brother looked ashamed of him.

I'm alive, Jimmy told himself. That's something.

The bus went slowly up Broadway by fits and starts. It passed Canal Street, which looked for all the world like a stationary carnival. It passed Third Avenue at Cooper Square. It passed Fourth Avenue at Union Square. Jimmy glanced at Klein's, a famous outlet store, and recalled the story about a sale they had on mink coats which had caused a traffic jam of chauffeur-driven Rolls Royces. He wondered what the Communist orators who held forth on the Square had thought of that. It crossed Fifth Avenue at Madison Square. It crossed Sixth Avenue at Herald Square, made

famous by the cut-rate department stores, Gimbel's, Macy's
and Sak's 34th Street. It crossed Seventh Avenue at Times
Square, the world renowned hurdy-gurdy of movie theatres
and restaurants built around the old triangular Times building. It crossed Eighth Avenue at Columbus Circle, where
naked children bathed in the fountain at the entrance to
Central Park and were chased across the grass by red-
faced, embarrassed cops. Cutting Manhattan on the bias.

Jimmy watched the city scene go past, he looked at the
faces of the people, white faces mostly, sprinkled with a few
black and brown faces everywhere, and wondered how many
of them were scared too.

He tried not to think. He didn't want to think. But he
couldn't help himself. The street scenes faded from his
vision as he relived those minutes of terror. What had
happened between Walker and the fellows? he wondered.
What could they have done or said to make him mad
enough to kill them? Was the man a homicidal maniac? Or
had he just been in a homicidal rage? All he knew was
what he had been told by his examiners, and that was nothing.

He was overcome by such a sense of dread that he began
to shiver. The gray-haired woman sitting beside him asked
in alarm, "Are you sick, young man?"

He looked at her stupidly, he'd forgotten her presence.
He tried to smile. "No, ma'am, just a foot stepped on my
grave." He saw she didn't understand and explained, "It's
an expression when one shivers suddenly."

She seemed relieved.

He tried to keep himself under control. But he was still
in a daze of dread when he alighted at 145th Street. At the
corner of 149th Street there was a bar-restaurant which
catered mostly to colored people, called Bell's. He stopped
at the lunch counter for coffee and toast. Even that early
in the morning jokers were playing the jukebox in the adjoining bar and putting out their big loud voices: "Maaan, listen
here to me, I worked them mother-raping dice 'til they come
red-hot," crowed one voice and another voice, "An' w'en I
ate up the last foot, my old lady jumped salty. . . ."

He listened and slowly relaxed. Everything was sane and
normal as he knew it. His appetite grew. He ordered more

coffee and a stack of flapjacks. Another customer was having fried country sausage so he ordered some too. He ate ravenously, cleaning his plate. Still he wasn't filled. He ate a slice of apple pie and a scoop of vanilla ice cream and told himself that was enough.

He paid and went outside. Something drew his gaze. He saw detective Walker standing on the far corner of 149th Street, hands in his trench coat pockets, watching him from his opaque blue eyes. His stomach turned over and all the good food he'd just eaten went suddenly sour. Panic exploded in him. He felt as he had when Walker had first shot at him, naked and defenseless. One part of his mind urged him to run as it had done then. It took all of his will to fight down the impulse and reason with himself. This was in the street, he told himself; there were people going and coming. The man wouldn't dare shoot. But then maybe the son of a bitch was crazy, his mind whispered. Maybe he was shell-shocked, one of those war psychos. Maybe he was a member of some rape-fiend racist group, dedicated to violence. White men had murdered those civil rights workers in Mississippi, bludgeoned them into pieces. But this was New York City. Hell, what difference did that make? his mind asked. There had been that psycho over in some city in New Jersey who had taken an automatic army rifle and had gone down the street, shooting people he had never seen before. He had killed thirteen before the police disarmed him. White cops were always shooting some Negro in Harlem. This was a violent city, these were violent people. Read any newspaper any day. What protection did he have?

He broke out into a cold sweat. But he forced himself to walk normally toward the entrance to his building. He cut diagonally across 149th Street to avoid Walker as far as possible. Walker watched him, unmoving. His body felt as fragile as spun glass, his feet seemed nailed to the ground.

He got into the entrance hall without looking around. The hall was deserted. He pushed the button for the elevator. He was afraid to take the stairs, afraid he couldn't make it, afraid the detective would catch him on them, shoot him down. No one would hear the silenced shots; few people

ever used the stairway, it was closed off from the hallways
and the doors were kept shut. He stuck his thumb against
the button and held it. The elevator had been at the top; it
came slowly. . . . Come on, mother-raper, he raved in
desperate silence. Come on, goddammit, do you want me
to be killed? . . . Over his shoulder he watched the entrance,
expecting Walker at any instant. Usually when he wanted
the elevator there were so many residents waiting they
couldn't all get on. Now it was just his luck—

A shadow fell across the glass-paneled front door. A
man entered, wearing a trench coat. Jimmy's heart tripped;
the air froze in his lungs like a drawing coldness passing
through his chest. His stomach constricted in a small ball
of terror. Then he saw the black face looking out from
beneath the pushed-back hat. His bones wilted as he sucked
in air. Relief gagged him. There had never been a black
face more welcome.

The elevator came and he got on; the colored man followed. He felt his heart beating sluggishly. He felt the man
looking at him. He started making up a story. But the man
got off at the third floor.

He tightened up again the instant he was alone. He was
trembling by the time he reached the fifth floor. His hands
shook as though he had the palsy as he fumbled with the
keys to his apartment. He kept looking over his shoulder
down the empty hall. Finally he got the door open, got inside, and stood for a moment in the dark hall to regain his
composure.

Once he had been amused by Mr. Desilus' distrust of the
colored people of Harlem, as though he lived in fear of
someone breaking into his apartment. What did they have
that anyone would want to steal? he had asked himself. But
now he was infinitely grateful for all the locks on his front
door. There was a lock at the top and one at the bottom
and two in the middle. One of the middle locks had a chain
and the other was attached to a long bar anchored to the
floor.

He locked all four locks. They could be opened with keys
from the outside. But he hesitated before fastening the bolts
at the top and bottom edges of the door because the family
was out—Mr. and Mrs. Desilus were at work and Sinette

was in school—and he didn't want them to come home and find themselves bolted out. But on second thought he fastened the bolts too. They'd just have to understand.

He went through the gloomy hall to his front corner bedroom. It was a large room furnished with a bedroom suite of oak veneer—a specialty of the credit stores—which consisted of a double bed, dressing table, chest of drawers, two small bed tables and a green imitation leather ottoman thrown in. Mrs. Desilus had given him a large deal table for a desk. It held his books and papers and an old-fashioned upright typewriter. There was a large rag rug on the polished oak floor.

He paid fifteen dollars a week rent.

His girl, Linda Lou, had added feminine touches: two stringy black Topsy dolls flanking the dressing table mirror, which she had dared him to remove; clear nylon see-through curtains and flowered paper drapes to brighten the room and give more light; a chintz cover for his armchair and a foam rubber cushion for his desk chair.

It was a light, pleasant room with windows on both Broadway and 149th Street. On clear days he could look down the steep incline of 149th Street to Riverside Drive, the Hudson River, and the New Jersey shoreline in the murky distance. But there was nothing pleasant about it at the moment.

He closed and locked the door on the inside. Now there was no way for the killer to reach him. Neither of his windows opened onto fire escapes and only a bird or an insect could get at him. He sighed deeply and slowly the panic and the terror left him. At least he was safe there, if only temporarily. But that was all he could think of at the moment, just to stay alive.

He threw his hat on the bed and hung his duffel coat in the closet. Then he remembered it was bad luck to put your hat on the bed. He moved it onto the table. He only drank alcoholic drinks at what he called "social occasions" and never kept liquor in his room, but he wished at the moment he had something to drink. He needed something to blunt his thoughts, they kept too near the edge of panic. But there was nothing to relieve them and he tried to assess his predicament realistically.

I've got to give this situation some thought, he told himself. I'm in a dangerous position. What could have stopped that maniac from coming inside down there and shooting me dead and walking off without anyone seeing him?

He strolled to the window looking out on Broadway as he racked his brain trying to recall every detail of the minutes when Walker had been shooting at him, trying to surprise a clue. But he couldn't think of a single acceptable reason for the murders.

Absently he drew aside the nylon curtains and looked down at the small drab park running up the center of Broadway. An old woman was sitting on a green iron bench, feeding bread crumbs to a flock of pigeons on the crusted snow. Suddenly he felt a taste of bile in his mouth as though his gall bladder had burst.

Walker stood to one side of the old woman, his open trench coat flaring in the wind, both hands stuck into his pockets, hat pushed back from his maniacal face, staring up at the front of the building with a steady intensity. He stood with his feet wide apart and his shoulders hunched. He appeared statuesque in his immobility.

Jimmy dropped the curtains as though they had turned red-hot, stepped back from the window, gasping for breath, trying to subdue his shock. Now he knew for certain, knew beyond all doubt, that the detective was shadowing him, searching for an opportunity to murder him. The dread and the terror came up in him in waves and he felt too weak to stand.

He dropped into the armchair, twisting his head to watch the immobile figure in the park below.

What could he do? He didn't feel safe anymore. Should he telephone the police? What would they do? What could he tell them? They hadn't believed anything he had said. Why would they believe him now?

Then he thought of Hanson, the attorney. He went to the closet and fished Hanson's card from his duffel coat. The telephone was in the master bedroom and Mr. Desilus did not permit him to make outside calls, only to receive calls and that grudgingly. But this was an emergency and besides, Mr. Desilus was not there.

He unlocked his room door and went down the hall. For

an instant his stomach went hollow for fear the bedroom might be locked, and he didn't dare leave the apartment. The bedroom door was open but the telephone was locked by a padlock on the dial.

"These goddamn people don't even trust themselves," he muttered bitterly.

He found a bowl of hairpins on the dressing table and took one and tried to pick the lock. But it bent out of shape. He tried another. It was a cheap lock and he got it open with his sixth hairpin. The room was tightly closed with the curtains drawn and the windows barred and felt almost airless. By the time he got the lock open he felt as though he were suffocating.

Finally he got Hanson on the phone.

"This is James Johnson, Mr. Hanson. You told me to call you if there was any trouble—"

"Yes, Jim, what is it now! What kind of trouble are you having now?" His voice was brisk and impatient.

"That detective, Walker—"

"The one you pointed out this morning? What about him now?"

"He's following me. He's waiting to get a chance to kill me. He's—"

"I think you're exaggerating, Jim. I watched him this morning after you had left. He showed no sign of any interest in you. He did not follow you and he did not—"

"Maybe he didn't follow me but he was up here at the corner of 149th Street when I got home. I kept away from him as you advised—"

"Are you certain it was Walker whom you saw? You're not imagining all of this? When I saw Walker last he was leaving the courthouse in the company of another detective."

"That could be so, but I'm certain of this. I'm not imagining it. He's still up here. I got inside the building and came up to my apartment and locked myself in. Then for some reason or other I looked out the window—I have a window overlooking Broadway—and I saw him down there in the park staring up at the building."

"You are certain of this? You're not leading me on any wild-goose chase?"

"Yes sir, there's no way I can be mistaken."

A sigh came over the phone. "All right, Jim, don't be alarmed. There's nothing he can do to you. Remain in your room and ignore him." Hanson paused.

Jimmy was silent. He didn't know what to say.

"What was he doing?" Hanson asked. "Was there anything threatening in his behavior?"

"There never was. The first time he shot at me there wasn't anything threatening in his behavior; he just aimed at me and fired."

"All right, all right," Hanson said as though he didn't want to hear about it. "Now what is he doing?"

"Nothing. He's just standing down in the park staring up at the front of this building. But I'm scared. What's to stop him—"

"All right, I'll tell you what I'll do. I'll have the commissioner's office send someone up there to find out what he's doing."

"Yes sir, but they won't believe me."

"There won't be any need for them to talk to you at all. I will tell them what you have reported to me and ask them to investigate. You go right ahead with your studies or whatever you're doing as though nothing had happened. Okay?"

"I may as well tell you, Mr. Hanson. I know the man is waiting to kill me."

"All right, Jim, all right. But you're safe. Nothing is going to happen to you, so try to take it easy. And give me your telephone number. I will phone you when I hear from the commissioner's office and tell you what they have found out."

Jimmy thanked him and read the telephone number from the dial. He hung up, relocked the padlock and went back to his room to keep an eye on Walker until the men from the commissioner's office arrived, whoever they might be.

But Walker was nowhere in sight. His frantic gaze searched the park and the other side of the street, then with growing alarm he raised the window and leaned out to search the sidewalk below. But the dreaded figure had disappeared. He was more terrified by Walker's disappearance than he had been by his presence.

He went back to the front door to make certain it was

locked and bolted. Then he went into Sinette's room, which opened onto the fire escape, to see that the iron grille over the window was closed and locked. When he returned to his room he locked his own door again. He sat at the table and opened a textbook and tried to force his mind to concentrate on the printed page. But the print blurred in his vision and he saw only a tall demoniac white man standing at the top of some stairs, aiming a pistol at his heart and firing without warning, without a change of expression in the tight angular face.

What did a man do when he knew someone was going to kill him? Kill the killer first? That was what men did in the western movies. But this wasn't a movie. Not even a gangster film. This was real life.

He got up and started pacing the floor. His legs kept buckling, his mind felt dead, beaten to death by his fear. But he forced himself to keep moving. At least the movement helped contain his panic.

Finally, he didn't know how much later, the telephone rang. He unlocked his door, went cautiously through the hall to the master bedroom and answered it.

"Mr. Hanson?"

"Yes . . . Jim?"

"Yes sir? Did the commissioner's men find him? When I got back to my room after telephoning you, he was gone."

"I see. . . . The telephone is in another room and you cannot see the street from that room?"

"No sir, it's a back room that looks out over the courtyard. My room is on the front."

"I see. . . ." There was a long silence. Jimmy swallowed and waited. "The commissioner sent two members of his staff uptown to your vicinity," Hanson finally went on. "They drove up and down Broadway on both sides several times, then toured all the side streets. But they didn't see Walker."

"Then he must have seen me standing at the window at the same time I saw him. Then he came into the building. He must be hiding somewhere in the building. Did they search the building?"

"No, they returned to headquarters and put out a police call to have Walker picked up. Walker heard the broadcast

and telephoned the commissioner's office. He had been in
the detectives' room at the Homicide Bureau on Leonard
Street since shortly after we both saw him on Centre Street
this morning. Another detective had been with him all of
the time and several other detectives, passing through, had
exchanged greetings with him."

"But that's impossible," Jimmy said.

Hanson remained silent.

"I don't mean I doubt your word. But there's something
very strange going on. I saw him. I know I saw him. He
was up here. It was just like I said. He was standing in the
park down on Broadway staring up at this building . . ."
Jimmy knew that he sounded hysterical. But he couldn't
help it. He felt hysterical. "Listen, Mr. Hanson, I'm being
framed. Everything I've said about that detective is true."

"*You're* being framed?" Hanson echoed. "No one has
accused you of anything. You are doing all the accusing."

"I mean there's some sort of conspiracy to make it sound
as though I'm crazy."

Hanson let the silence run until it revealed his disbelief. Then he said with a flat unemotional deliberation,
"Johnson, if I were you I wouldn't make that charge in
public." His voice sounded strange to Jimmy, as though he
were talking through a pipe or from under water. "I wouldn't
charge the police with conspiring to show that you're insane. I wouldn't touch that angle if I were you. My advice
to you is to drop all these accusations against detective
Walker until you have incontrovertible proof. You have put
yourself in an indefensible position. It's regrettable from
both your position and ours that you made the last charge
against Walker. . . . Okay?"

"But he was here!" Jimmy said, almost sobbing. "I saw
him standing at the corner of 149th Street. I came from the
restaurant. He was standing there. I cut across the street
to avoid passing close to him. And I saw him later standing
down there in the park on Broadway when I looked out of
the window. That's the God's truth, Mr. Hanson."

"The difficulty is, Johnson, that he has proof that he
was someplace else. He has reliable witnesses." Hanson's
voice sounded very strange to Jimmy; it sounded more pitying than anything else. "In fact, Johnson, his claim that

he was in the detectives' room at homicide when you claim to
have seen him uptown is irrefutable."

"Yes sir," Jimmy said. "Irrefutable." The receiver had
grown so heavy in his hand he could barely hold it. "I'll
take your advice. Thank you for letting me know."

"Don't mention it," Hanson said.

It was a relief for Jimmy to put the heavy receiver down.

12

Linda Lou was washing lingerie in the kitchen when the
doorbell rang.

"Shit!" she exclaimed irritably.

She was wearing an old nubbly maroon bathrobe she
wouldn't have been caught dead in, over a cotton flannel
gown she wore only to sleep in privately, and a pair of
worn-out mules. She had scarcely awakened and hadn't as
yet washed her face. Her short crisp hair looked more
kinky than curly and her face bore the stolid, slightly sullen
look of early morning stupidity. She glanced at the kitchen
clock and saw that it was past three in the afternoon but
didn't take the trouble to notice how many minutes past
three. She hadn't even had coffee. She'd gotten up and
started washing lingerie as she always did after a troubled
night. Jimmy worried her.

The doorbell rang again, long and insistently.

Maybe it's the numbers man, she thought, adding men-
tally, I hope.

She had a small two-room apartment on the third floor
rear. She wiped her hands on her robe as she went through
the living room to open the front door, her hips moving
with a lazy roll.

Jimmy stood in the doorway.

"Oh, honey, it's you!" she exclaimed, half in exasperation
and half in joy. Her hands flew quickly to her matted curls
but one feel was enough to know they were hopeless. She
laughed fatalistically, and moved aside. "Well, come on in."

Jimmy entered and started past her. His face bore the
fixed expression of a sleepwalker.

"I know I look like hell, but you can kiss me, can't you?" she complained. "Just for old times' sake."

He kissed her absently, frowning at his thoughts.

"Well!" she said, put out. "I asked for it." Then she noticed his expression. "My God, what's happened? You haven't broken out of jail, have you?"

He didn't smile. "No, I was released this morning."

"I was just going down to see you when I'd finished washing."

"Well, you're shut of that chore," he said bitterly. "They let me out. They decided I wasn't the murderer after all."

"Hush," she said, putting her hand over his mouth. "Come on back to the kitchen while I make coffee."

"I don't want any coffee," he said.

"Well, I do," she said irritably, turning toward the kitchen.

"I'm sorry, I wasn't thinking," he apologized, following her meekly. "I'm kind of upset."

She pushed him down into a straight-backed chair beside the table. "You just sit there and tell mama about it."

In age she was but a year older, but in experience she was his mother.

"I know you're going to think I'm crazy—" he began, but she stopped him.

"Well, if it's like that you'd better wait until I've had some coffee 'cause otherwise I can't do any kind of thinking."

He relaxed a little. "This is a dangerous city," he said, sighing. "Dangerous and indifferent and cynical."

"You just think too much," she said, dumping coffee from a can into the strainer of a battered aluminum percolator. "New York is not for thinkers, it's for stinkers. You're too nice to be a stinker. You let it get you down. You haven't learned yet to take it as it comes." She moved about as she talked, running water into the pot through the spout, saying apologetically, "I do everything ass backwards, don't I?" She put the pot on the stove and turned on the gas, then reached for the matches and found the box empty. "Shit!" she said and turned off the gas until she found a book of paper matches on the shelf over the stove.

It was a small compact kitchen, incredibly dirty, with cosmetics and curling irons and half-eaten sandwiches

lying about with dirty dishes, empty milk bottles and cans.
The white enameled stove and refrigerator came with the
apartment, but the tubular steel table with the yellow plastic-
bottomed chairs belonged to her.

She caught him looking at her and said defensively, "I
know I look sloppy and talk sloppy. My mother always
told me Never let your sweetheart see you in the morning
before you get dressed up in your airs—"

"You look fine," he said.

"Fine," she mimicked. "Shit!"

He'd been thinking how sane and normal life appeared in
that dirty little kitchen. Dripping wet stockings hung from
the clothes rack lowered from the ceiling; the rest of the
washing was in the sink. Outside, across the gloomy courtyard, was the grimy brick wall of another wing of the building with the dirty windows shut against the cold afternoon.
It looked so safe and peaceful it seemed incredible that
there was a maniac walking the streets bent on killing him.

"I mean it," he insisted.

She laughed deprecatingly. "Who're you kidding? If I
looked that fine you'd have thrown me on the bed."

"I'm just worried," he said.

"I know, baby, I'm just kidding." She rubbed his head.

The pot started percolating, filling the room with the
tantalizing coffee scent.

"I think I'll have some coffee after all," he said.

"I thought you would," she said, searching for two clean
cups in the cupboard. She got a half-used can of con-
densed milk from the refrigerator and placed it on the table
alongside a bowl of sugar cubes. Then she served a carton
of cinnamon toast and a stick of butter wrapped in tinfoil.
"Well, I guess that's enough for afternoon tea," she chat-
tered on. "So let me sit my big ass down."

"Don't talk so vulgarly," he said. "You're always trying
to be hard-boiled."

"Listen to the man!" she exclaimed as she poured the
coffee. "You think I'm trying to shock you? I'm just rattled,
that's all. You come in here and catch me looking like the
morning after and expect me to be beautiful and demure."

She knew he was going to tell her something she didn't
want to hear and she was trying to head him off.

But it was seething in his mind and came out with a bang.
"That detective is trying to kill me," he said.

She had her coffee cup almost to her lips. Her hand
froze and her eyes brimmed with tears. "Well, you might
have let me drink my coffee," she said. "At least get the
first sip in peace."

He jumped to his feet, looking like a hurt child. "I'm sorry
I bothered you. I should have known better. You don't believe me either. No one believes me. The only way anyone
will believe me is for me to wind up dead."

She put down her cup, sloshing coffee over the table,
jumped up and ran around the table, knocking over a
chair, and gripped him by the arms. She had a wire-tight,
bone-dry look of fury.

"Sit down!" she shouted, wrestling with him, trying to
force him back into the chair. "You're going to sit down
and drink your coffee if I'm going to have to make you
beat me up."

"If you're not going to believe me what's the use—"

"Shut up!" she fumed and kept struggling until she got him
seated again. "You're a hundred percent imbecile and baby
on top of that. I feel like killing you myself."

"I just got to talk to somebody about it," he said. "I got
to make somebody believe me."

She kissed him on top of the head and went back to her
own seat, righting the overturned chair on the way.

"I believe you," she said, looking steadily into his eyes
across the table. "Now tell me what it is that I believe."

He gave the first little smile. "No, go ahead and drink your
coffee," he said. "In peace."

When they had finished he told her about seeing the
detective on 149th Street and in the park on Broadway and
his conversation with the lawyer, Mr. Hanson.

"But why!" she exclaimed. "Why does he want to kill
you?"

"Because I'm the only one who knows he killed the others.
I'm the only witness against him. He's afraid I'll find some
proof."

She nodded understandingly. "If you just knew why he
killed the others."

"That's what really worries me. I can't think of any reason

on earth why he'd kill either Luke or Fat Sam. Unless he's a
real psychopathic. And that's what I think he is, a homicidal maniac. That's what scares me most. If he's a psycho,
he didn't need any reason to kill them."

"But how can you be so sure of that? There might have
been an argument or a fight. They might have attacked him
for some reason or other. You said he was drunk—"

"No, there wasn't any sign of a struggle of any kind."

"Well, maybe not a real fight. But if he was drunk like you
say, there could have been a real dirty argument. You know
how some white men are toward colored men when they
get drunk; they get dirty and abusive and start saying things
the average colored man up North won't take—"

"No, neither Luke nor Fat Sam were like that," he contended.

"How do you know what they were like? You've only been
working with them for a little over four months. You just saw
them on the job. You never saw them away from work. You
don't know how they'd react in that kind of situation. You
never saw them being cursed out by a drunken white man."

"But I'd be willing to bet my life neither one of them
would have gotten into a serious fuss with a white detective.
Both of them were kind of Uncle Toms in different ways.
Luke was one of those even-tempered slow-thinking kind of
people—"

"He'd be just the one to blow his top when he really got
mad," she argued.

"Maybe. But I doubt it. Luke had been working for
Schmidt and Schindler too long to lose his head with a
white drunk. He'd been with the firm more than twenty years,
and in that time he must have come up against scores of
white drunks who were abusive."

"Well, what about Fat Sam? You told me he'd been a
preacher. And you and I both know preachers who've got the
temper of a devil. I once knew a preacher back home who'd
beat the living hell out of every man he thought was a sinner;
he'd knock them down in the street, kick them unconscious.
He sent more than one suspected sinner to the hospital—"

"I know, but Fat Sam wasn't that kind. He wasn't a devil-
fighting preacher. He was a chicken-season preacher, one
of those jive ministers. He only preached when the chickens

were fat or during hog-killing time. A drunken white man couldn't have made him mad enough to fight, no matter what he said. He'd pop his eyes and quote the Scriptures and if the white man kept on he'd start ducking and dodging like a minstrel man."

"Anyway, it was Fat Sam the detective saw first, you said."

"After he went into the store."

"That's what I mean. You don't know what happened between them."

"I doubt if anything—"

"But you don't know. Maybe he'd already killed Fat Sam when Luke went inside. You couldn't have heard anything outside, loading the garbage truck, could you?"

"No, but—"

"Then maybe Luke found Fat Sam dead and he killed Luke too. You said you went down to the basement on the elevator. You couldn't have heard the shots, could you?"

"If it had been a regular pistol. But I figured it out afterwards he had a silencer on his pistol. That's why I couldn't hear when he shot at me. At first I thought I was just too scared to hear—"

"Do the police know he used a silencer?"

"Oh sure. They know the pistol had a silencer. And they know it was the same pistol that shot me that killed Luke and Fat Sam. But as they told you, they can't find the pistol or any record of it. At least that's what they say!"

"A dirty cop like him could have that kind of pistol," she said. "But that doesn't help us any."

"There's another angle. Luke said he accused him of looking out while somebody stole his car. But in the statement he made to the D.A. he claims his car wasn't stolen until after he'd come into the other building and found me shot. He claims the car was stolen while he was inside helping with the investigation."

"Maybe we should talk to the D.A. about that," she said excitedly. "The D.A. told me they were convinced the detective had been in the store earlier, just like you said. Maybe if they knew he had accused you-all of stealing his car—"

"But they know all of that," he cut in bitterly.

"But that would give him the motive," she contended.

"I've told them all of that. They just won't believe me.

They say there isn't any proof." He paused, then went on despondently, "It's just that he's a cop—pride of the City of New York. He's a white detective and I'm just a poor colored porter."

"But you've got Schmidt-Schindler behind you."

"They're behind me, all right. Way behind me. They're so far behind me I'm going to be dead before they catch up."

"You're not going to be dead, honey," she said, reaching across the table to capture his hand. "You just be careful and no one's going to kill you."

"Listen, baby, do you know how easy it is to kill a man?" he said. "I read all about Murder Incorporated when the story broke but I never thought anything about it until now. Do you know all a man's got to do to murder someone and go scot-free? All he's got to do is catch him alone somewhere, anywhere, and shoot him dead, stab him in the heart, knock out his brains, and just walk off—just like that maniac could have caught me alone in the hall downstairs. That's all, just kill him and walk away."

Blood drained from her face, leaving a greenish pallor beneath bloodless yellow skin, as the terror came up from her constricted stomach.

"You're not just trying to scare me, are you?" she asked in a small scared voice.

"No, I'm just trying to show you how easy it is. All that detective's got to do is just keep on following me about until he catches me alone—downstairs, upstairs outside my door, on any street between here and 116th when I go to my classes, at any time of day or night, and shoot me dead with that silenced pistol. He can wait for me any night when I get off the subway at Herald Square—"

"You never told me how you go to work."

"I take the IRT on Broadway at 145th down to 59th then change over to the Sixth Avenue Independent. I come up on 35th Street in front of Macy's and walk over to Fifth Avenue and 37th. And anywhere along that way he can shoot me down. All the stores in that section are closed by then and there are a hundred places where he can shoot me without being seen."

"Can't you get a Fifth Avenue bus on Riverside Drive and get off right in front of the store?"

"What's going to stop him from shooting me while I'm walking down 149th Street in the dark to Riverside?"

"But they'll know it was him."

"That won't help me any," he pointed out.

Her face burned with a reddish-brown blush. "That was stupid," she confessed.

"And if they can't prove a motive and can't find the weapon, what can they do to him, even if they feel certain that he killed me?"

She realized she'd been crying and wiped her cheeks with her hands. "It's hard to believe there's anyone like that loose in the world," she said.

"It's not hard for me to believe," he said. "What about that psycho over in New Jersey who shot those thirteen people? What about that colored boy in Brooklyn who went down the street with a butcher's knife and stabbed seven people to death? What about that drunk in the Bronx who shot those two couples in a booth in a crowded bar, two men and their wives, shot them to death, because they wouldn't accept drinks from him? You're telling me it's hard to believe? In this violent city? The papers are filled with stories of senseless murders every day. What's one more murder in a city like this? If they ever caught all the murderers in this one city alone they wouldn't have space in the jails for them. These people look on a killing like a circus performance. A man like him hasn't got any more compunction about killing than taking a drink of water. As long as he doesn't get caught. What cop in this city gives a good goddamn about killing somebody? I don't *believe* he's trying to kill me. I *know* he's trying to kill me. It might sound fantastic, but I know what I'm talking about. If I want to keep on living I'd better not let him catch me alone."

"Then I'll go with you whenever you have to go any place," she said.

"You can't go with me everywhere."

"Why can't I? We both work at night. I don't have to be at the club until eleven. That gives me plenty of time to go with you to work at nine and get back to 125th Street in plenty of time to eat before going to the club. Then I can pick you up at six every morning. I can wait outside the lunchroom on 37th Street."

"But you get off at four. What will you do until six?"

"Oh, the club stays open until then, sometimes until seven or eight. It's just that the acts finish at four, but you know the jazz musicians congregate there after-hours for jam sessions and they'd be glad if I stayed."

"No," he said. "I don't want you to get killed too."

"He wouldn't shoot me," she contended. "It's you he's after; he wouldn't bother me."

"You don't know this man. He's a psycho. He'd kill you as quick as he'd kill me if he got the opportunity. One more killing wouldn't make any difference to him."

"He wouldn't take the chance. A woman screams. He'd have to kill you first and I'd be screaming so loud all of New York would hear me. You've never heard me scream. You've only heard me sing. But I can scream, honey. When it comes to screaming, I can wake up the dead."

"No," he said. "I'll go alone. I'll take my chances."

"No you won't," she said. "I'll go with you."

"Well, not now. I'm going back to my room now, where it's safe."

"Wait, I'll come with you."

He grinned. "It won't be safe then."

She bridled. "Why not! You think I'm going to rape you? I'm not that hard up."

"It's just you don't know Mr. Desilus," he said.

13

Walker squeezed into the place at the jammed bar the big man in a dark gray coat and dark green hat had been holding for him.

"Thanks for covering for me, Brock," he said.

"Don't mention it," Brock said.

A bald-headed bartender with a heavily lined face and a cynical expression approached and swabbed at the bar with a damp towel.

"Rye and water and salami on rye," Walker said.

"How about another tongue on rye for me, Junior?"

Brock said, then drained his glass and added, "Another bourbon on the rocks."

It was eight o'clock at Lindy's and the cocktail hour was verging into dinner. Behind them, across the expanse of crowded tables, curtained windows veiled the sight of packed pedestrians fighting for passage along the sidewalk and the dense traffic clogging Times Square. The place was filled with newspaper columnists taking a fling at kosher cuisine, Broadway racketeers, here and there a Brooklyn gangster and his retinue, and a smattering of $100 call girls making themselves available for potbellied executives from the garment industry five minutes south by taxi.

"You kept the commissioner off my ass," Walker said.

"Glad to do it," Brock said. "But I'd like to know what for. Just a matter of habit. I'm one of those inquisitive sons of bitches that want to know why I do what I do."

Walker glanced at him. "It's with that Schmidt and Schindler business where the dinge fingered me."

"Naturally." Brock showed his teeth in what was supposed to be a grin, but his eyes didn't change expression. "But all I know about that business is what I read in the newspapers."

"Oh, come off it," Walker said.

"Sure," Brock said.

The bartender served their sandwiches and Brock bit off half of his. Walker drained his glass at a gulp and tapped on the bar for a refill. The bartender reached for the bottle he'd just returned to the shelf and poured without interest. Brock finished his sandwich with his second bite.

"Well, hell," Walker said defensively. "After the other dinges were found dead, I couldn't admit having been in there, could I? What would this district attorney do with that, riding the department as he is? All he'd want is to tie some charge like that onto one of us."

"Sure," Brock said, finishing his bourbon on the rocks.

Walker glanced into the mirror behind the bar, studying the faces in the room.

"It's safe," Brock said. "That's why I chose here. Don't no one here listen to anyone but themselves."

"I know it's safe," Walker confirmed. "It's my beat. I was just looking for stoolies."

"The stoolies split when I showed," Brock said.

Walker swilled his rye and banged on the bar for another. When it came he looked into the bottom of the glass as though it were a crystal ball.

"It was just my rotten luck," he said. "Just my rotten luck. When I left that whore's pad it was the only joint close by where I could get some coffee. I just went inside to get some coffee from those dinges."

Brock looked away. "I ain't asking you for it, you know. You don't have to feel obliged to tell me anything."

"Hell, I don't mind telling you," Walker said. "I'm as innocent of any crime as a newborn babe."

"Sure," Brock said, looking at the glasses behind the bar.

"I'd have leveled with the lieutenant if that punk district attorney's assistant hadn't been there. He wouldn't have understood."

"Sure, what makes you think I'll understand?"

"Won't you?" Walker asked appealingly, looking at him with a frank, open expression.

"Well, go on then, if you want, but I ain't asking you for it."

Walker sucked air silently, as though he had been holding his breath. "I'd been with the whore, naturally—" He had a certain youthful appeal, like a college boy confessing an indiscretion.

"Naturally," Brock grunted.

Walker looked piqued for a moment as though he might challenge Brock's sarcasm, but he decided to pass it. "I'd gotten so loaded I didn't know where I was anymore. Then while I was wandering around trying to remember where I'd left my car, I saw this joint with the dinge porters working and went in for some coffee."

"Sure."

Brock's tone of voice galled Walker but he tried not to show it. He picked up his glass and emptied it.

Brock looked at him disapprovingly. "You should eat more if you're going to drink like that," he advised.

Dutifully, Walker bit into his salami sandwich as though it were rank poison.

"Hey, Junior," Brock called to the bartender. "How about some gefüllte fish and a dill pickle!"

"Rye bread?"

"Pumpernickel." He thumped his glass. "And a refill."

"Right, boss."

"All right, all right, I'm a goy." Brock acknowledged the slur. "I like gefüllte fish, so what?"

"So nothing, boss."

Brock snorted. Walker seemed absorbed in his thoughts. They waited in silence until he was served. He cut off a slice of gefüllte fish, slapped it onto a slice of pumpernickel and bit it off. Then he bit into the dill pickle.

"How do you figure the porter fingering you?" he asked Walker through a mouthful of food.

"Just rotten luck, that's all. Just my rotten luck. The bastard recognized me."

Brock looked steadily ahead, chewing like a camel, and kept silent.

Walker threw him another quick look but his blunt profile told him nothing. "I've been playing with his gal," he went on. "A little brown piece who does a gig up in the Big Bass Club in Harlem."

"Sure, I see how it is," Brock lied. "But he didn't know your name, so he said."

"It don't figure that she was going to tell him either," Walker said. "But he knew me all right. He'd seen me up there in the club and he knew how it went."

"Sure, I see that much," Brock lied. "But after that I'm blind."

"Well, hell, after I got my coffee I left," Walker said irritably. "Those killings took place after that. The bit about the Negro dressed as a porter sending me in there to look for the burglar is straight."

"Sure," Brock said. "It sounds screwy enough to be straight."

"Maybe he's the one who did it. I'd know him again if I saw him, that's for sure."

"Sure. But you didn't remember what he looked like when Lieutenant Baker questioned you. How is that?"

Walker's gaze moved around a bit and he swallowed. "I didn't think it was important then," he said. "Anyway, he didn't ask."

"Well, maybe he didn't," Brock had to admit. "I don't remember."

Walker relaxed. "I don't remember, either, to tell you the truth. But I've been thinking about it a lot since. And the only way it adds up, it's a home job, strictly a dinge affair."

Brock looked up. "A dinge with a silencer on his rod?" he questioned with raised brows.

"Why not?" Walker argued. "These folks are getting modernized. Sawed-off shotguns and Molotov cocktails. But anyway you figure it, it must have been someone from uptown. Might have been gal trouble—"

"With a silencer?"

"Well, maybe not," Walker conceded. "When a dinge shoots another about his gal, he wants to hear the gun go off. But it might have been anything. You can never tell nowadays about a Harlem affair. It might have been something to do with the numbers, a religious wingding; maybe some cat took a powder with a payoff—they might have been running a numbers' drop in there."

"Sure," Brock said. "For the ghosts in that area?"

"Hell, it wasn't any ghost that shot 'em."

"That's for sure."

"The man we're looking for is good and goddamn alive. And a goddamn smart son of a bitch or else he'd left a clue."

Brock stared at him without expression. "Whoever killed those porters is a maniac," he said.

"Maybe," Walker said, appearing to think about it. "Maybe not. There might be something behind those killings bigger than we think."

"Such as?"

"Well, one of 'em might have been a connection for the H-ring. It's an ideal setup. They could keep the shit there for distribution to the pushers. One of 'em could have done it without the others knowing anything about it. Or they all could have been in it together." He showed a certain youthful ebullience as he enthusiastically developed his theory. "It would have been easy as pie. Whatever it was, that dinge knows who made the hits. He *knows* him," he contended dramatically. "You can bet on that. And he's scared to

name him. He's scared if he names him his own number
is up—"

"He named you," Brock reminded mildly.

Walker brushed it off with a gesture, and went on: "He's
so scared he's shitting in his pants. So he fingers the first
man he sees. And that happened to be me," he finished with
a spread of his hands.

"Sure," Brock said admiringly. "You oughta been on the
stage."

"You don't believe me?" Walker asked with genuine aston-
ishment.

Brock looked at him curiously. "Sure. It's just that you
said a moment ago he fingered you because of his gal."

Walker flew into a rage. Red spots burned in his cheeks
and his blue eyes went opaque. "What the hell, goddammit,
are you conducting an investigation?"

Brock shrugged his massive shoulders. "I told you I
wasn't asking for it."

Walker rapped for another drink, gulped it down, and
relaxed. "Good old Brock. Forget it. I'm just touchy. Can't
blame me for that, can you? All this brass riding my ass. I'm
telling you just how it was. It was just a coincidence. I was
coming out the whore's pad, just like I told you, and ran into
this Negro dressed like a porter, and when I stopped him to
question him, he says he's looking for a cop because there
was a burglar in the basement."

"I remember you saying you'd just left her pad when you
stopped in the lunchroom for some coffee, and all the porters
were alive then; or is my memory just bad?"

Walker put on a sheepish look. "I didn't tell you all of it,"
he confessed. "You see, the whore had clipped me for a
couple of C's and I had gone back for it."

"Sure. I see," Brock lied. "But I keep thinking you said
you didn't remember where she lived."

"Well, hell goddammit, you think I was going to admit
knocking off a piece while I was supposed to be on duty and
being clipped like a lain to boot? That's why I went with
the Negro to look for the burglar, to give myself an alibi for
being off duty half the night."

"Sure, I see," Brock lied. "That was when your car was
stolen?"

"Some time during then. I didn't miss it until after the bodies were discovered and I went back to look for it where I'd parked it on 36th Street. Just like I told the lieutenant—if you remember."

"You sure hit a jackpot of coincidences," Brock said.

"Don't you believe in coincidences?" Walker challenged.

"Why not?" Brock conceded. "They always figure in murder cases. We're working on the same angle ourselves."

"What angle?"

"Coincidences."

Walker shot him a quick, baffled look. "I was just going to ask what you homicide men were working on, but if it's top secret and all that—"

"I told you. Coincidences. And speaking of coincidences, like I said before, I'm still wondering what you wanted me to cover you for this morning."

"Oh that." Walker shrugged it off. "I've been shadowing that third dinge. Someone killed those other two dinges—"

"Like I said, that's for sure."

"And I figure whoever did it is going to kill this third one and level it off. So I'm keeping tab on him. More for my own sake than for his. If the killer comes out into the open, I've got him. And if it's the one I'm thinking, I'll know him. I'm going to have to get him to get clear myself."

"Sure. We figured that angle too. About the killer coming out into the open to get the third man."

"Well, if you homicide men are shadowing him too, then I can let up," Walker said.

"We're not shadowing him, if that's what you want to know," Brock said. "We're just at the figuring stage right now." He looked at Walker inquiringly. "You were shadowing him this morning when he went home?"

"Yeah. He must have spotted me and reported to the Schmidt and Schindler shyster. I figured he saw me when he looked out of his window. That's why I rushed downtown and looked for you. But you were out. So I telephoned you. I figured the commissioner was going to get in touch with you."

"I see you've been doing a lot of figuring too."

"What the hell's the matter with you!" Walker exclaimed

angrily. "I'm in a jam. I've got to figure. And all you can do is be sarcastic."

"I want to help you," Brock said.

"Why don't you act like it?"

"I am acting like it. I'm just curious about how you knew his window."

"That bastard has fingered me for murder. Remember?" Walker said flatly. "I know everything there is to know about a bastard who fingers me for murder."

"Sure," Brock said. "Including his gal. So what do you want me to do? You said when you phoned you had another favor to ask."

"I want you to find the whore I picked up that morning so I can get an alibi for the first time I went into the joint."

"I thought you just said you knew where she lived."

"I didn't say any such a goddamned thing."

Brock thought that over for a moment and decided finally he was wrong. That hadn't been what Walker had said. "You think she'll give you an alibi?" he asked.

"She'd better," Walker said.

"Sure," Brock said. "How you want me to go about it?"

"Just put some pressure on these pimps around here and make them spill. Some of them know where she's holed up. They all know I've lost my shield for the now, and I don't want to have to hurt any of 'em."

"How long are you suspended for?"

"Until the investigation is over."

"That might be forever," Brock said. "A murder investigation is never over until the murderer has been brought to trial."

"You don't have to tell me."

"All right, Matt, maybe I can help you," Brock said. "We're looking for her too."

Walker glanced up sharply. "What for?" he asked suspiciously.

"Just a coincidence. We want to give you an alibi too," Brock admitted. "What are you going to give me to go on?"

Walker strained at his memory. "Not much," he conessed. "All I draw is a blank from the time we had our irst drink over at the Carnival bar."

"Did she slip you a Mickey?"

"No. I just changed from rye to Pernod."

"I see. I thought you went back to get the money she clipped you for?"

"I didn't find her. She had already split."

"I see."

"All I remember about her is she's new on the stem. Too tony for a Times Square hustler. Felt at home in the plush joints. Called herself Cathy. Dyed blonde, brown eyes, five feet four-or-five inches, about one hundred and twenty, twenty-five pounds, twenty-eight to thirty years old, slightly bucked teeth, molars full of amalgam fillings of recent date, scar from Caesarean on belly—no other marks."

Brock studied him curiously. "You looked at her good enough," he remarked dryly. "That'll help if we find her corpse."

"I think of them as corpses," Walker said.

"Sure," Brock said, commenting idly. "She must have lived a fairly decent life until she got into the trade."

"Must have," Walker conceded indifferently. "I know she wasn't from New York. Probably from London. She spoke English."

"What about her place, apartment, room, whatever it was?"

"I keep thinking of a room, but it doesn't have to be *her* room. You know how whores' pads run together in your mind after a time, like a bad dream. You can't remember them apart anymore."

"You're a real gay dog, aren't you?"

"Well, hell, you know how it goes on my beat."

"Sure. All the vice you want for free. So what do you want me to do when we find her?"

"I want to talk to her first."

"Maybe I can arrange that, if I'm the one who finds her."

"Well, thanks, Brock." Walker called the bartender and settled his bill. "How is Jenny?" he asked Brock.

"Fine. Did you ever find your car?"

"I thought you knew. They found it the next day. Down by the Armory on 34th Street. The thief must have used it for a job and ditched it there."

"An accommodating thief, wasn't he? Brought it right back to the vicinity where he lifted it."

Walker shrugged carelessly.

"Was it locked?" Brock asked.

"I forgot to ask," Walker said indifferently. He turned to leave. "Give my love to Jenny."

"Right." Brock looked at him blankly, thinking, It's a damn good thing you're my brother-in-law. But he only said, "Take it easy, Matt. Watch out for coincidences." It was all he could do to keep the disgust from his voice. He beckoned to the bartender. "What you got for a belly-ache, Junior?"

14

Walker noticed that it was 9:15 when he emerged onto the street. He should have stayed with Brock longer, he realized, until 10 at least, but he had let Brock get on his nerves with all his sly insinuations. Well, to hell with that. Brock was all right, he told himself. Good old Brock. He was going to find it damn difficult to digest that story of his. But if he had to plead insanity, Brock would make a good witness.

Times Square was lit up. The lights filled him with a pricklish titillation. All these thousands of people searching for a thrill. I've got your thrill, dear, he said silently to a good-looking woman who passed. Ah well, he thought. That's life.

His car was parked in a *no-parking* zone at the curb. It was a big silver-gray coupé. During a vacation in Germany several summers before he had heard the big American cars referred to as Land Cruisers. Those envious Krauts, he thought. He was reminded fleetingly of Lieutenant Baker's pointed reference to its cost—"a lot of car for a first-grade detective." Well hell, did anyone think he bought it out of his salary? He just played the angles, that was all. If whores wanted to sell pussy and there were men who wanted to buy it, they had to pay the law-enforcement officers. That was no more than right and just. People couldn't expect their vice for free, that was illogical.

There was a traffic violation ticket tucked beneath the windshield wiper. He plucked it off and stuck it carelessly into his trench coat pocket. Then he got in and eased into the north-bound traffic on Broadway, thinking, Now I'm in the Manhattan fleet.

He kept up Broadway to Columbus Circle and took Central Park West to 110th Street and followed Convent Avenue up to 145th Street, passing through the campus of New York City College, his old home grounds, on the way. He was feeling melancholy when he turned over to pick up Broadway again. He made a U-turn at 150th Street, easing to the curb across from the apartment building where the porter lived, and sat studying the window.

The shades were drawn but slivers of light showed about the edges. The bird hasn't flown, he thought.

He got out and went into a corner bar run by people of Italian descent. A couple of colored prostitutes with dyed red hair sat at the bar, but all the male customers were white. He kept on through to the back and looked in the telephone directory. He found a Linda Lou Collins at the right address, put a dime in the slot and dialed the number.

"Hello . . . Jimmy?" He heard a note of anxiety in the contralto voice and it made him sad.

He hung up without answering.

When he came out he noticed how the neighborhood had changed since his school days at City College. Colored people were moving in and it was getting noisy. Already Harlem had taken over the other side of the street. This side, toward the river, was still white, but there was nothing to stop the colored people from walking across the street.

His thoughts intensified his feeling of melancholy. Poor colored people, soon they'd have to live on riverboats, he thought.

He drove slowly south on Broadway. South of 145th Street the Puerto Ricans were taking over, crowding out the Germans and the French. who'd gotten there first. It was like a dark cloud moving over Manhattan, he thought. But it wasn't his problem; he'd leave it to the city planners, to Commissioner Moses and his men.

The red light caught him at 125th Street. To his right was a ferryboat moving away from the pier bound for the New Jersey coast across the Hudson River. Looking eastward was Harlem, extending across the island to the

Triborough Bridge. Those poor colored people; they had a hard life, he thought. They'd be better off dead, if they only knew it. Hitler had the right idea.

The light changed and he shook off the thought and continued down beside the iron stanchions of the subway where it had come out of the ground at 129th Street.

They weren't dead, he thought, and that was a fact.

On sudden impulse he turned west off Broadway at 121st Street and went up the hill past International House. He came out on the winding Riverside Drive and passed the Greek letter fraternity houses of the Columbia University students and farther down, the modern apartment buildings interspersing the old stone houses of a former grandiloquence.

He felt as sad as he had ever felt in all his life.

But when he passed the Yacht Club basin at 77th Street the sadness began to leave him, and when he turned on 72nd Street and came to Broadway again, it was gone. He was back among the pimps and the prostitutes, the racketeers and the horseplayers, the has-been actors and actresses, cheap hotels and cheap people, the tag-end of Times Square. He began feeling like the Cock of the Walk.

Now he was a man of purpose again; a man with a purpose.

He kept down Broadway to Madison Square and turned east on 23rd Street to First Avenue, and south into the landscaped streets of Peter Cooper Village. He parked in front of a modern red brick apartment building which looked much the same as any other building in the Village and went inside.

He was feeling sorry for himself, thinking how unlucky he was. If he hadn't accidentally pulled the trigger and killed Fat Sam, the whole incident would have been just a joke. Now it was double murder; and that wasn't the end.

He rode up in the big silent elevator to the third floor, unlocked the polished pine corridor door of an apartment, and passed through a right-angled alcove into a large pleasant sitting room, the outside wall of which was one glass window closed off by bright yellow drapes. Handwoven scatter rugs decorated the polished pine floor, and the maple furniture was made to order.

A woman lay stretched out at full length on a long divan, watching a color television program on a built-in screen between two modernistic bookcases filled with books in the French and German languages. She wore a man's purple silk dressing gown and red pumps with heels like the stems of champagne glasses. In the soft white light from a parchment-shaded reading lamp, her skin had the dull gleam of polished ivory and her long black hair hung loosely over her shoulders like the folds of a mantilla.

"What is the trouble with you?" she greeted Walker. "You have gotten your mouth pulled down like the mouth of a fish." She spoke textbook English with a European accent. Her eyes were eloquent with passion, but she didn't move.

"You're a gorgeous piece, Eva," he said, looking at her with unveiled lust.

"Am I not?" she said. "But you did not answer me."

"I feel blue and depressed," he said. "Let's go to bed."

"Oh la-la." Her green eyes smiled indulgently. "You are like the men from my native Yugoslavia," she said, sitting up with slow, indolent movements. "Always sad and passionate. But you do not look like them, you look more Germanic and tortured, like the characters from Wagner's operas."

As though angered by the allusion, he said roughly, "You talk too much." He took her hand and pulled her savagely to her feet. "Go get undressed."

"You are too rough," she protested.

"Goddammit!" he exclaimed, dragging her into the bedroom. "Just be my whore and shut up."

He began stripping off his clothes as though in a blind rage, tossing them to the floor about the room. She was so frightened she undressed quickly also. But he was nude and groping for her before she had time to arrange herself beneath the bedcovers. He handled her brutally, taking her as though in a raging fury, gritting his teeth and mouthing obscenities while making love, as though any instant he might choke her to death.

His behavior terrified her. She could scarcely breathe.

Afterwards they lay panting and exhausted, without tenderness or rapport.

"You hate me when you make love to me," she accused. "Why is that?"

He didn't reply. He closed his eyes and turned away from her.

"You rape me each time," she said. "I think always you are going to murder me."

Suddenly she realized he was asleep. He had gone to sleep instantly.

Sighing, she got up and went into the big modernistic bathroom adjoining. She ran a hot bath and lay in it, thinking, I'd better get away from him. There is something wrong with him. He is not quite human.

He slept for about fifteen minutes and awakened abruptly, refreshed and alert. He heard her splashing in the tub and leaped from bed nude and went into the bathroom to take a shower. He was in the best of spirits, humorous and charming and almost playful.

"Don't get your hair wet," he said. "It feels funny when I kiss you."

She tied her hair into a ball atop her head but the ends were already wet.

"You are a funny man," she said.

"What's funny about me?" he asked in genuine surprise.

"Strange."

"Mm. . . . But you like me?"

"Sometimes."

He laughed and went into the glass-enclosed shower which was separate from the tub. He turned on needles of hot water and then cold. When he stepped out he was pink-skinned and goose-pimply. She was drying herself with a big wrap-around towel.

"Don't you have any *bidets* in America?" she asked. "Anywhere?"

"I don't know," he confessed, laughing. "I've never seen any."

She thought he was joking. "What do women do?" she asked.

"Get in the tub, I suppose."

"Every time?"

"There are not all that many times," he said.

"But suppose it is day and they do not have much time? Or they are in the man's place?"

"Wear contraceptives, I suppose."

"It is not for that, I ask. How do they clean themselves?"

He laughed so hard she began to laugh too. But after a moment, seeing him strap on his service revolver, she became sober and frightened again.

"You are not permitted to wear that anymore," she objected. "You will get into trouble."

"Who said so?" He spoke offhandedly as he continued dressing.

"You do not have your badge. You told me so yourself, and I also read about it in the newspaper, that you have been suspended."

"I've been reinstated," he said airily. He reached into his pants pocket and took out a duplicate badge. "See, here's my shield."

She looked at it suspiciously, suspecting a trick. She never knew when he was serious, and his strange, mirthful mood made her apprehensive. It frightened her badly to realize how much she feared him.

While putting on his trench coat he said, "Get the package I asked you to keep for me."

"Is it not too late?" she questioned. "You told me it was evidence, and you have taken it out before."

He stood stock-still and looked at her with speculation. The opaqueness had closed over his blue eyes and there were bright red spots on each of his high cheekbones.

But he said only, "You must remember I work at night."

"But of course," she quickly conceded and went into a small adjoining dressing room.

He stepped out into the sitting room to wait and relaxed by practicing drawing his service revolver. Then he realized she was taking too long. Soundlessly he opened her bedroom door and slipped inside.

She stood beside the unmade bed in the dressing gown she had put back on after her bath, her shoulders hunched, her head cocked slightly to one side. Hearing him in back of her she gave a violent start, and turned involuntarily to look at him. Her face was stark white and pure terror looked out from her wide green eyes. She began trembling from head to foot.

His gaze went directly to the unwrapped package on the bed. The long blue steel .32-caliber revolver with the silencer attached gleamed dully in the dim light from the single bed lamp.

He smiled at her sadly. "You looked," he said. "Like Lot's wife."

She backed slowly to the distant wall.

"Oh God," she whispered sobbingly. "You are the one who killed those men. You shot them with this pistol."

"You shouldn't have looked," he said and began moving toward her.

She would have run but she found herself cornered and the strength went out of her bones. She opened her mouth to scream and her lips worked convulsively but no sound came forth.

"I'm sorry you looked," he said.

He put out his left hand slowly and clutched her by the lapels of the dressing gown. She didn't resist; she didn't have the strength to raise her arms. She was immobilized, like a bird charmed by a snake, rendered powerless by the look of pure malevolence in his distorted face.

He began slapping her with his right hand; her left cheek with his open palm, her right cheek with the back of his hand. He slapped her steadily, as though in a dream; with an expression of detachment he watched her terror-stricken face pivot back and forth, as though it might have been a punching bag.

She kept her eyes open; she was too terrified to close them; and slowly they became senseless. Her head rang with a continuous tolling sound and her face became numb. She lost her sense of balance and the room began to rock. But he held her upright and kept on slapping her as though he'd forgotten what he was doing.

Finally she found enough voice to whisper, "You are going to kill me."

The words shocked him back to his senses. He released her abruptly and stepped back, exclaiming, "I don't want to hurt you."

She crumbled to the carpet, but still kept her gaze on him. His tall figure wavered in her vision and the floor seemed to rock wildly beneath her. But she didn't care anymore.

"You must kill me," she said in a faint, lisping voice. "Because I am going to tell that you killed those men."

He looked at her reproachfully. "If you do that, I will tell them that you're a Communist spy," he said.

She tried to laugh but couldn't. "They know I am not a spy," she lisped. "They have investigated me so often they know I am not a spy. But you are a murderer and I am going to tell them."

"Then I will tell your compatriots that you are a capitalist spy," he said. "You speak seven languages and you have often been seen with me. If I tell them you are a capitalist spy, they will believe me. Your people will believe you are a capitalist spy quicker than my people will believe that I have murdered two dinges. It's just a matter of what people want to believe. Do you want to believe me?"

She began to cry, her prone body convulsed with sobs. "Kill me," she begged in her faint lisping voice. "Please kill me. You will be safe then. Do not accuse me please of being a spy. It will make much trouble for me with everyone."

"I can guess," he said sadly.

"Please," she begged. "I will not tell. I will do anything you say. I am not a brave person. Please do not say I am a spy. I will not tell on you."

"I didn't think you would," he said matter-of-factly, looking at his watch.

It was midnight.

He picked up the silenced revolver from the bed, examined it to see that it was loaded, slipped it carelessly into his trench coat pocket and gave her a sad smile.

"You shouldn't have looked."

She sobbed without replying.

"I'll be back later," he said.

She didn't answer.

He went out through the sitting room and the front hall and walked down the corridor toward the elevator. His vision was slightly out of focus but he felt sober physically. It was his mind that felt drunk. He was going to kill the third dinge and go scot-free. If he had to plead insanity, she'd make another witness for his defense. But the beautiful part of it was if he could just keep his nerve he could do it in such a way that it could never be proved against him. Everyone might think he had killed them, but no one would be able to prove it. And he'd go right back on the police force as though nothing had happened. Because they wouldn't fire him if they couldn't prove him guilty.

15

The Big Bass Club was on 125th Street near Eighth Avenue, right in the heart of Harlem. It had the likeness of a bass violin inlaid in the tiled front wall identifying itself. In the glass-enclosed frame beside the entrance doorway there were numerous glamour photos of the entertainers. In her picture, Linda Lou Collins looked so much like Pearl Bailey as to arouse suspicions of the management's integrity.

The entrance opened into a public room with a bar curved like the side of a bass viol and booths along the opposite wall. The murals were composed of eight bars of various blues hits painted on the walls.

A curtained doorway at the back led to the private club where money was the only requisite for admission. It was another world, a Harlem nightclub for home folks, like nothing else on earth.

The atmosphere was both sensual and animal, thick, dense, odorous, pungent and perfumed. Bulls herded their cows. They were domesticated bulls but they were dangerous. Every man had his knife and wore his scars of conflict. Every bull had his cow with heavy udders filled with sex, smelling of the breeding pen, cows that had been topped again and again and wanted to be topped again indefinitely. Most times they were as orderly as bulls packed into any corral. But violence always lay cocked and ready in the smoke-filled, whiskey-fumed air.

It was a hangout for people whose business was vice—pimps, gamblers, racketeers, madames and prostitutes.

Aside from the Negro middle class, they were the only ones who could afford it. The prices were too high for working people. However, Negroes of the middle class—businessmen and professionals, doctors, lawyers, dentists and morticians—came when they were in the mood for slumming. The entertainment was good, but it was adapted for colored people. It had to be good.

The guests just sat and drank and listened and ate fried chicken when they got hungry and were entertained. There was no provision made for dancing. If they wanted to dance, the manager told them to go to the Savoy Ballroom where they had the space for it.

No one flirted with other men's women or other women's men. It was not a place to change partners, make dates or play eyesie and footsie with former bedmates. Everyone kept their passions in their own backyard and tended strictly to their own business. Yet sex was the most predominant factor of the overall atmosphere.

When Walker pushed through the curtained doorway, Linda Lou was singing: *"Come to me, my melancholy baby, cuddle up and don't you cry . . ."*

She was standing in a baby blue spotlight beside a white baby grand piano at which sat a slim dark man with shiny conked hair, making the soft run of notes sound like falling rain.

She was singing in that copyrighted Negro woman's blues voice which lies between soprana and contralto, and is husky on the deep notes and plaintive on the high notes, and has that slightly whiny sexy intake between breaths.

She wore a show-through scarlet evening dress that looked violet in the blue-tinted light; underneath, her wide-shouldered voluptuous body shook as though held in a passionate embrace.

She was singing directly to Jimmy, who sat enthralled at a ringside table beside a numbers banker—a squat dark man—and an overdressed "showgirl" who were complete strangers to him.

Her gaze flickered briefly to the white man seen dimly in the entrance, but he didn't interest her. Lots of white people visited there, musicians, racketeers and thrill-seekers, but they went unnoticed.

The manager was a big black rugged man who had for-

merly been a policeman. He went over toward the curtain
to head off Walker. He didn't welcome unescorted white
men who were strange to him.

"If you're looking for girls, friend, you won't find
nothing here but trouble," he greeted. "Why don't you try
the Braddock or Apollo bars?"

Walker smiled and showed his shield. "It's a free
country, isn't it?"

The manager studied his face.

"Looking for anybody in particular?"

"I just want to see the show, buddy boy," Walker said.
"Is there any law against that?"

"Nope. Go ahead and enjoy yourself," the manager said
evenly. "Just don't call me *buddy boy* is all."

Walker stepped past him and looked over the room. A
girl showing a lot of skinny brown shoulders combined with
an overpainted mouth in a way she thought was sexually
exciting leaned from a cubbyhole and said musically,
"Check you hat and coat, kind sir?"

He looked at her. Her eyes got bright with promise. He
looked away without replying and the promise left her eyes.
When he had spotted Jimmy, he moved toward the back,
still wearing his hat and trench coat.

The manager beckoned to his bouncer, a big black man
bigger than himself, who looked exceptionally hard-used
for his size. "Keep an eye on that chappie," he ordered.

"Shamus?" the bouncer asked.

"No, a city dick, but he's got a sad look, and I don't
trust cops with a sad look about them. They ain't sad for
nothing."

"That's no lie," the bouncer said.

Walker noticed them whispering and smiled to himself.
He could damn near guess what they were saying. He kept
moving along the back wall until he reached a place where
it was almost dark and stood leaning back against the
wall with his hands in his trench coat pocket, gently patting
the silenced revolver. The people at nearby tables glanced
up at him briefly, then paid him no further attention.

Linda had seen the whole play. Her attention had been
drawn again when the manager spoke to the white man,
and she had noticed his exchange with his bouncer. She

watched the white man through the corners of her eyes. When her act was finished there was a smattering of applause. She knew it didn't mean they didn't like her singing; these people just didn't believe in applause.

During her break she went over and sat beside Jimmy. The Jive Fingers, a rhythm group, took over.

Without asking their permission, the numbers banker ordered champagne for all four of them and tried to start a conversation.

"You sounded mighty good, Miss Linda Lou."

"Why don't you catch this act?" Linda said coolly, giving him the brush-off. "They're good."

" 'Scuse me," he said. "I didn't mean nothing."

Jimmy couldn't tell whether it was an apology or a rebuke. But Linda put her finger to her lips for silence, then leaned over and whispered in Jimmy's ear, "There's a strange-looking white man standing in back—against the wall. He keeps looking at us. Wait for a moment, then look around and see if you know him."

Jimmy felt his intestines knot. His voice stuck in his throat like a bone. He knew who it was without looking around. He started to look anyway, his head pivoting involuntarily, but she stopped him. "Not now! He's watching us."

"Let him watch!" he whispered fiercely.

But she clutched his arm, restraining him, alerted by her intuition. "No, don't let him see that you've seen him."

"Goddamn, Linda," he muttered, but obeyed her.

The numbers banker had his ears cocked, trying to follow their conversation. Linda caught him and gave him a furious look. He took a sudden interest in the act.

A waiter approached Walker and asked him to sit down. "It's against the rules to stand up in here, chief," he said.

When Walker turned his head to reply, Linda whispered, "Now!"

Jimmy gave a quick look, his gaze stabbing the dark shadows with the beginning of panic. He felt foolish and cowardly at the same time for being influenced by Linda to peep. But the instant he saw Walker's profile, he turned away quickly and was overcome by a strange sense of resignation that left him unnaturally relaxed.

"It's him," he said, forgetting to whisper, relapsing into a state of fatalism.

The numbers banker had resumed his interest in their affair and was peering toward the rear to see the man in question. But neither of them noticed. Jimmy had drawn into himself and sat with bowed shoulders and downcast eyes. He had built up such apprehension at seeing Walker again, he was left with a sense of letdown by his fatalistic mood.

"It's him all right," he repeated tonelessly. "The maniac."

"Listen," Linda whispered tensely. "Will you do what I tell you?"

"Why not?" he said.

"Then I want you to get up as though you haven't seen him. Kiss me good-bye, then stop at the checkroom and get your coat and hat as though you were going home. Then take a seat out at the bar. You'll be safe there. I want to see if he follows you."

Jimmy looked at her for a long moment. "You never have believed me, have you?"

"Oh, daddy, let's don't quarrel. I've got a plan."

"All right." Jimmy stood up and leaned over and kissed her. "I hope your plan works—whatever it is," he said and left her.

But the numbers banker had finally got the man spotted. He turned to Linda and said, "I don't want to interfere in your business, Miss Linda Lou, but if it's that white sport back there what's bothering you and your gentleman friend, I'll take care of him for you."

Linda watched Jimmy stop at the checkroom for his coat and hat, turning over possibilities in her mind. She decided to confront him and get it straight to her satisfaction once and for all.

"If you want to do me a big favor," she said to the numbers banker, "let me have this table for a while."

"Sure thing," he said, standing. "But I'll be around."

"Where am I going to sit?" his showgirl friend complained petulantly.

"Sit on you thumb, baby," he said, laughing at his joke.

She gave him an evil look but she got up to follow him. "You ain't as funny as you think you is," she said.

The next instant Linda had forgotten them. She turned back to watch Walker and saw him move casually toward the exit as though the show was boring him. She looked around and located the manager and when she caught his eye beckoned to him. He came over to her table.

"Who's the white man who just left?" she asked.

"A city dick. Is he bothering you?"

"Not me. He's shadowing my boyfriend. I want to talk to him."

He looked around. Walker was nowhere in sight. "He's gone."

"No he isn't. He's outside at the bar. He thought Jimmy had left but I told Jimmy to stop at the bar."

"Okay, little sister, I'll give him over to you," he said. "But if you can't handle him, give him back to me."

She gave him her glad smile reserved for special friends. "Thanks, General."

When Walker found Jimmy sitting at the bar, he was momentarily confused. All the seats at the bar were taken and the booths were occupied. He stood in the center of the aisle and let the black people move around him.

General came from the club and said, "A lady wants to talk to you, friend."

Walker was beginning to feel drunk. "What lady?" he asked thickly.

"The lady who sings. Linda Lou."

Jimmy heard him and it required all of his willpower to keep from looking around. Walker glanced once in his direction, then suddenly came to a decision.

"Right," he said and followed the manager back into the club to Linda's table.

"Sit down," she ordered.

He sat down and looked at her with a sympathetic expression. The manager still lingered. The Jive Fingers began harmonizing on one of their own songs called "Don't Blow Joe," and all over the place big and little feet began patting time.

Satisfied that Linda had the situation under control the manager left them.

"Take off you hat," Linda said to Walker.

He looked surprised but removed his hat obediently. His rumpled blond hair gave him a youthful, devil-may-care look.

She studied him openly, torn between curiosity and loathing.

"Why don't you let him alone?" she said in a tense, furious voice. "If you did it, like he says, you've already got away with it. So just let him alone."

"I don't know what you mean," he said.

"The hell you don't!" she flared. "You're following him about. He thinks you're trying to kill him too."

"Don't get excited," he said.

"Don't try to scare me too," she warned in a blinding rage. "I'm covered. Look around you. If you try to hurt either one of us you'll wind up dead. These people in here don't give a hoot in hell for who you are. If I tell them you're trying to hurt me they'll cut your throat and leave your carcass in some dirty gutter." She stared at him challengingly, breathing hard. "Don't you believe me?"

"I believe you," he said sadly. "That's what it all comes down to. Who believes who."

"Then get wise to yourself!" she raved. "Get up off of him. If you just hurt so much——" She caught herself. "What was that you said?"

"I said that's all it is, who believes who," he repeated dutifully. "You believe him. He says I'm tryin to kill him. So you believe him. You're his girl. Why not? What kind of girl friend would you be if you disbelieved him? But have you thought of the possibility that he might be lying?"

"He's not lying," she denied automatically.

He just looked at her. The voices of the Jive Fingers filled the silence: *"I'm gonna sit right down and write myself a letter, and make believe it came from you . . ."*

"Did you hear that?" he asked. "That's all it amounts to—*make believe.*"

"Shit!" she rejected scornfully. "Those two men are making believe they're dead?"

"But you're worrying about *who* shot *him,*" he argued. She stared at him without replying. "Someone right up here in Harlem," he said.

The suggestion jarred her but she rejected it from a sense of racial loyalty. "I don't believe it."

He sensed that he had shaken her. He pressed his advantage, "Look at it objectively. I'm the first person he saw when he regained consciousness after being shot. The first thing he said was that I shot him. *Me*! I had just come into the building from the street. One of the janitors unlocked the door to let me in. The charwoman saw me enter. The building superintendent was standing right there when I came inside. They took me down into the basement of a strange building and showed me into a room. A man I had never seen before was lying unconscious in a pool of blood. The first thing he says on opening his eyes, was, 'That's the man who shot me.' I doubt if he could even see me distinctly, he had lost so much blood. And you believe him. Does that sound reasonable?"

"Why couldn't you have shot him before?" she asked. "That's the way he tells it."

"That would have been impossible," he said evenly. "I was with a woman when he was shot. The police know this. The woman will swear to it. And there are other witnesses. Do you think I would be free if what he said were true? Do you think the police are imbeciles?"

He saw the doubt flicker in her eyes. "Then what are you following him around for?" she asked.

"I'm trying to keep him from getting killed." He sounded sincere.

She wore a puzzled frown when the manager came to tell her she was on again.

"Wait 'til I come back," she told Walker.

The manager followed her backstage. "How's it going?" he asked with concern.

"I don't know," she confessed.

She began with an old favorite, *"If this ain't love it'll have to do . . ."* Jimmy heard her over the amplifier in the bar and went back into the club to listen. But he saw Walker sitting alone at her table and stopped beside the checkroom, numbed by a strange bewilderment. He felt lost in a situation which he did not understand. What did she have to say to him? What was he telling her? He felt his legs trembling. He listened to Linda's twangy voice and watched her shaking body, but he couldn't meet her eyes. She looked at him from across the floor and tried to capture his gaze to tell him that she loved him with her eyes. But she couldn't reach him; he had turned away from her. Tears leaked into her voice.

The checkroom girl thought he was being two-timed and looked at him pityingly, but the next moment she was staring longingly at Walker's angular profile. That's life, she thought.

Someone in the audience cried for "Rocks in My Bed" and she took it and gave out. When she'd finished her act, she tried once more to find Jimmy's eyes but couldn't find them, and went slowly back to the table where Walker waited.

Jimmy turned away and went back to his seat at the bar. The manager came out and patted him on the shoulder. "Brace yourself, pops," he encouraged. "She's in there pitching for you."

Jimmy felt flooded with shame. She'd made it a goddamn community project, he thought bitterly.

Inside the club, Walker greeted Linda on her return, "Listen, lady. What do you know about him? What do you really know? How do you know he wasn't pushing H, or fingering for car thieves, or picking up for prowlers? How do you know what he was doing down there all night?"

"He wasn't doing nothing but working," she said. "I know him."

"How long have you known him?" he pressed.

She hesitated for an instant, then said defiantly, "Almost ever since he's been in New York."

"How long has that been?"

"He came up here the first of July," she answered reluctantly.

"A little over six months," he said derisively. "You haven't even known him for a year."

"I know him just the same," she declared. "It doesn't take long to know a man—if you ever know him. And I know he wasn't involved in anything crooked."

"Maybe *he* wasn't," he conceded. "But what about the other two? What do you know about them? Can you truthfully tell yourself that they weren't involved in some kind of dangerous activity?"

"Maybe, but I don't believe it," she argued.

"All right, say you don't believe it. That's what I told you at first. It's just a matter of what you want to believe." He sounded so earnest and sincere she found herself sympathizing with him, but she quickly put it from her mind and his next words brought back her suspicion. "But consider the possibility. They were involved in some racket. Someone from up here went down there for a showdown. Whoever it was shot them. Your friend witnessed the shooting, or accidentally appeared at the wrong time—"

"How do you know that?" She caught him up quickly.

"I'm just imagining," he said. "Whoever it was had to kill your friend because he was an eyewitness. But your friend got away. Whoever it was, your friend knows him. But he's scared to name him. He knows the minute he names him, his number is up. It might be someone sitting right here in this room."

His intense voice made Linda look about at the familiar colored faces: pimps, gangsters, numbers men, thieves. Could any of them be the murderer? She knew several men present who were reputed to have killed someone.

Doubt grew slowly in the back of her mind, and with it his image slowly changed. He looked so fresh and boyish in that atmosphere of crime and sex. He smelled of out of doors. She visualized him with a sweetheart somewhere. She'd be a nice girl who thought of marrying him. She'd rumple his shiny blond hair and caress him. But she mustn't be sentimental about him, she told herself sternly. Only it was so difficult to think in that atmosphere.

An instrumental trio—piano, bass and drums—had taken over and were knocking themselves out with a vulgar, old-time tune . . . "Yass-yass-yass!" some loud-mouthed drunken madam shouted. The joint began rocking and jumping, reeling and rolling. . . . It didn't make sense that this rawboned, bright-eyed young white man wanted to kill her Jimmy, or that he had murdered those other two colored porters in cold blood, Linda thought. . . . The instruments thundered and another drunken woman screamed uncontrollably, "It's your ass-ass-ass!" . . . It didn't make sense.

Wearily she brought her suspicion back into force. "Then what are you following him around for?" she asked.

"I could say what I told you before, I'm trying to keep him from getting killed," he said. "But I'd be lying. Look at it from my point of view. Your friend put the finger on me. He got me suspended from my job. He's put me under suspicion. If I was Jesus Christ from heaven, I couldn't love him. I hate him. But I don't want to hurt him. All I want to do is catch the killer. Look at it reasonably. I've *got* to catch the killer. Until I catch the killer, I'll be under suspicion. I'll never be reinstated on the force. There will always be people who'll think I'm a murderer. So I'm going to keep on following him until the killer shows himself. And the killer's going to try to kill him the first opportunity he gets. You can bet your sweet life on that."

The fear came up into her loins like sexual torture. Because if that was the way it was, she knew she couldn't help him. Someone had to help. Suddenly Walker appeared to be her friend.

"What can he do?" she asked desperately, tears welling into her eyes. "He can't just go on like this and get himself killed."

"The only thing he can do to help himself is to tell who the killer is," he said in a positive tone of voice.

Her face clouded again with suspicion and perplexity. "He'll only just say it was you."

"That will get him killed for sure," he said.

She put her face in her hands to hide her terror. "If only I knew what to believe," she sobbed.

The colored guests studiedly ignored them. The girl was in trouble, they concluded; that was obvious. That was the only reason a white man could make her cry. But it wasn't their business. Never butt in on an argument between a colored woman and a white man, was their maxim. The woman might turn on you.

Walker leaned forward and gently removed her hands from her face. He looked into her eyes intently and said in an intense, sincere voice, "Listen, Linda, you're the only one outside of himself who can help him. Make him tell you who the killer is. Swear to secrecy if you have to.

Do anything you have to do, but make him tell. Then you tell me."

"Oh, I couldn't do that," she said spontaneously.

He drew back. "It's his funeral."

She gasped sobbingly. "But what will you do?"

"I'll fix him so you won't have to worry."

"If it was that easy he'd have already told," she argued.

"You're missing the picture," he said earnestly. "He's scared the police can't help him. He knows if they arrest the killer, there will be someone else to do it. He figures the only chance he has is to keep buttoned up and maybe the killer will let him off. As long as he keeps fingering me, he figures he's safe. He saw the killer. Don't forget that." He hammered his statements into her mind. "He's got to name someone for the police. He can't say he didn't see the killer because the killer shot him in the chest. Do you understand that?"

She stared into his bright blue eyes as she listened to his hypnotic voice. She felt as though he were casting a spell over her. She tried to maintain a sense of logic, to keep thinking straight. But he was such an appealing man. She felt a strange desire to touch him. And he looked so innocent.

"What will be the difference if I tell you who the killer is?" she asked.

He leaned forward again and held her gaze. "I will kill him," he said.

She shuddered with a thrill of horror. It flooded her with sexual desire. She was repulsed by him and at the same time irresistibly drawn to him. He would kill a man, she thought. She looked into his eyes and trembled from a strange bewilderment. Their eyes were locked together, his subduing hers. She felt naked and powerless before him.

"If I get him to tell, how will I get in touch with you?" she asked submissively in a small breathless voice.

"You can telephone me." He gave her a number with a SPring exchange. "If you forget, I'm in the telephone book. Matt Walker, 5 Peter Cooper Road. Phone any time of day or night. I'll come up to your apartment "

She sighed. "I just hope I'm doing the right thing," she whispered doubtfully, as though speaking to herself."

"You're trying to save your friend's life," he said. "That's all you can do."

"I hope so," she murmured.

After a moment he asked, "How are you going home, Linda?"

"I'll get someone here to drive us. The man who was sitting with us. He's a numbers banker; no one will bother us if we ride with him."

"Numbers banker!" he repeated. "How do you know he isn't the killer?"

She shivered. "Please," she protested. "I can't suspect everyone."

"That's all right," he indulged her. "I'll follow you in my car. If you still believe that I'm the killer you'll be safe with him."

"Oh no!" she cried, covering her face again.

"If it happens that he really is the killer," he continued, "then you'll be safe with me following you."

Her hands dropped into her lap, the strength gone from her arms. Her eyes told him that she put her fate in his hands.

"One more thing, Linda," he went on. "Your friend will go home with you. He'll want to know what we've been talking about, what I've said to you. Don't tell him. Continue to act as though you believe him implicitly. Do you understand?"

She nodded meekly.

"Then you start working him around to being sensible. You know how to do it. As much woman as you are, you could make any man tell you his secrets. Work on him. Put that lovely body of yours on him. You know how to do it. In the meantime I'll park across the street on Broadway. When I see a light in his room, I'll come up to your flat to see what you've found out. Okay?"

She wanted to tell him not to come, but she found herself saying. "All right," against her will.

The Jive Fingers had just come on again and were giving out in a frenzy with: *"It ain't what you do but it's the way that you do it . . ."*

16

It was past five o'clock in the morning and it was close and still and very hot in her small sitting room crammed with junky furniture. She sat in a red-and-white silk upholstered imitation Louis Quinze love seat which had cost her a fortune in a third Avenue antique shop. She hadn't changed from her working clothes but her Persian lamb coat was flung carelessly across an overstuffed chair which had come from the Salvation Army secondhand store.

He stood in the middle of the red carpeted floor with his head bowed dejectedly. He still wore his duffel coat, buttoned up despite the heat, on which snowflakes had melted into glistening water drops.

"I just wished you hadn't talked to that murdering son of a bitch," he said once again.

She had her legs tucked underneath her and her shoulders were bowed as though in resignation. But she looked at him with an expression of intolerable frustration.

"That's all you've been saying since we got home," she charged angrily. "You act as if I wanted to talk to him; as if I had enjoyed it."

"It just looks like I'm hiding behind your skirts," he said.

"Why should you care how it looks? I just did it for you."

"I know," he admitted, looking cornered as though by his own knowledge. "I know you did."

On sudden impulse he went over and knelt on the floor before her, overcome by a sudden wave of tenderness. He seized her hands and kissed them and was engulfed by the smell of woman and perfume.

"You're all I got," he said. "If you don't believe me, who will?"

"Don't say that. You have your mother and your sister. You talk as if they were dead."

"Dead to me anyway. They're in another land."

She too was overcome by a sudden wave of tenderness. She stroked his kinky hair. It felt stiff and electric to her touch, inspiring an indefinable thrill.

For a moment neither spoke. It was as though they were enclosed in a tomb. No sound came from the sleeping building or penetrated from without. The double windows opening on the back courtyard were closed and curtained with heavy green drapes.

"I believe *in* you," she said stroking his hair. "That's more important."

He got quickly to his feet.

"Listen, Linda, this isn't a matter of semantics," he said. "This man is trying to kill me and he's killed two other men besides."

She sighed feelingly. "I'm sorry I'm not as educated as you are," she said reprovingly.

"Goddamn!" he exclaimed, scrubbing his face with the palm of his hand. "Now you bring that up, as though I'm the one who's guilty."

"It'd just make it easier for us to get a case against him and get others to believe you too if he looked more like the type who'd do such a thing."

"If he *looked* like a murderer?" he exploded. "What's a murderer supposed to look like?"

"I mean if he looked vicious," she said defensively. "Like some of those Negro-hating sheriffs in the South. It'd make more sense. But he doesn't act as if he's got any prejudice at all."

"Jesus Christ, I believe he's got you half convinced I'm lying," he accused.

"That just isn't so," she flared. "You started all this just because I asked you how well you could see the man who shot at you."

"Not *shot at me, shot me,* you mean," he corrected angrily. "And he's *the man.* I saw him as well as I see you."

"Well, from the way you first described what happened it didn't sound as if you hardly saw him at all."

He wheeled about and stared at her.

"You mean because I ran?"

"You said he starting shooting at you before you'd hardly seen him, without giving you any warning. You were coming up the stairs and the first thing you knew somebody was shooting at you—"

"Not somebody—*him*! And let me tell you something,

Linda. You don't know what it's like to have a man shoot at you without warning. There's no such thing as calling for help or shouting for the police or trying to reason with him to find ·out what it's all about. You don't think about justice or the courts of law or retribution or anything else like that. All you think is, *Run, man, run for your life.* But you see him all right. You see him in a way you'll never forget him."

She could just stare at him; he had almost convinced her again.

Then he added, "That legend on the county court building, *the true administration of justice is the firmest pillar of good government,* is just so much shit when a man is shooting at you."

It was something Matt might say, she thought, recalling his boyish looks, his intense voice and earnest blue eyes, and it didn't seem possible. *He'd kill the killer,* he had said, but she couldn't believe he'd murder two defenseless colored men and shoot at Jimmy without warning.

"Did he look like he looked tonight?" she asked. "You said the man who shot you didn't look angry or anything, didn't show any kind of emotion. Is that possible? For him to shoot you without any reason at all?"

"White men've been killing colored men for years for no reason you'd understand."

"In the South."

"It's still America."

"And anyway, they always had a reason—at least a reason that other white men understood, even though it didn't justify it. But no one can think of any reason for him to have done it."

"He had a reason. He's a schizophrene. Do you know what a schizophrene is?"

"Somebody with two personalities, one good and one evil."

"No. A schizophrene doesn't have any personality. He's out of contact with reality, with morality too. He could kill you in cold-blood murder and smile while he did it."

She shuddered. "If he's that far gone, wouldn't they know about it in the police department? Don't they have to pass psychiatric tests? They don't hire crazy men for policemen."

"They wouldn't have to know. That's the hell of it. He could pass the kind of tests they give. And maybe he was all right when he first went on the force. Maybe something happened to him since he's been a detective. Some of them can't take it. There are men who go crazy from the power it gives them to carry a gun. And he's on the vice squad, too. There's no telling what might happen to a man's mind who constantly associates with criminals and prostitutes."

"Wouldn't someone know? His wife, or his sweetheart if he's not married. His relatives, or somebody?"

"Not necessarily. It might have just broken out."

"I don't understand that," she confessed.

"He might have just gone crazy the night he killed Luke and Fat Sam. Something might have happened that all of a sudden sent him crazy, made him lose contact with reality. Some little thing. It didn't have to be anything big."

"Couldn't you explain that to the district attorney? Wouldn't he understand it?"

"I've already told the police of the Homicide Bureau. They think I'm too intelligent for my own good."

"Then what about the lawyer from Schmidt and Schindler? He's with a big firm. They must have a lot of influence to represent Schmidt and Schindler. Tell him what you told me. Ask him to have Matt—"

"*Matt!* You're calling him Matt now," he caught her up.

"He said that was his name," she snapped. "I'm not in the South. What difference does it make what I call him anyway? Why don't you listen to what I'm saying?"

"I am listening."

"Then ask the lawyer to have his brain examined— What do you call it when they test to see if you're crazy?"

"Psychoanalyzed. But you can't have a man psychoanalyzed against his will unless he's officially charged with a crime— and pleads insanity."

"Well, you can ask him, can't you?" she insisted. "It'll give him something to work on. All those lawyers he's with—they must be able to do something, all the gripes they have to handle for Schmidt and Schindler. You told me they serve a half a million people a day—"

"Yes, and do you know what those lawyers would say?"

"No, and you don't either."

"Listen, you know what you've told me about the white agents you've had. You ask them to try to get you into a certain spot—say the King Cole room at the St. Regis, or rather not that big, say some night spot in the Village. You think you'd be a hit; you're certain you can put it over. You have the voice, you have the experience, you have the looks and you have the personality. They know all this. It would look like they'd want to advance you for their own ten percent—"

"Twenty-five percent," she cut in. "That's what my agent takes."

"All the more reason," he went on. "But they say, no, you're a blues singer. As if a blues singer can only sing in blue joints for blue people. You say, Lena Horne sang there. They say, *Lena,* but you ain't Lena, baby, you're for the blues. You told me that you kept fighting with your agent for two years to get booked into that nightclub in the Village. It wasn't that the management didn't want to give you a trial —your agent just wouldn't book you. Two years before you could get him to do it. So after he's done it, he makes up your repertoire. You're not allowed to sing what you want, or what you sing best, or even what might make the biggest hit. No, he says, sing a spiritual, then a slave chant, the blues for an encore, then a social protest ballad, and another blues encore. Then after he's done this great thing for you, he wants you to pay him off with your body. And why? Because you're a colored singer and they think of a colored singer in just one way. They think that all a colored woman has is a voice to be directed and a body to be used. That's the way it would be if I go down and ask them to have this schizophrene psychoanalyzed. They'll think instinctively that I'm getting beyond myself, being too smart for a nigger, or that some white person put me up to do it, or that I'm trying to cover up something—my own guilt, perhaps. Chances are they'll think I don't know what I'm talking about. They'll try not to laugh in my face, and save it for a lunch table joke. You say yourself he doesn't look like a schizophrene. You don't even believe me yourself, because of how he looks—"

"That just isn't so," she denied.

"The hell it isn't so! Don't deny it. It is so! He doesn't look like a killer to you, and you're colored like me. How do you think he looks to them, who're white like he is? They'll

think I'm the one who's a schizophrene. Maybe you're beginning to think so too, since you've talked to him."

"Oh God Jesus Christ!" she cried. "Are you going to harp
on that all night? I've got a splitting headache."

He drew suddenly into himself. "I'll go then."

"Oh, don't be so touchy," she said, trying to control her
exasperation. "I want to help you—if I can. If you'll just
let me help you without keeping on throwing accusations in
my face every minute."

"You could help me, if you believed me," he said solemnly.

"Don't go into that again, please," she begged. "Just tell
me what to do and I'll do it."

"If I knew what to do, I'd go ahead and do it," he said.
"What I thought was, maybe we could figure out some way
to get him out into the open. Schizophrenes like to boast if
they have a sympathetic audience. Maybe you could get him
to confess to you—since you've got to know him so well.
Play on his vanity. I can't tell you how, but you ought to
know how, much experience as you've had."

She gave him an angry look. "Oh God, Jimmy, why don't
you try being honest yourself for once?" she said.

He turned to stone. "So you think it's me who's lying?"

She felt at the end of her patience. She buried her face in
her hands and stifled a sob. "I don't know what to think
anymore," she confessed.

He stepped over to the lamp table and picked up his hat.
He moved slowly, like an old man. He felt as though she had
betrayed him.

She scrambled to her feet and clutched him by his arms,
held him and made him look down into her eyes. "Stay with
me, honey," she pleaded. "Hold me in your arms. I need
you as much as you need me. Don't run out on me."

He held himself rigid and aloof. "I need you too, but
you've already run out on me," he accused.

Tears streamed down her face. She sobbed chokingly.
"You're asking too much of me. I'm not one of the strong
people. I'm just a singer of the blues."

"I'm just asking you to believe me," he said.

"You don't know how I feel," she said sobbingly. "I feel
as if my emotions had been taken out and beat with a stick."

"It's not how you *feel*," he said. "It's what you *believe*."

"I *want* to believe you," she declared, releasing his arms for a moment to wipe away her tears with the palms of her hands. "But we don't always believe what we want to," she added.

He stepped back out of her reach. He felt broken up inside. "I wish you hadn't said that," he said. "You've *got* to believe me—or we're finished."

"How can I believe you when what you say is so un-believable?" she cried hysterically.

He turned and started toward the door. "Good-bye," he said.

She ran after him and clutched him about the waist, trying to hold him back. "No. Don't say good-bye like that. I'll go up to your room with you—it'll be safer."

He shook her off roughly. "Goddammit, no!" he shouted. "I'll go my way alone."

17

Walker had brought the elevator up to the third floor; he had switched off the light and shut off the power. The doors could be opened but the elevator couldn't be moved.

He stood inside the darkened elevator and surveyed the darkened corridor through the Judas window. He had to stand close, with his eyes almost glued to the tiny diamond-shaped pane, in order to see the door to Linda Lou's apartment at the end of the corridor. He had been standing there for a long time. No one had appeared.

It was nearly six o'clock when he saw Jimmy rush into the corridor and slam the door behind him. He took the revolver with the silencer attached from his trench coat pocket and held it loosely in his right hand.

Jimmy headed toward the elevator, moving like a sleep-walker, looking neither to the right nor left. He felt castrated, impotent, horsewhipped. He was afraid to think, afraid of what he might do. He tried to draw in his emotions and nail them down. He was so tight inside that he felt wooden and his breath wouldn't go any deeper than his throat. But the emasculating notion persisted: His girl had turned against him for a white man, for a schizophrenic murderer who had already murdered two colored men and was trying to kill him too.

Halfway to the elevator was the green door to the service stairway. Impatience jerked him in that direction. His raging frustration wouldn't tolerate waiting for the elevator to come up from the ground floor where it always stayed that time of morning.

He snatched the door handle and jerked open the door as though he would pull it off its hinges. He was muttering curses under his breath and his head roared with such a fury of anguish and chagrin that he didn't hear the elevator doors being hastily opened.

Walker ran silently down the corridor on the balls of his feet, caught the door to the stairway before it had completely closed on its hydraulic hinge. He held the revolver shoulder high, muzzle up, in the pose of a marksman prepared to shoot at any angle.

But Jimmy had taken the stairs three at a time, goaded by his insufferable humiliation. He had turned at the landing and was already out of sight.

Walker leaped toward the stairs in headlong pursuit. He landed on the second step and tried to take the next three in one stride. His foot slipped on the iron tread and he fell to his hands on the landing. The revolver butt struck the concrete stairs with a metallic clatter.

"Goddammit!" he cursed softly.

Jimmy wheeled about on the fourth floor landing like a startled cat and looked down over the banister. For a brief, frozen moment his panic-stricken gaze locked with Walker's opaque blue stare. Again the maniacal face looked nine feet high. His mind exaggerated every sight. His eyes stretched as though they were bursting in their sockets and popping from his head. Then cold terror swept him in a freezing wave as he saw Walker swing the muzzle of the revolver up and around.

The next instant he was running. He was leaping up the stairs. He was running for his life.

He heard Walker scrambling to his feet. It urged him to greater effort. He strained his muscles to their limit. But it seemed to him as though he had never moved so slowly. He died with every step.

He rounded the corner as Walker rounded the corner below.. He ran crouched over and close to the wall. The instinct to live had subdued his panic. He was cold-headed now and his thoughts came crystal clear, like scenes lit by lightning. He knew he couldn't leave the staircase to turn into the corridor. Walker could catch up and shoot him before he could reach his door and get it open. On the stairs he could keep far enough ahead to keep out of range. But the stairs ended at the door to the roof above the sixth floor. If the door was open he'd still have a chance. He'd have the rooftops to run on, the parapets to duck behind. Maybe he'd find another door to another building unlocked and be able to get down the stairs to the street. But it all depended on the door above being unlocked.

As he leaped toward the fifth floor landing the door opened from the corridor and a colored man appeared. The man was grumbling to himself. "It's the fourth time this week that elevator's been stuck in the mawning—" Jimmy burst upon him so abruptly his eyes bucked wildly with terror. But Jimmy was just as terrified. Without stopping or breaking his stride, he wrapped his arms about the man and propelled him back into the corridor.

The man wrestled instinctively to defend himself. "What you tryna do, man, what you tryna do?" he shouted as though to subdue his enemy by the loudness of his voice.

"I'm not trying to hurt you, man, I'm not trying to hurt you!" Jimmy shouted in reply, trying to reassure the man of his peaceful intentions by the loudness of his voice.

For a moment they fought silently in panic-stricken fury. The service door closed slowly on its hydraulic hinge. Walker had caught up in time to hear the desperate conflict taking place in the corridor. He stopped and let the door close while trying to make up his mind whether to kill them both or wait for another chance.

"Turn me loose, man, turn me loose!" the stranger panted threateningly. "I'll take my knife and cut your throat."

"I'm not fighting you, man," Jimmy gasped. "You got to protect me."

His words spurred the man to frantic effort. "You tryna rob me, man, I know," he gasped.

"I'm not trying to rob you!" Jimmy shouted.

"Turn me loose then!" the man demanded.

But Jimmy had wrestled him down the corridor in the direction of his own door. Now the problem was how to keep him there while he got it unlocked.

"Can't turn you loose," he hollered at the top of his voice. "Unless you promise to come inside with me."

"Come in your house?" The man was outraged. He had relaxed a little but now he got buck wild again. "I don't play that stuff!" he yelled.

"It's not like you think," Jimmy kept hollering, hoping he'd wake up the neighbors. "I just want you to stand here."

"I ain't going for that right here in this hall," the man began shouting again.

"Man, goddammit, I'm being pursued," Jimmy shouted back. "Can't you see that? I just want you to stand here and protect me until I get into my house."

"Pursued?" The man looked up and down the empty corridor. "You being pursued?" He gave Jimmy another wild look and his eyes bucked white. Then he wrenched himself free in a burst of superhuman strength and ran toward the stairs.

Frantically Jimmy got out his keys. It seemed as though he would never get all the locks unlocked. He broke out in cold sweat at the sudden thought that the door might be bolted on the inside. As he fumbled with the locks he expected Walker to appear any moment. He couldn't turn his head because the various keyholes claimed his attention. He cursed his proprietors. All those mother-raping locks would get them all killed on their threshold some day, he thought in rising panic. Then suddenly the last lock clicked and the door swung inward. He rushed inside and wheeled about and didn't pause until he had all the locks securely locked again.

Then he leaned against the wall in a state of nausea while cold sweat trickled down his hot body like sluggish worms.

Walker had returned the revolver to his trench coat pocket and leaned against the wall of the staircase, feeling letdown and intolerably thwarted. It was just his goddam rotten bad luck, he was thinking. The black son of a bitch was a bad omen, like a carrion crow.

He was still leaning in the same position when the door into the corridor was flung open and a colored man came tearing through, his eyes bucking wildly and his skin powdered with gray. At sight of him, the colored man drew up short and his eyes seemed about to fly from their sockets. The man had started down the stairs but curved in mid-motion and went up instead.

Walker heard him run out into the corridor on the sixth floor. Then after a while he heard the door being opened again cautiously. He knew the man was up there listening for a sound of movement. Probably peering furtively over the banister.

He pushed from the wall and went slowly down the stairs. May as well let the Negro get on to work, he was thinking. None of them had long to be here. On the third floor he went into the corridor and kept on back to Linda Lou's apartment door.

Linda was expecting to see Jimmy when she opened the door. She was nude underneath a sleazy kimono. She wanted him to make love to her and was afraid he might refuse again. Her emotions were braced against another scene. At sight of Walker, her unbearable tension broke in a flood and she became instantly hysterical.

"Oh, it's you, the villain," she said in a gaspy voice.

He tensed for an instant, but relaxed when she went into a fit of hysterical laughter.

"I'm the monster," he agreed, smiling at her sadly.

He came in without being asked and closed the door behind him. His opaque eyes made a quick professional scrutiny of the junky room.

"Don't mind me," she said chokingly. "This is my natural manner. Just pull up a chair and make yourself at home."

She's light-headed, he thought.

She groped blindly toward the love seat and sat on the edge and buried her face in her hands. Her smooth brown thighs were exposed but she didn't notice. Her bowed shoulders shook convulsively.

He went and stood beside her and stroked her shaking

shoulders, slowly and soothingly. He could feel her vibrant flesh beneath the flimsy nylon kimono.

"You shouldn't have quarreled with him," he said.

"*Me* quarrel with *him!* My God!" she sobbed. "I hardly had a chance to say a word."

"You should have expected it the first time," he said, continuing to stroke her shoulders. "You shouldn't get upset."

"I shouldn't get upset! It isn't every day a girl has her sweetheart walk out on her."

The heavy revolver with the silencer in his trench coat pocket bumped gently against the arm of the love seat as he soothingly stroked her shoulders. He felt his palm getting electric.

"He'll come back," he said. "He hasn't got anywhere else to go."

The thought intensified her crying.

His legs grew weak from standing and he felt himself growing dizzy in the close hot room. He looked about for a seat but her fur coat occupied the only chair which looked reliable. He saw the worn ottoman beside the television table and brought it over to sit on. He removed his hat and sat down in front of her and took her left hand and began stroking it slowly and soothingly from fingertips to wrist.

She looked down and noticed her bare thighs were exposed and drew her kimono closed.

"Did you get him to talk at all?" he asked.

"Talk! How he did talk!" she exclaimed, bursting into hysterical laughter again.

"Don't worry about that now," he said, lengthening his stroke from her fingertips up her smooth bare forearm to her elbow. "Don't think about that now. We'll find some way to save him."

She became conscious of his hand gently stroking her bare arm. It sent tingles through her body like slight electric shocks. She wiped at her cheeks with her other hand and tried to control her convulsions. But her body kept shaking as when she put sex into a song.

"If he was only more passionate," she complained, her voice still choking slightly on the words.

"You're a passionate girl," he said in a low intense voice, and began stroking the upper part of her arm and shoulder. "You've got too much passion for the average man."

He had leaned so close to her that she could smell his damp ruffled hair. Her free hand touched it involuntarily and a shock went through her body.

Suddenly his hand closed over her breast.

She shuddered spasmodically.

His lips found hers in a hot blind kiss.

She put her arms about him and pressed her breasts against his coat. She felt the room going away in a stifling flood of desire.

An arm went underneath her legs and he stood, picking her up, and carried her into her bedroom.

It was like taking candy from a baby, he thought.

She didn't pay the slightest attention when he uncoupled the shoulder holster of his service revolver. She didn't appear to see him until he stood nude, then she said, "Oh," and when he lay in her arms she said "Oh" again. Then she matched her passion against his and hers was the greater.

She was already asleep by the time he had dressed.

He staggered from the apartment, pulling the door shut on the Yale snap lock, and found the elevator as he had left it. His legs kept buckling and he felt as though he had reentered a dream he had dreamed a thousand times before. It gave him an insufferable sensation of being outside of his own emotions.

At first, when he left the building, he couldn't remember where he had parked his car. He had forgotten entirely his reason for being uptown.

He began walking up the incline toward Amsterdam Avenue. Needle-fine snow slanted against his hot face and his coat flapped open in the wind. He'd gone half the long block before he remembered having parked his car on Broadway. He turned about and retraced his steps. When he passed the entrance of the apartment house again he suddenly remembered why he had come uptown.

He began feeling unlucky again. He felt intolerably depressed when he climbed into his car and began driving south on Broadway. He kept on down to 23rd Street, intending to return to his apartment in Peter Cooper Village, but as he neared it he thought of Eva and kept on past and turned north into Roosevelt Drive on the East River. He drove up past the UN building and entered the approach to the Triborough Bridge before reaching 125th Street.

His head felt as though it were ringed in steel. The left side felt definitely heavier than the right. He had to fight down the almost overpowering inclination to steer the car to the left, into the stream of oncoming traffic. It was so strong he had to grit his teeth and grip the wheel with all his might to control it. Still he felt as though he were driving on a road that slanted to the left and he had to keep the wheels turned sharply to the right to keep from sliding off. His teeth were on edge and there was an acid taste throughout his mouth.

He kept on turning on the clover-leaf bridge, feeling as though he were sliding down a scenic railway, until he came to the exit for the Bronx River Parkway.

It was a big superhighway split down the center by a continuous park, heading straight north toward Westchester County, cutting the Bronx in half. The limit was fifty miles an hour but the north-bound traffic was light at that hour and he eased the big Buick up to ninety, a hundred. The speed relaxed his tension slightly and by the time he turned off into Bronxville his nerves had quit jerking him about.

He kept on through the winding residential streets and stopped in front of a small ranch-type house made of plate-glass panels and natural pine with a huge fieldstone fireplace jutting from one end.

A blond, blue-eyed woman of about thirty-five, wearing a flowered plastic apron over a wool tartan dress, answered his ring. Her eyes flooded with compassion at sight of him.

"You're sick, Matt!" she exclaimed.

"Not sick, Jenny, just beat," he said, entering the front hall. "I want to go to bed."

They never kissed or indulged in any gesture of affection. But their casual instinctive understanding of each other showed they were very close. She wanted to ask questions but was restrained by the same undemonstrative trait.

"Take the guest room, it's made up," she said. "I'll fix some toast and coffee while you're bathing. How do you want your eggs?"

"I don't want anything to eat," he said rudely, heading toward the bar in the sitting room. He poured a stiff drink of rye. "Where's Peter and Jeanie?"

"They're in school, of course," she answered in surprise.

"Didn't realize it was so late," he muttered, gulping another drink.

"I'll fix you something to eat anyway," she said, containing her disapproval with an effort.

"Don't want anything to eat," he said crossly, like a little boy. "My head won't stand it." Then, in an offhanded manner, he asked, "Where's Brock?"

"Oh, he hasn't been home from work," she said innocently. "He stayed in the city last night—some special detail he's on."

"You know," he said slowly and deliberately, like a little boy telling his big sister a dirty secret, "Brock believes I murdered those two dinges."

He watched the horror flood into her face.

"Oh, don't say a thing like that!" she cried. "He's going crazy trying to get you reinstated."

He smiled at her sadly. "He does though."

"I won't hear it," she said sharply. "You go on to bed. You're sick and upset. I'll bring your breakfast as quick as I can."

She turned away and hurried toward the kitchen before he could say anything else. But he had said all he wanted to say. He took the bottle of rye and kept on through the sitting room to the guest room at the other end of the house.

He put the whiskey on the night table and peeled off his trench coat. Then, on sudden impulse, he took the revolver with the silencer from his trench coat pocket and went through the connecting bathroom into the master bedroom. It contained a double clothes closet with a hat shelf. He wrapped the revolver in a handkerchief and shoved it back into the far corner of the hat shelf, behind stacks of seldom worn hats and odds and ends of summer things. Then he returned to the guest room and finished undressing.

He was asleep when she brought in his breakfast tray. He was twisting and turning and gritting his teeth as though

in the thralls of a nightmare. She got a damp towel from
the bathroom and wiped his sweating forehead.

Poor Matt, she thought compassionately. He should
never have been a cop.

18

Where can I get a gun?

The one thought had possessed Jimmy's mind from the
instant he had stood trembling behind the locked door.

Four hours had passed. He hadn't undressed; he hadn't
even taken off his hat and overcoat.

He got up and left the house and went searching for a
bar on Eighth Avenue which he remembered having heard
was a hangout for muggers and stickup men, and where one
could get a hot rod. He found the bar and kept on through
to the back and sat on a stool.

A big fat black bartender with popeyes and a perpetually
surprised expression came down and swabbed the bar in front
of him.

"I want to buy a pistol," Jimmy said, lowering his voice.

The bartender jumped as though he'd been prodded with
a shiv and his already popping eyes bugged out.

"This ain't no hardware store, man!" he exclaimed in a
loud outraged voice, moving his arms theatrically. "This here
is a respectable bar. We sells gin, whiskey, brandy, tequilla,
rum, wine, cordials, light and dark beer and ale. Nothing but
alcoholic refreshments. Just name your drink and we got it."
He frowned with dignity. "Now what you want to drink?"

"I'll have a Coke," Jimmy said.

The bartender looked shocked all over. "Is you come into
my bar looking for trouble, man?" he asked challengingly.

"What you so mad about? What's wrong with drinking
Coke?" Jimmy asked.

With silent disapproval the bartender served the drink,
then stalked toward the front of the bar like an offended
rooster.

Jimmy twisted about on his high wooden stool and looked
for another soul-brother to approach about buying a pistol.

Several ragged alcoholics stood at the front end of the long mahogany bar, nursing empty shot glasses, but the back end, where he sat among the stools reserved for the elite, was deserted. Two loafers posing as businessmen sat at a front table beneath the small, diamond-shaped, stained-glass panes, reading halves of the morning *News*. In one of the booths along the wall, a drunken prostitute slept; in another a blind beggar sat drinking cognac, his seeing-eye dog half asleep on the floor beside him. None of them appeared to him as likely hot rod peddlers.

He turned his attention back to the rows of flyspecked bottles on the mirror-backed shelves behind the bar. In the center was a faded sign reading:

DON'T ASK FOR CREDIT
HE'S DEAD

Through the corners of his eyes he noticed the bartender looking at him furtively, trying to case him.

Time passed. He sipped his Coke. The bartender started inching slowly back in his direction. He took his time. He swabbed the bar in front of imaginary customers. He wiped off a bottle and polished a glass. He tried the spigots in the sink to see if they were still working. He rinsed out his towel. He acted as though he wasn't giving his Coke-drinking customer a thought in the world. Slowly he worked his way back like a purse-snatcher stalking a sucker in a crowd. He stopped in front of Jimmy and looked down at the Coke with a jaundiced expression.

"You oughtn't to drink that stuff this early in the morning," he said. "It'll ruin your stomach."

Jimmy swished the liquid about in his glass. The bartender reminded him of a schoolteacher he'd had as a youth down South.

"What ought one to drink in the morning?" he asked dutifully.

"Gin," the bartender said. "It calms the stomach nerves."

"Okay, put some gin in it," Jimmy said.

Slowly, with a great show of hesitation, the bartender took the gin bottle and stood it on the bar.

"You don't want it in that Coke," he stated more than asked.

"Why not?"

"If it's for tonic you want to drink it, you oughtn't to mix it," the bartender informed him patiently. "Gin and Coke is an after-dinner liqueur, like all them French cognacs—fixes you up for the sport."

"What kind of sport?"

The bartender's brows shot up in a look of amazement. "*The* sport."

"Oh, you mean women," Jimmy said.

The bartender shot him a supercilious look. "What other kind of sport is there?" he asked condescendingly.

He replaced the gin bottle on the shelf and stalked off again, looking disgusted by Jimmy's ignorance. But he didn't go far this time. He only went far enough to swab an imaginary speck from the chrome-plated beer tap. Then he came back like a precinct cop giving the third degree.

"Who sent you here, fellow?"

"No one," Jimmy said. "I just heard I could get one here."

"Who told you that?"

"I don't remember."

"You ain't thinking about some other place, is you?"

"No, this is the place. This is the Blue Moon Bar, isn't it?"

"What's left of it," the bartender admitted cautiously. Again he took down the gin bottle, put two shot glasses on the bar and filled them to the brim.

"I don't want but one," Jimmy said.

The bartender's eyes popped. "Can't you see me, man, big as I is?"

"Excuse me," Jimmy said. He lifted his shot and toasted, "To your health."

The bartender picked his up and emptied it with a swallow. "Cheers," he said, smacking loudly and licking his lips. "You're new here, ain't you?"

"Yeah, practically," Jimmy admitted. "I've been here about six months. I came from Durham."

The bartender thought this over. "North Carolina?"

"Yes."

"There's a good show at the Apollo," he said. "It's a matinee today."

"What about it?" Jimmy asked.

"Good show is all," the bartender repeated noncommittally. "You ought to catch it."

"What for?"

The bartender studied him carefully. "It's got some acts what might interest a man like you from Durham, North Carolina," he said just as carefully. "Got one act by two comedians you ought to like. One of these comedians says where can I buy a gun? Other comedian says you ought to go to the Apollo, man. First comedian says what for, man? Second comedian says you want to buy a gun, don't you? First comedian asks, they sells guns at the Apollo? Second comedian says naw, man, that's a theatre where a man can get a seat way up in the back row in the balcony, all by himself, nobody to bother you, nobody sitting on either side of you. First comedian asks how come all of that just to see a show? Second comedian says you want to buy a gun, don't you? First comedian says sure. Second comedian says that's the way I like to see shows."

The bartender looked hard at Jimmy to see if he had got it.

Jimmy had got it.

"Right," he said. "I'd like to see that show."

"I thought you would," the bartender said. "The price is right. Twenty bucks."

"Twenty bucks," Jimmy said. "That's all right."

"Best time to be there is around three-thirty," the bartender said.

"Three-thirty," Jimmy echoed.

The bartender lifted the bottle of gin. "Big or little?" he asked.

He lost Jimmy then. Jimmy looked at the shot glasses and looked at the bartender. "The same as before is all right," he said.

The bartender put down the bottle and stalked away in overwhelming disgust.

Suddenly Jimmy got it. "Hey," he called to the bartender.

The bartender returned with a great show of reluctance.

"Not too big, not too little," Jimmy said.

"That's what I always say," the bartender agreed, looking

relieved. "Give a woman that's not too old and not too young. Thirty-two is the age I like best in a woman."

"You and me both," Jimmy said. He motioned toward the empty glasses. "What do I owe you?"

The bartender filled the shot glasses again without replying.

"*Salut,*" Jimmy said, emptying his.

The bartender's brows shot up again. "Cheers," he said and emptied his. He licked his lips and said, "A buck, twenty."

Jimmy gave him two dollar bills, picked up a half dollar of the change. He slid from his stool and said, "I'm sure going to see that show."

The bartender smiled indulgently. "Have your sport, sport," he said.

Outside, a sand-fine snow drifted through the gray morning, stinging Jimmy's face. It wasn't yet eleven o'clock and he had to find some way to kill the time until his rendezvous. But he had decided when he left home that morning not to return until he had a pistol in his pocket.

He turned up his coat collar and walked down Eighth Avenue to 125th Street. Turning the corner toward Seventh Avenue, he came unthinkingly upon the entrance to the Big Bass Club. He was shocked by the sudden memory of the nightmare horror he had lived through since leaving there less than six hours ago. But he no longer felt helpless now that he knew he'd get a pistol.

"God helps those who helps themselves," his mother had often told him.

On passing a shoeshine parlor he turned in on sudden impulse and took a seat in the row of elevated chairs. A sign on the wall announced that shines were priced:

Regular—15¢
Special—20¢
Deluxe—25¢

"Regular," he said to the shoeshine boy.

The shoeshine boy gave him the silent treatment reserved for cheapskates and began dabbing liquid cleaner on his brown shoes as though thinking of more pleasant things.

In the back was a record shop presided over by a slim

brown girl with a petulant expression. It was too early for her customers and she leaned on her elbows on the glass-topped counter, leafing through a Negro picture magazine with a bored air.

Jimmy's thoughts went to Linda as the shoeshine boy worked with the electric brush. He felt contrite for having left her as he did. She'd probably been so worried she couldn't sleep, he thought. And if she'd happened to go up to his room and found out he'd left without notifying her, she'd probably be terrified. Maybe he ought to have slept with her, he thought. She became so frustrated when she went without loving. But goddammit, she always thought she could solve all of life's problems in bed, he thought resentfully.

The shoeshine boy gave the cloth a final pop.

"C'est fini," he said.

"Vous avez fait du bon travail," Jimmy replied.

The shoeshine boy's dark face flowered in a sudden white smile. "You was stationed there too, hey, man? In gay Paree?"

"No, I was in Versailles," Jimmy lied. He had never been out of the States.

"That's what I like about the army," the shoeshine boy said enthusiastically. "They'd just as soon station you in them palaces as not."

Damn right, Jimmy thought. Someone else's palaces.

But he gave the boy a quarter and told him to keep the change. He hadn't eaten that morning and the two shots of gin on an empty stomach had made him light-headed and ravenous.

Frank's Restaurant was across the street, but the lunch-hour waiters were mostly white, old-timers left over from the time it was a Jim Crow place catering strictly to a white trade, and he didn't like their condescension. So he kept on walking toward Seventh Avenue, past the solid front of grocery stores, drugstores, shoe stores, hat stores, butcher shops, notion stores, and Blumstein's, the biggest department store uptown. Across the street, bars abutted bars, all selling the same liquor and all doing good business. The doors of the two theatres—the Apollo, which interspersed a B-movie between shows by big-name Negro bands, singers, and a blackface minstrel act; and Loew's 125th Street, which dished up a double feature of western and gangster films—were closed and the ticket booths empty. Loew's would open first, at one o'clock; the Apollo at two-thirty.

The Theresa Hotel occupied the corner site. On its ground floor corner was a snack bar called Chock Full O' Nuts. Jimmy passed it. He'd never decided whether it meant the place was chock full of nuts, or the food, or the customers felt as though they were chock full of nuts after eating the food. He couldn't imagine anything more disagreeable than being chock full of nuts.

He passed the hotel entrance and turned into the entrance to the hotel grill adjoining the lobby. Sitting on a high stool at the counter, he ate a breakfast of fried country sausage, scrambled eggs, hominy grits swimming in butter, two slices of buttered toast, and coffee with cream, served by a sleepy-eyed waitress. It was a good breakfast for 90¢ and he tipped the waitress a dime.

The clock over the counter read 11:30 when he'd finished. Still four hours to go.

He went out and stopped next door to read the titles of books by colored authors in the showcase of the hotel book-store. *Black No More,* by George Schuyler, he read; *Black Thunder,* by arna bontemps; *The Blacker the Berry,* by Wallace Thurman; *Black Metropolis,* by Cayton and Drake; *Black Boy,* by Richard Wright; *Banana Bottom,* by Claude McKay; *The Autobiography of an Ex-Colored Man,* by James Weldon Johnson; *The Conjure-Man Dies,* by Rudolph Fisher, *Not Without Laughter,* by Langston Hughes.

Suddenly he felt safe. There, in the heart of the Negro community, he was lulled into a sense of absolute security. He was surrounded by black people who talked his language and thought his thoughts; he was served by black people in businesses catering to black people; he was presented with the literature of black people. *Black* was a big word in Harlem. No wonder so many Negro people desired their own neighborhood, he thought. They felt safe; there was safety in numbers.

The idea of a white maniac hunting him down to kill him seemed as remote as yesterday's dream. If he had seen Walker at the moment he would have walked up to him and knocked out his teeth.

It was a funny thing, he thought. He'd told the truth about the murders to a number of people. He'd told his girl; he'd told the D.A.; he'd told all the various police officials who'd questioned him; he'd told the lawyer representing Schmidt and Schindler. And none of them believed him. But he could walk up to any colored man in sight on that corner and tell him, and the man would believe him implicitly.

Looking up, he saw his silhouette reflected in the plate-glass window. Hair stuck out beneath the brim of his hat like wool beneath a sheep's ears.

"If I don't get a haircut I'll soon look like the original Uncle Tom," he said to himself, and turned in the direction of the barbershop south of 124th Street.

It was a big place with modernistic décor, six new chairs, and the latest in tonsorial equipment. It seemed specifically designed to make the customer defensive. All six chairs were occupied and most of the waiting seats were taken. The smartly uniformed barbers all had glossy straightened hair. Two manicurists were at work with their trays attached to the chair arms.

A brisk young woman in a glass cashier's cage asked, "Do you have an appointment, sir?"

"No, I don't," he confessed. "Do I need one?"

She gave him a patronizing smile, but a barber signaled that he'd take him on next, and she put away her smile.

He hung up his coat, put his hat on the rack and sat down and began absently leafing through *Ebony* Magazine. Prosperous people looked out from the pages. None looked as though they had anything to fear. Suddenly he began thinking about the killer and the horror returned. He wondered again what had happened to set him off; what had Fat Sam done or said? Or had it been Luke? The police admitted there'd been no sign of a struggle. So it had to be something that was said. But what could either one of them have said to get the both of them killed in cold blood? Jimmy knew that Walker was bent on killing him because he was the only one left to identify him. But what about them?

He was so engrossed in his thoughts the barber had to come over and get him when his chair became vacant. He slipped into the nylon gown and the barber wrapped a sheet of tissue paper about his neck.

"Just a haircut," he said.

The barber edged his hair with the electric clippers and feathered the neckline with the shears.

"Take some off the top," he said.

"You ought to have it straightened," the barber suggested. "You have just the right kind of hair; it's thick and coarse."

"You'd never get my die-hard kinks straightened out," Jimmy said, laughing.

"Oh yes," the barber said. "It'll come out soft as silk and straight as white folks' hair. I'll put a wave in it for you if you want."

Jimmy looked about at the other men with straightened hair. One man had his marcelled like a woman's. Then suddenly he thought of the detective sitting in the Big Bass Club talking to Linda, his thick blond hair shining in the dim light. Maybe it was the son of a bitch's hair that had caught Linda's fancy, he thought; maybe· that was what had made her think he looked so innocent. Colored women were simple-minded about straight hair anyway, he thought.

"How much will it cost?" he asked.

"Seven dollars. That includes the cutting. But it'll last you for a couple of months," the barber said. "You'll just have to come in and have it trimmed every two weeks."

"Okay," Jimmy decided. "Give it the works."

The barber wrapped a bath towel about his neck, then daubed gobs of heavy yellow Vaseline into his hair and massaged it into the scalp.

"That's to keep from burning you," he explained as he went along. Then he took a large jar of a thick white emulsion and began applying it with a wooden spatula. "This here stuff that does the straightening job is liquid fire."

"What is it?" Jimmy asked.

"I don't know exactly," the barber admitted as he began slowly working the straightener into the Vaseline. "Some say it's made out of potato flour and lye, others say raw potatoes and lye. Anyway, it's got lye in it."

Jimmy felt his scalp begin to burn through the heavy coating of Vaseline. "Damn right," he said.

Using a fine-toothed metal comb with a wooden handle, the barber kneaded the smoldering paste slowly back and forth through Jimmy's hair until the hair was killed to the roots. Then he combed it back and forth until it became as straight as threads of silk.

When the straightening procedure was finished, he took Jimmy to one of the row of bowls at the back of the shop and washed his hair in hot soapy water until it was thoroughly clean. What had been a thick mass of kinky hair was now a mop of dull black hair so straight it stuck to his head. The barber took Jimmy back to the barber chair and massaged his hair with petroleum hair oil to give it a gloss. After that he carefully combed it and set it in big rolling waves. He tied a net about his head and put him beneath the hot-air drier to one side while he began on another customer. When his hair became dry, the barber removed the net and Jimmy had a head of sleek wavy locks. The operation had required two hours.

He stood and looked at himself in the mirror. Having straight hair gave him a strange feeling. He felt that he was handsomer, but he was vaguely ashamed, as though he'd turned traitor to his race.

The barber stood smiling, waiting for a compliment, but Jimmy couldn't meet his gaze. He tipped him a dollar from a sense of guilt, paid his check at the cashier's cage, and hurried from the shop.

But the big two-faced clock atop a pillar in front of the corner jewelery store told him there was still an hour to go before the Apollo opened. He crossed 125th Street, stopped in the United Cigar store and bought cigarettes, and kept on up Seventh Avenue.

He found that he was hungry again. He had a yen for some good home cooking, southern style: pig's feet and lye hominy; hog maws and collard greens; stewed chitterlings with black-eyed peas and rice; roasted opossum and candied yams; crackling cornbread; fried catfish and succotash; and some blackberry pie; or even just some plain buttermilk biscuits with blackstrap sorghum molasses.

He'd always heard that one could find anything and everything in Harlem, from purple Cadillacs to underwear made of unbleached flour sacks. But he hadn't found anything good to eat. The big chain cafeterias had come in and put the little restaurants out of business. All you could get in one of them was grilled chops and French fried potatoes; roasts and mashed potatoes; side dishes of creamed spinach and Harvard beets, green beans and plain boiled rice; all kinds of cockeyed salads—crab salad and tuna fish salad and chicken salad and egg salad. The salad dressing manufacturers must have started that salad craze, he thought. Tomato and lettuce salad with Thousand Island dressing. What kind of turds would that make? They'd made a salad spread where you didn't even need the salad anymore—you just spread the spread on two slices of bread and you had a salad sandwich.

He wanted some good heavy food that stuck to the linings of a man's stomach and gave you courage. He was tired of eating Schmidt and Schindler food, luncheonette-style food, no matter how good it was supposed to be.

He came to a dingy plate-glass, curtained-off storefront which held a sign reading: HOME COOKING. It looked like a letter from home. He went inside and sat at one of the five empty tables covered with blue-and-white checked oilcloth. To one side a coal fire burned in a potbellied stove. It was hot enough in there to give a white man a suntan.

He chose hog maws and turnip greens with a side dish of speckled peas. He splashed it with a hot sauce made from the seeds of chili peppers. The hot dish with the hot sauce scorched the inside of his mouth and burned his gullet as it went down. Sweat ran down his face and dripped from his chin. But after he'd finished, he felt a hundred percent better. He felt mean and dangerous and unafraid; he felt as if he could take the killer by his head and twist it off.

He sat there sweating and drinking cup after cup of boiled coffee strong enough to embalm the Devil, until it was time to go.

The doors of the Apollo were open and two uniformed colored cops were standing in the lobby when he arrived.

Only a few people came for the movie which preceded the stage show. With the exception of five teen-agers down in the front row, smoking marijuana, he had the balcony to himself.

A gangster film was showing. It looked like a grave-robbing job done on the corpse of the ancient movie, *Little Caesar*, by a drunken ghoul.

Near the end of the movie a young colored man came in and wormed down the row and took the seat beside him. He was dressed in buttoned-up, belted trench coat and a snap-brim hat pulled low over his eyes. It was almost pitch-dark in the balcony but he wore dark sunglasses which looked as though he had glass spots in his black skin. He might have come straight out of the movie that was showing, Jimmy thought.

"You the man?" he asked in a husky whisper.

"Yeah," Jimmy replied in a whisper. "I'm the man."

He spoke so authoritatively the young man stiffened, thinking for the moment he might really be *The Man.*

"You the man what want a woman?" he asked.

The question startled Jimmy. He'd been expecting the man with the pistol. "What kind of woman?" he asked angrily.

It was the other's turn to be startled. "You *is* the man, ain't you?"

"Not if you're trying to sell me a woman," Jimmy said.

"Well, how old a woman would you buy if you was buying a woman?" the young man tried again.

"Oh," Jimmy said, getting it at last. "A thirty-two-year-old woman."

The other breathed in relief. "You is the man," he acknowledged.

With a pageantry of caution, he took a package wrapped in brown paper from beneath his coat and handed it to Jimmy.

Jimmy started fishing for his pocketbook, but the other said, "Go ahead and look at it, man."

Jimmy opened the package. A blue-steel .32-caliber revolver gleamed dully in the dim light. It had an iron butt with a corrugated grip and the replica of an owl's head imprinted on one side. Brass shells looked like dead birds' eyes staring from the cylinder chambers. It looked deadly in the dim light.

"It looks fine," Jimmy said.

"It'll kill a rock," the other said. "If you're close enough to it."

Jimmy paid him twenty dollars. The young man stored it away in some inside pocket beneath the buttoned-up trench coat and said, "See you, man," and left just before the lights came on.

Jimmy sat looking at the gun in the light. There was no

one near enough to observe him. Suddenly he felt secure.
He'd lay for him in the downstairs hall of his apartment
house, he thought. He'd wait until the son of a bitch drew
the pistol with the silencer, then he'd kill him. He wasn't
apprehensive or excited. He wasn't scared of what might
happen to him afterward. He looked at it objectively, as
though it concerned someone else. He'd kill the son of a
bitch with the pistol in his hand, and then they could all believe whatever in the hell they wanted to believe after that.

He had a pistol too now. He had evened up the difference. He stuck the pistol against his belly, underneath his
belt, and buttoned up his coat. He got up to go.

19

Linda was in the downstairs hall of the apartment house
when Jimmy arrived. She gripped him by the arm.

"Don't scare me like that," she said tensely. She looked
furious. "I've been waiting here for hours, afraid to move."

"What the hell for?" he said roughly. "You don't believe
I'm in any danger."

"You fool!" she said.

He tried to move her hand from his arm. She wouldn't let
go.

"No," she said. "You're coming with me."

They rode up in the elevator in silent conflict, neither
looking at the other.

When the elevator stopped on the third floor, she tugged
at his arm. He pulled back. She backed against the door to
keep it from closing.

"Goddammit, come on!" she cried. "I'm going to put you
to sleep. When I get through rocking you you'll want to go
to sleep and never wake up."

"You're the one who's a fool," he said, but he left her drag
him from the elevator.

She held to his arm like a cop making an arrest and didn't
let go until she had her key in the lock.

It was dark in the apartment. She switched on the overhead

light and closed the door. Then she turned and gripped him by both arms as though she would shake him.

"Now you listen to me—" she began. She broke off and stared at him appraisingly. "You look different," she observed. "You got a haircut. While I was worrying myself sick there you were—" She stopped. Her eyes widened. She took off his hat. "Oh, daddy, you've got new hair!" she exclaimed rapturously. She ran her fingers through his oily locks, rumpling his waves. "It's soft as silk." She gave him an adoring smile and cooed, "Daddy, you look beautiful."

Then she went as sweet as sugar candy. Her big brown eyes got limpid and her mouth got wet. Her body folded into his. He could feel her pointed breasts through the thickness of their coats.

He pulled her tight against him. His lips melted into hers. Right then he would have given everything to be free of his horror and fear and the terrifying knowledge that a mad killer was stalking him. He peeled back her coat and buried his mouth in her neck. He could hear her gasping.

Her hands fumbled with the buttons of his overcoat as she pressed her body hard against his. She got it open and opened his suit coat. Her hand moved down from his chest. It touched the handle of the .32-caliber revolver stuck beneath his belt. She said "Oh!" Her hand closed about the grip. She said "Oh!" again in a different tone of voice.

Her body stiffened. She jerked her body from his embrace, flung open his coat, and pulled the pistol out.

"Jesus," she said in sudden cold shock.

"Give it here," he said and reached for it.

"No! No! No!" she cried, holding it out of his reach.

"Goddammit, give it here!" he shouted and lunged toward her, clutching at her wrist. "That isn't any plaything!"

"You fool!" she muttered.

She twisted sideways, holding the pistol extended, and bumped him with her hip. He grabbed her by the shoulders and tried to turn her around.

"That thing's loaded," he warned.

She wrenched loose from his grip and butted him with her solid hips, knocking his feet from under him. She tried to run but he grabbed her about the neck like a drowning man clutching at a log. She kept running and carried him half-

way across the sitting room as he hung on. His weight made
her stumble and fall to her knees, and she was unable to
brace herself because she still held the pistol extended. He
landed heavily on her back, flattening her to the carpet.

"You can't have it," she panted as she squirmed about
beneath him.

He clung to her neck and tried to inch up her back. Their
heavy coats hampered their movements and their bodies began to steam in the close hot room.

She made a sudden turn and rolled over beneath him. He
grabbed at the love seat with one hand, trying to get an-
chorage, but missed it, and she slipped from his grip. When
she tried to stand up he made another sudden grab for her
wrist. He got hold of her coat sleeve and pulled her down
again. She kept twisting and they smashed into the spindle-
legged lamp table and knocked it over. A leg broke with a
crashing sound and the alabaster lamp thudded on the floor.

Her struggles ceased automatically.

"You're breaking up my furniture!" she screamed.

"Goddamn your furniture," he muttered and lunged toward her like a swimmer.

Before she could move again he had captured both of her
wrists.

"Goddamn you!" she grated in a raw fury. "You broke my
table."

She tried to hit him in the face but couldn't free her hand.
She twisted beneath him in a blind rage, threshing about
like harpooned fish. He pinned her wrists to the floor, flattening her on her back, and sat astride her stomach. She
ceased struggling and spat in his face.

"I'll pay you back," she said through gritted teeth. Her face
was swollen with rage.

"Let it go, goddammit," he muttered.

She released her grip on the pistol. "All right, go ahead
and take it," she grated. "And I hope you get yourself killed."

He knocked the pistol out of reach and started to get up.
But something about the way she lay touched off his passion
like an electric shock. Her skirt had hiked up to her sky-blue
nylon panties, exposing a smooth brown sheen of legs
above her stockings. The violent exertion had opened her
pores and a strong compelling odor of woman and perfume

came up from her like scented steam. He felt his mouth fill with tongue and his stomach drain down to his groin.

"I'm going to take it all right, goddammit," he mouthed, and reached down and opened her legs.

It didn't need any force; they opened at his touch.

They made love in a sweating rage, as though trying to kill one another. They uttered strange guttural sounds as though cursing one another in a savage tongue. When they had finished, neither could move. They lay waiting for strength to return, panting for breath.

Then he stood up and buttoned his clothes and straightened his overcoat. He picked up the pistol without looking at her and stuck it back into his belt. The air was fecund with the mating smell. He didn't speak.

She stood up then and began shaking her skirt down like a pullet rustling its tail feathers. Her attention went first to the broken table. She tried to stand it up before removing her coat. But it wouldn't stand on three legs.

"You've broken my favorite antique," she said accusingly, but she didn't sound angry anymore.

"It's more of an antique now," he said unsympathetically.

She threw him a reproving look. But she was drained of rancor. She felt almost light-hearted with a warm afterglow.

"You'll have to have it fixed," she said and propped it against the wall.

"Of course," he said.

She picked up the alabaster lamp and set it on the table close to the wall so it wouldn't topple off. Then she switched it on to see if it was broken. She acted as though she'd forgotten all about the pistol.

The light came on, shining up into her face, highlighting her softly molded features in exotic relief. Sweat was beaded on her upper lip.

Finally she sighed. "Now I suppose you want to take your pistol and go out and shoot him," she said, half in derision. "Or have I got some sense into you?"

"He's got his pistol and I've got mine," he said stubbornly. "That makes us even now."

"Come on and go to bed," she said. "I'm not going to let you go until you've got some sense."

"To you that's the only thing that makes any sense," he said harshly.

"Well, isn't it?" she said.

He didn't answer.

She took off her fur coat and threw it carelessly across the armchair. "I'll make us some drinks," she said and started toward the kitchen.

"I'm not going to stay," he said.

She turned and looked at him tentatively. Then she walked up to him, cupped his face in her hands, drew it down and kissed him, forcing her tongue between his teeth.

He pushed her away and picked up his hat from the floor.

"Leave the pistol here," she pleaded.

"Hell no," he said.

"Two wrongs don't make a right," she argued. She still felt she could persuade him to give her the pistol.

But she only infuriated him. "Goddamn the morality of it!" he flared. "We can stand here and argue all night about what's right and what's wrong. You've got your opinion and I've got mine. You can't convince me and I can't convince you. People have been arguing a thousand years about right and wrong. I'm finished with that. I'm going to kill the schizophrenic bastard and keep on living myself."

The warm afterglow left her and her loins turned icy cold.

"You sound more like a crazy killer than he does," she charged. "You sure it's not you who is persecuting him, instead of the other way around?"

"I ought to slap you in the mouth for that," he said.

"Go ahead and slap me," she taunted him. "Draw your big pistol and shoot me. Everybody is persecuting mama's boy and he's got to knock everybody around. Next thing you'll be saying is that I'm trying to kill you too."

His neck swelled from holding his temper. He gave her a long, appraising look. "You know, Linda, you don't sound like a colored woman," he said thoughtfully. "You've been taking up for this white bastard ever since you talked to him."

"You don't think I'm colored do you!" she exclaimed and began tearing off her clothes in a fury of defiance. She didn't stop until she was stripped to her stockings and garter belt. "Do I look like I'm white, or do you want to see some more?"

His hair-trigger passion flared again, but he held himself in. "Listen," he said slowly. "Last night when I left you here he was laying for me in the hall outside. I took the stairs just on impulse instead of taking the elevator. I'm sure he was hiding in the elevator and if I'd stepped inside of it he'd have shot me. As it was he followed me up the stairs and if he hadn't slipped and made a lot of noise I'd be dead right now."

"He's admitted he's following you," she said without bothering to put her clothes back on. "He's just trying to trap the killer, he says. If that doesn't make sense, why hasn't he killed you before now?"

"He hasn't had a chance, that's why."

"Then why didn't he kill you last night—or this morning rather? Just because he slipped and you saw him shouldn't have made any difference, the way you tell it. He'd have been glad for you to see him shoot you, according to your story."

"Because I ran, that's why. Because I lit out and ran for my life, just like I did the first time. He had the pistol in his hand. The same one with the silencer attached. The one he killed Luke and Fat Sam with. And shot me with. Listen, I'm going to tell you just exactly how it happened."

She felt herself turn to ice all over as she listened to his story. If what he said was true, she'd slept with Matt right after he'd tried to kill him.

"I can't believe it," she said in a horrified tone of voice.

"I'm not trying to make you believe it anymore," he said and put on his hat. "And I'm not going to run anymore. I'm through with that shit."

He walked out and slammed the door behind him.

She rushed into her bedroom and snatched the telephone from the night table as though to rip out the cord. Her fingers trembled as she dialed Walker's number.

"If I find out he's telling the truth I'll stab out your heart myself," she raved, speaking aloud to herself.

Walker's number didn't answer.

Her imagination began to work. Maybe Walker was somewhere in the building still. If Jimmy ran into him he might shoot him on sight; she wasn't sure any longer what Jimmy might do. But Walker was more used to handling pistols than

Jimmy. If he saw Jimmy draw, he'd beat him to the draw. She imagined them in a gun duel on the service stairway. One falling dead, rolling head over heels down the stairs. Which one?

Sudden terror sent her flying to the bathroom. Then she went into the kitchen and drank a glass of gin. She sat down but she didn't feel the cold plastic seat on her bare skin. Panic kept coming up inside of her like the taste of vomit.

Suddenly she jumped up and ran into the sitting room. She'd have to find out whether Matt was in the building. She started out of the door without realizing she was undressed. A man was coming from the apartment across the hall. His eyes bucked as though he'd hit a hundred-dollar jackpot. His gaze focused on one point of her anatomy.

She drew back and slammed the door in his face. She grabbed her clothes from where she'd thrown them on the floor. She was frantic with haste. She had started out again when she got on her dress, then stopped and slipped into her fur coat.

This coat will be worn out before I get it paid for, she thought absently.

Outside, the man from across the hall was waiting patiently. She made for the elevator. He followed her. She rode up to the top floor and walked to the service stairs. He kept following her. She started down the stairs. He closed up and took her by the arm.

"How about my apartment, sugar, it's cozier," he said.

She swatted him in the face with the palm of her hand.

He backed away and felt blood dripping from his nose. He took out his handkerchief to staunch the blood. She continued on down the stairs. He called after her, "You is crazy, sure enough. I thought you was crazy."

She kept down the stairs to the entrance foyer, walked to the back of the hall and tried the door leading to the basement stairs. It was locked. She went to the front of the hall beside the entrance and sat down on the hard wooden straight-backed bench beside the door.

People came and went. Married couples eyed her furtively: the husbands with secret longing, the wives with secret envy, each hiding it from the other. Single women eyed her jealous-

ly. Most of the single men made passes at her, and several
of the single women. Some sat down beside her, but the atmosphere was too cold for comfort.

She sat there for an hour in a cold numb panic, scarcely
noticing the people who spoke to her. She was watching for
Walker.

Suddenly it occurred to her that Jimmy might not be in
his room. He might have gone out looking for Walker.

She jumped up and took the elevator back to her apartment and telephoned Jimmy's apartment. The girl, Sinette, answered. She said she would see if Jimmy was in his room. A
moment later she said, "He hasn't come back since he went
out this morning. Is that you calling, Miss Collins?"

"Yes," Linda said. "When he comes home have him call
me at once, please."

She started to go back to the bench beside the entrance and
take up her watch again. Then she realized it would be use-
less. She might be able to stop it from happening for a time,
but as long as Jimmy had the gun and Matt kept following
him about, one of them was certain to be killed.

She felt herself going dead inside. She went back to the
kitchen and swallowed four shots of gin in rapid succession.
Then she went into her bedroom and dialed police headquarters.

A tired voice said, "Central Police."

"I'd like to talk to someone in the department that in-
vestigates murders," she said.

"About what?" the voice asked indifferently.

"I'd like to talk to the person who's investigating the murders at the Schmidt and Schindler luncheonette at—"

"You mean the automat murders," the voice said, taking
on a slight interest. "Just hang on, I'll turn you over to
homicide."

The voice from homicide told her to come down to the
Homicide Bureau on Leonard Street and ask for Sergeant
Peter Brock.

20

When Walker awakened, the room was dark. The shades were drawn. He had no idea what time it was.

He felt a sudden sense of danger. He became alert in every nerve, tense in every muscle. He lay still without breathing. He strained his ears to listen.

But he heard only the muted sound of the television from the adjoining sitting room. Then he heard Jeanie scream with laughter, and Peter Junior shout, "Hush!"

He knew that Jenny had told them to keep quiet because he was asleep in the guest room. He sensed that they resented his presence. But the sense of danger was something different. It was imminent, as though a reckoning were closing in upon him.

Finally he moved his arm and looked at the luminous dial of his wristwatch. The radiant hands pointed to 6:31. He had slept all day. He felt as though he had wasted precious time.

He switched on the reading light and felt along the floor for the bottle of rye. His hand encountered nothing. He turned over on his side and craned his neck to peer over the edge of the bed. He saw nothing but the dark green carpet. He leaned over to look underneath the bed. It was gone. That was more of Jenny's doings.

He felt the need of a drink bad. But there was no way of getting to the liquor cabinet in the sitting room with the children there. He damned Brock's children to hell.

With an abrupt movement he stood up. He'd slept nude but there was a fresh pair of pajamas and a bathrobe hung across the back of a chair. They were Brock's, he knew. He thought of that saying that came out of the war: Kilroy was here. Only it was Jenny who had been here.

But it wasn't that.

He put on the robe. It was too big for him. He hadn't realized Brock was so much thicker than himself.

He kept looking about the room. His sixth sense kept sounding the danger alarm. But it was something he couldn't see.

His clothes had been hung up, he noticed. His holstered service revolver had been hung from a chair back by the strap. That was strange. Jenny didn't like the sight of pistols. He knew that she had come in and straightened up while he was asleep.

But it wasn't that.

He opened the clothes closet and looked into his coat pockets for cigarettes and his lighter. His sixth sense sounded danger like a burglar alarm. He stiffened. Suddenly he knew his clothes had been searched. He didn't know how he knew it, but suddenly it was fact. The presence of the searcher was as strong as a scent.

"Brock," he muttered softly to himself. "What the hell is his game?"

He felt the danger closing in. It was as though he were being cornered by hounds of retribution.

I'll have to finish it tonight, he told himself. It can't go on any longer. I'll have to finish off the last Negro and ditch the gun.

It was as though the pistol had turned red-hot. It was the pistol that would hang him.

He went quickly into the bathroom and put his ear to the panel of the adjoining door. He could hear the muted sounds of the television, but nothing else.

They'd all be eating soon, he reckoned. They usually ate dinner at 6:30 in the winter, but they were probably waiting on him to awaken. Jenny would no doubt be in the kitchen. She fixed the meals herself and had the colored girl serve. By now Brock should be home. He always thought of Brock by his family name. But Brock would probably be downstairs in his workroom.

He knocked gently on the door panel. There was no answer. He knocked louder. He didn't expect an answer, but he wanted to make sure. Silently he turned the knob and pushed. The door didn't budge. He pushed harder, then leaned his weight against it softly.

"Bolted from the other side," he muttered.

Never to his knowledge had they locked the bathroom door.

That smart son of a bitch! he thought.

He wondered how much Brock knew. His teeth clenched and the taut muscles rippled down his jaws. He had to fight down the rising panic. Had Brock found the gun, or was he just guessing?

There was a door from the guest room to the sitting room on one side, and to the adjoining bath on the other. Brock's and Jenny's bedroom opened into a hall that ran in back of the sitting room to the dining room and another short hall that led to the kitchen and the garage. In order to get into their bedroom with the bathroom door locked, he would have to pass through the sitting room and dining room.

"The clever bastard," he said softly.

He'd have to wait until they were all at dinner and then find some excuse to leave the table for a moment. It would have to be a good excuse because Brock would be watching him. He could act as though he were suddenly nauseated and had to rush to the toilet. That would be crude, but it would be believable.

He got under a cold shower and stayed as long as he could bear it. The tension didn't leave him but the panic subsided. While he was toweling himself he heard someone open the bedroom door. His stomach knotted.

"Matt." It was Jenny's voice. He realized he'd been holding his breath.

"Yes, Jenny."

"Hurry up. Dinner's on the table."

"Coming right away."

He heard her leave and close the door behind her.

He dressed hurriedly. He was in a frenzy of haste to see the expression in Brock's eyes.

The sitting room was empty when he passed through. Two television stools sat side by side, facing the dead screen. He kept on through to the dining room, bracing himself to meet his brother-in-law.

Everyone was seated. Brock sat at one end of the table, Jenny at the other. There was a place for him across from the two children.

A sepia-colored girl was serving grapefruit halves.

As he walked behind the children to get to his place, he rumpled Peter's hair. Peter was nine. He moved his head in a gesture of displeasure.

" 'Lo, uncle Matt," he said grudgingly.

His hand moved on to Jeanie's head. She was eleven and wore her hair in pigtails. She reacted to his gesture like a kitten, smiling up at him.

He took his seat and unfolded his napkin. Finally he met Brock's gaze. There wasn't anything in Brock's eyes.

"Jenny said you were working all last night," he said.

"Yeah," Brock said. "On the automat murders."

Jenny's face contorted with revulsion. "Do we have to talk about that at the dinner table?" she said sharply.

They finished their grapefruit in silence. The girl removed the plates and brought in a leg of lamb and serving dishes containing peas and carrots, whipped potatoes and a sauce. Brock carved and served the roast and Jenny the vegetables as the plates circled the table. The girl served individual plates of mint gelatin salad. There was a napkin-covered basket of poppyseed rolls. The children drank milk with their dinner; the grownups water.

Matt forced down a mouthful of the roast.

"How do you feel now?" Jenny asked.

"Fine," he said. Then he turned to Brock and asked, "No word of my girl friend as yet?"

"Not that one," Brock said. "We ran across another one."

Matt knew the answer but he had to ask anyway. "What one was that?"

The children stared at him with silent curiosity.

"Eva Modjeska," Brock said.

"She must be a foreigner," Peter piped up.

"Children should be seen and not heard," Jenny rebuked him sharply.

Matt felt the tension growing in his chest and tried to control his breathing. "How did you run across her?" he asked between breaths.

"Coincidence," Brock said. "Somebody called homicide and said there was a murdered woman at that address."

The breath turned rock hard in Matt's chest.

"If you're going to discuss murders, you'll both have to leave this table," Jenny said angrily.

Brock showed his willingness to keep silent but Matt blurted out, "Was she dead?"

"No," Brock murmured. "Somebody beat her up bad; but she wouldn't say who."

Jenny turned furiously on Matt. "I mean it," she said.

"Uncle Matt's getting sent from the table," Peter said slyly.

Jenny wheeled on him. "Another word out of you and you'll get sent to bed."

Matt forced a grin and stood up. Now was his chance to get the pistol from her closet. "My stomach was turning flip-flops anyway," he said.

"Sit down, Matt," Brock said. It was said cordially enough but it sounded almost like an order.

Matt jerked a look of sudden rage at Brock. For an instant their eyes locked. There still wasn't anything in Brock's eyes.

Then Jenny said, "Oh, sit down and finish your dinner and quit acting like a child. You should know better than to talk about such things before the children."

Matt was caught. His face had flushed crimson but it didn't look as though it was caused by his stomach. He sat down reluctantly and riveted his gaze on his plate. He didn't want Brock to see the murderous rage in his eyes.

They were all saved from embarrassment by the telephone ringing.

Brock started to get up to answer it but Jenny stopped him. "Let the maid answer it."

The maid passed through from the kitchen to the telephone stand in the back hall.

"Mr. Peter Brock's residence," they heard her say in a proper voice. Then after a moment she said, "I will see if he is here."

Brock got up and went to the phone. "Yeah," he said. "Yeah . . . Yeah . . . Hold her, I'll be right down."

He came back into the dining room but didn't sit down. "I'm sorry, Jenny," he said, "but I have to leave. Something important has come up."

"Can't you finish your dinner first?" she said.

"No. There isn't much time," he said.

Matt winced. He felt time closing in on him.

"Want me to go along with you?" he asked in a breathless voice.

"You'd better stay here," Brock said, without giving him an opening to ask about the call.

Matt waited until he heard Brock back his car out of the

drive. Jenny was saying something but he didn't know what. Then he said, "Excuse me," and got up.

"You haven't had your dessert," Jenny said.

"Another time," he said.

He went down the hall toward hers and Brock's bedroom. He knew that she heard him and wondered why he went that way to get to the guest room. But it didn't matter what she thought. She wouldn't follow him and if she did, that wouldn't matter either.

He had to get the pistol and get going. Get it cleaned up. Brock was right. There wasn't much time.

21

The name on the stainless-steel doorplane read: MATHEW WALKER.

Jimmy pushed the bell button and heard the distant sound of muted chimes. He felt the pistol beneath his belt pressing against his drum-tight belly. It reassured him. But there was no need drawing it now.

He waited. No one answered. There was no Judas window in the door. No one could see him from the inside. He pushed the button again.

He knew what he was going to do. He didn't feel nervous but he noticed that his hands were trembling. He breathed in short jerky gasps.

Still no one answered.

He turned and walked back down the red flagstone floor of the well-lighted corridor past other identical polished pine doors spaced along the pale blue walls. He felt his knees buckling from nerve tension.

The main thing was to keep his head, he told himself. Just don't get panicky. If Walker was at home and had spotted him through some unseen peephole in the door, then everything was fine. Walker wasn't going to shoot him in the back right there in the house in Peter Cooper Village where he lived.

A woman came from one of the doors and looked him over appraisingly. She seemed intrigued by what she saw.

She appraised him further while they waited for the elevator.

She was a dark-haired woman with a bony, interesting face, dark eyes and a big mouth splashed with red. She wore a white knitted scarf over her head and a black cloth coat with an extremely wide flare. She looked about thirty-five and well-sexed.

They had the elevator to themselves. She smiled at him.

"Are you looking for someone?" she asked.

On sudden impulse he said, "Listen, if I get killed down here by someone it'll be detective Mathew Walker who did it. Remember that."

She shrank into the far corner and gave him a horror-stricken look. When the elevator stopped on the main floor she hurried out, giving him a swift frightened glance over her shoulder before disappearing toward the exit.

Jimmy didn't follow her. The elevators were situated on the corridor which ran parallel to the street. There was a pine-paneled waiting room beside the entrance.

He took a seat beside a reading table where he could see everyone who entered or left the building. Shaded wall lamps gave the room an intimate air. An artificial fire burned brightly in the English-type fireplace. A man and a woman on a nearby settee were talking in low intense voices. There was an atmosphere of quiet, genteel respectability.

Jimmy wondered how a killer like Walker fitted into that picture. But he didn't want to think about it. He didn't want to think about anything. He knew what he was going to do, and there was no need of any further thought.

The well-dressed people who had gone to work that morning were returning, singly and in pairs, with slightly wilted looks and lines of weariness in their faces. They gave Jimmy scarcely a glance.

Jimmy waited. His legs trembled. The handle of the pistol jabbed into his stomach. He cleaned his fingernails with a penknife. Time passed. White faces swam past his vision. Ordinarily he would have felt ill at ease, out of place. But he felt nothing.

Walker came in hurriedly. His hat was slanted to the back of his head and his hands were dug into the pockets of his flapping trench coat. Red spots burned in his high cheekbones and his face had a murderous expression.

He saw Jimmy and did a double take. Shock showed openly in his opaque blue eyes. Then came a flicker of fear. An instant later the opaqueness closed in again. He took a seat on the other side of the fireplace and looked at the artificial fire with a sad expression. He sat with his legs stretched out and both hands in his coat pockets as though time meant nothing to him.

He's got the pistol in his pocket, Jimmy thought. His drawn-up legs began jerking from nerve tension. He stood up and went toward the exit, walking stiff-jointed, his shoulders high and braced and his back flattened like a board.

Walker got leisurely to his feet and followed.

Jimmy stopped in the doorway and looked up and down the street. Snow covered the plots of grass and lighted windows dotted the surrounding buildings. His plan was to make Walker follow him uptown and kill him in the hall of his own apartment house. But first he had to get safely on the bus. And it was four blocks to the nearest bus stop at the corner of First Avenue and 23rd Street.

A couple came from the building and went down the steps to the sidewalk. When they turned in the direction of First Avenue, Jimmy leaped down the steps and passed them and slowed to a walk a few paces ahead.

Walker came down and followed a few paces behind.

The couple crossed the street. Jimmy crossed ahead of them, Walker behind. They came to a side street for pedestrians only. The couple turned off and left Jimmy walking in the empty road. His heart jumped into his mouth. What was to stop Walker from shooting him in the back and turning into the next building? No one would see him; no one would hear the shot.

He wheeled about, facing Walker across the street, and sprinted after the departing couple. The man heard him approaching and turned defensively.

"Pardon me, sir," Jimmy gasped. "I'm looking for a man named Mr. Williamson." The man eyed him suspiciously. "He asked me to come down and see him about some work," he continued hurriedly. "I've been looking all over this place and I can't find the address."

They were a middle-aged couple and the man looked patient. "What address did he give you, boy?" he asked.

"He said the first house on the first walk off Peter Cooper Road, but I haven't seen anything down here but streets."

The man smiled tolerantly. "This is the first walk so it must be one of these two houses facing each other."

Jimmy saw Walker loitering in front of the house across the street. He said, "Thank you, I'll try this one."

The man waited for him to enter the building. The entrance hall was deserted. He made a show of looking at the nameplates over the mailboxes. Through the glass-paneled doors he saw the couple moving off; then Walker sauntering across the street. He unbuttoned his coat and gripped the handle of his pistol.

It was a tight spot. If he shot Walker down there and they didn't find the murder pistol on him, he could offer no defense. If Walker shot him without anyone witnessing it, there'd be no way to tie it to him.

A woman entered from the street, carrying a shopping bag. He went quickly ahead of her to the elevator. The elevator was empty and they boarded it together. She looked at him suspiciously and tightened her grip on her purse. She got off at the fourth floor. There were push buttons for eight floors. Jimmy pushed the button for the top floor. When it reached the top he opened and closed the door and pushed the button for the second floor. His plan was to get off and try to find some other way out of the building if no one had boarded it by then. But people boarded it at every floor and it was crowded by the time it reached the bottom.

Walker was standing there as though waiting for the elevator when the doors opened. Their eyes met briefly. Jimmy's brown eyes widened in a look of pure hatred; Walker's blue eyes looked dispassionate.

People started toward the exit. Jimmy followed, keeping close.

At the bottom of the steps a big man in a loud tweed ulster stopped and tipped a wide-brimmed hat to a younger woman in a fur coat.

"I hope it'll be my pleasure to see more of you, ma'am," he said. "I'd like to have the pleasure of taking you to dinner."

The woman smiled coyly. "You have my phone number, Mr. Davis. Phone me tomorrow afternoon."

"That I'll do," the big man said.

"Tomorrow afternoon, Mr. Davis."

"Just call me Jim, ma'am. Jim Davis. That's the name. I'm not used to all this formality."

"All right, Jim," the woman said in honeyed tones.

"Until then," the big man said gallantly and turned in the direction of Peter Cooper Road, the woman in the opposite direction.

Jimmy closed in beside the man. "Pardon me, sir," he said, "but can you tell me how to get to the bus stop?"

The big man stopped and looked at him. "You're new here in New York, aren't you, boy?"

"Yes sir," Jimmy replied. "Just got here last week. Been down here to see a man about some work, but I don't know how to get out of this place."

"How you like it up here?" the big man asked.

Jimmy drew his shoulders together and shivered theatrically. "Sure is cold." He found the Uncle Toming distasteful, but it was necessary.

The big man laughed. "I'm from Texas—what part of the South are you from?"

"Georgia," Jimmy lied. "Columbus, Georgia."

"This ain't like Georgia, is it?"

"No sir, wish I was back."

The big man chuckled. "Come on, I'll show you where you catch your bus."

They walked side by side toward First Avenue.

"What I hate about this city is it's full of foreigners," the big man said. "In my town there ain't nobody but Americans and colored folks and a few Mexicans—Americans all," he added grandiloquently. "Here it's just like one of those European capitals."

Small stores fronted on First Avenue and it was brightly lit. When they'd walked a block, Jimmy said, "Boss, I think we're being followed."

The big man stopped abruptly and turned about. He spotted Walker immediately. "Yeah, that fellow in the trench coat looking in that delicatessen window. I saw him when I left the house."

"Yes sir, I saw him there too, standing in the hall."

The big man looked at Jimmy thoughtfully. "Is he following you or me?"

"He ain't got no reason to be following me, boss," Jimmy said. "I ain't done nothing to nobody."

The big man chuckled. "Maybe he's one of those sissies," he conjectured, staring at Walker a moment longer. But Walker seemed absorbed in a roast turkey. "Don't worry about him," he added. "I'm a sheriff in my hometown; I know how to take care of his kind."

"I sure am glad of that," Jimmy said.

The big man walked him to the bus stop and patted him on the shoulder. "Here you are, boy. Do you know how to get home from here?"

"Yes sir, boss. Thank you, sir."

The big man crossed the street to a taxi stand and got into a taxi. Several other people were waiting for the 23rd Street bus. Walker was nowhere in sight.

But as the bus appeared, Walker came suddenly from a tobacco store across the street. Jimmy was the third one to board; Walker waited until last. It was near the start of its run and the bus was practically empty. Jimmy chose an empty seat near the middle. Walker sat in the seat across from him. Neither looked at the other. The bus filled up.

Jimmy transferred to the Broadway bus at Madison Square. Others transferred, Walker among them.

They rode standing to Columbus Circle, then found seats. Neither showed the slightest interest in the other.

Jimmy alighted at 145th Street; Walker followed.

On one corner was a big chain drugstore; on the other a cafeteria of the Bickford chain. There were subway kiosks on all the corners. The intersection was well lit and crowded with people of all races.

Jimmy walked leisurely up Broadway, past the lighted front of the Woolworth store, the lobby of the RKO movie house. He was on his home ground. He was tense but he wasn't scared. He knew that Walker intended to kill him before he could get up to his room. But he wasn't worried. He was going to kill him first.

He kept close to other people, made a point of keeping

someone between himself and Walker, in the line of fire, all the time.

Pedestrian traffic thinned in the block between 148th and 149th Streets. Jimmy put himself in front of a big colored couple so that they practically walked on his heels. As he neared 149th Street, his stomach began to knot. It was like a film showing the countdown for an atom bomb. The hand was ticking off the seconds toward the zero hour. He had to get across 149th Street; then walk thirty paces on 149th Street to the entrance of the apartment house—he had counted them. Once he got inside the hallway he had to station himself so he would be out of line of fire from the street but facing the door, so he would see Walker first.

When he came to the curb he stepped out from in front of the colored couple and turned to look down the street to get Walker's exact position. He had gripped his pistol and had drawn it halfway from his belt.

Walker had disappeared. He was thunderstruck. He stood there foolishly for an instant, not knowing which way to turn. The street was momentarily empty in all directions. He was a perfect target. A sudden surge of panic shocked him into action.

Bell's Bar & Grill fronted on Broadway at the corner. Behind the curtained windows colored people crowded about the circular bar. The muted blare of the jukebox floated into the street. Parked cars lined the curb in front.

He ducked instinctively and broke toward the entrance to the bar. The bullet aimed for his heart hit him high in the left shoulder, and spun him about. He went off balance, falling in a grotesque stumble. The second bullet hit him in the back, beneath the right shoulder blade, went between two ribs and penetrated his right lung. He couldn't hear the shots and didn't know what direction they were coming from. He felt the tearing of the bullet's trajectory inside him. He tried to call for help but didn't have the breath. Nothing came from his mouth but blood. With one last desperate effort he jerked his pistol free and fired it at the pavement.

The shot hurried Walker. He was standing in the street between two parked cars. He had opened the hood of one and was bent over as though looking at the motor. His head and shoulders were shielded from view from all sides. He held the pistol with the silencer out of sight beneath the hood. He shot once more quickly, aiming at the head of the grotesquely stumbling figure, but missed.

Jimmy was unconscious when his body crashed heavily into the plate glass door of Bell's Bar.

The doors of the bar burst open and excited colored people erupted. The man in front did a hop-skip-and-jump to keep from stepping on the fallen body.

"My God!" a woman screamed, catching sight of Jimmy.

People came running from all directions, attracted by the sound of his one futile shot. From inside the bar a big bass voice blared from the jukebox.

Walker put the pistol into his trench coat pocket and sauntered calmly across the northbound traffic lane, skirted the dividing parkway, and crossed the traffic lane on the other side of Broadway. He didn't look back.

He was accustomed to scenes of violence. He knew that he wouldn't be noticed. There was always a period of from one to five minutes after a killing when the victim claimed everyone's whole attention. No one ever looked about for the killer until they had recovered from the shock.

He turned south on Broadway and continued walking casually toward the subway kiosk. He could have left the pistol in the motor of the car. That would have substantiated his story that some uptown racketeer did all three killings. But he wasn't finished with it yet. He had one more to go.

It had been a mistake to let her keep the pistol, he was thinking. He should have reckoned on a woman's curiosity. But there was no help for it now. She was the last witness who could appear against him. She had to be silenced and then it would be over. And then he would get rid of the pistol forever.

He knew it was going to look strange as hell for her to be killed with the same pistol that killed three Schmidt and Schindler Negro porters. The police might conceivably suspect him; they would know he had been often seen with her. Brock would know for sure. But that couldn't be helped. They couldn't convict him without the pistol because there wouldn't be any witnesses left. They could think whatever they goddamned well pleased.

He was going down the steps of the subway kiosk when the first of the patrol cars screamed around the corner into Broadway from 145th Street.

22

Brock stared thoughtfully at Linda across his desk. He fiddled with a 98¢ plastic stylo. In front of him was a memorandum pad on which he had written nothing.

"What are you holding out?" he asked.

Linda had told him, as near as she could remember, word for word, everything that Jimmy had said to her except that he had gotten hold of a pistol.

"Why do you think I'm holding something out?" she answered sullenly. "Why do you policemen always act as if everybody's guilty? You're jumping on me as if I'd done something."

"Sure," Brock said. "I'm jumping on you just because you're a defenseless little girl who wants to see justice done and got me up from my dinner table."

Linda puffed up with indignation but she couldn't meet his eyes.

Behind Brock's desk was a window reinforced by wire mesh. Through it Linda could see the picture windows of an apartment house toward the river. Lights showed in the windows. Behind the lights people could be seen, moving about, reading, watching television. White people. They looked safe and secure and protected.

"What would you say if one of those women in that big apartment house over there told you that a detective was trying to kill her husband?" she challenged.

"I'd laugh like hell," he said.

"You'd laugh like hell because you'd know it couldn't happen to a white man of his class. But Jimmy was shot. That did happen. Two other porters in the store were murdered. That happened too. And what are the police doing about it?"

"Sure," Brock said. "We're just sitting here and letting your boyfriend get murdered."

"You're doing more than that!" she flared angrily. "You're accusing me of holding something out. What do you think I'm holding out? Do you think Jimmy killed those other two men and shot himself? Maybe he swallowed the gun."

"Sure," Brock said placidly. "Somebody has swallowed the gun and that's a fact."

"You don't believe any of it?" she asked. "You don't even believe two men were murdered?"

"Two men were murdered is a fact," Brock said. "But Johnson told us practically the same thing you're telling us now. What's happened to make you get scared all of a sudden when you've had all this time to get scared in and you've been as calm as a statue."

"It was what he said happened this morning," she said. She shuddered involuntarily. "If he was telling the truth it was just by the hand of God he missed being murdered."

"Sure," Brock said. "If he was telling the truth."

"Why don't you try to find out whether he was telling the truth?"

"Suppose I believe his story," Brock said. "It's the same thing he said happened the time of the murders. The murderer laying in wait, the shot without warning, the flight down the stairs—the only thing different is the location. One thing is for sure, either your boyfriend has a single-track mind or else the murderer has."

"All right, go ahead and laugh," she said bitterly. "It's going to be even funnier if he gets killed."

"Sure," Brock said. "But what I'm trying to find out is what you're holding out that makes you so scared all of a sudden."

"I just started to believing him, is all."

Brock stared at her. "Sure," he said. "It took you quite some time to get around to believing him, didn't it?"

Her brown cheeks took on a copper-colored blush.

"It was just hard to believe at first," she said. "But I know that detective Walker was in the building this morning."

"We know that too," he admitted. "Walker claims he's following your friend Johnson to find the murderer. He's got his ready-made story just like Johnson has got his ready-made story. We're not a court of law. We can't decide on who's telling the truth and who isn't. We're just police officers. So what can we do?"

"You can stop him," she said.

"How?"

"You can hold him on suspicion or something, can't you? The police uptown are always picking up colored people on suspicion."

"Sure," Brock said. "We can hold him until his lawyers get there. That would be about an hour."

"It's horrible," she said with a sob in her voice. "Everybody's just waiting to see what he'll do next. It's just like watching a cat play with a mouse."

"If we had some charge to hold Johnson on, that would make it easier," he said. "That might give us the time we need."

"Well, you can hold him in protective custody, or something like that, can't you? You can always find a charge to hold a colored man."

"Not unless he asked for it," Brock said. "If we just picked him up, it would be the same as with Walker. We could hold him until the Schmidt and Schindler attorneys got there with a writ."

"That wouldn't help any," she admitted.

"I'm afraid not," he said. "But if I knew what you're holding out, maybe that would help."

"Don't start that again!" she exclaimed. "I'm not holding anything out."

"You women," he said bitterly. "What has Walker got that makes you women want to shield him?"

"I'm not shielding him," she denied.

"Not only you," he said; then he paused, struck by a sudden idea. "There's one thing we might try." He stood up. "I'm going to take you to see a woman."

Two other detectives at their desks looked up curiously as they passed.

He put her in his private car and drove her over to Peter Cooper Village. He parked in front of number 5, Peter Cooper Road, and they went up the short entrance hall past the waiting room with its English type fireplace where an hour before Jimmy had waited for Walker to appear. They rode up to the third floor in the big silent elevator.

The nameplate on the door said EVA MODJESKA.

Brock pushed the bell button. The muted sound of chimes came from within the apartment. He waited. No one answered. He pushed the button again. Still no one answered.

He said in his ordinary voice, "Miss Modjeska, this is detective Brock from the Homicide Bureau. I talked to you early this morning. I must talk to you again."

From the other side of the door a thick, lisping voice with a slight foreign accent said, "Why won't you let me alone? Why do you persecute me?"

"Either you open the door or I'll get the building superintendent to open it," he said.

The lock clicked and the door opened into a pitch-dark alcove.

"Pass in," the lisping accented voice said from the dark.

Linda hesitated.

"Don't be afraid," Brock said, steering her around the corner into the large sitting room.

The door closed and a vague shape followed them.

"Be seated, please."

Heavy drapes were drawn across the big front window and one dim night lamp burned on an occasional table in the far corner.

"Why don't we sit down?" Brock said. The two women ignored him. They all remained standing.

Eva noticed Linda staring at her and turned her face away. She wore a heavy red woolen robe buttoned up to the neck. Her hair hung loosely over her shoulders in a tangled mass. Both sides of her face were so swollen that her eyes had almost disappeared and her mouth formed a lipless indentation. Her skin ranged in colors from deep purple to bright orange.

"I have told you I do not know who attacked me," she lisped in a resigned, beaten manner. "He was a burglar. I came home unexpected and caught him in this room. He attacked me so suddenly I did not see his face."

"Sure," Brock said. He brought a chair and faced it toward the davenport. "Sit down."

She sat down as though accustomed to obeying orders.

"You sit down too," he told Linda.

Linda slowly sat on the edge of the davenport and stared down at her hands, horror overcoming her curiosity.

"Please do not humiliate me," Eva begged.

"Miss Modjeska, this is Miss Collins," Brock said. "Miss Collin's boyfriend works for Schmidt and Schindler's restaurants."

A flicker of fear crossed Eva's face. Brock gave no sign he'd noticed it.

"Early one morning last week her boyfriend was shot," he continued. "The other two night porters who worked with him were murdered. You must have read about it in the newspapers."

A violent shudder passed over Eva's body. "I know nothing of that," she lisped in a frightened voice.

"Sure," Brock said. "That's why I brought Miss Collins along, so she could tell you something about it."

"Does she have to?" Eva pleaded.

"I'm afraid so," Brock said, then turned to Linda. "Go ahead and tell her what you told me. And don't leave anything out."

As Linda told her story, Eva wilted. From time to time she shuddered convulsively. Brock sat on the arm of the davenport and stared at her.

"So you see," he said when Linda had concluded, "this man is very dangerous."

"Yes, yes, I know," Eva lisped. "But he is sick."

"Sure," Brock said. "That's why you didn't tell me he beat you up."

"You must stop him," Eva said, leaning forward tensely. "I did not know he was planning to kill the other man too."

"That's right," Brock said. "Now go ahead and tell me that you knew all along he killed the other two men."

Eva hid her face in her hands. "I didn't know until last night," she lisped in a muffled voice.

"Sure," Brock said in a tight voice. "You knew last night but you didn't tell me when I talked to you early this morning."

"I wanted to tell you," Eva lisped sobbingly. "It was I who telephoned the police and told them there was a murdered woman at this address. I planned to tell you then but I was afraid."

"You were afraid all right," Brock said tightly. "You were afraid he was going to come back and kill you. That's why you telephoned the police. Now go ahead and spill it all," he said roughly. "How did you find out he was the murderer?"

"I saw the pistol," Eva confessed in a terrified voice. "I had read about the murders in the newspapers. It was said they were committed with a pistol that had a silencer attached. When I saw the pistol had a silencer attached to it I knew that he was the murderer."

"Stop shuddering," Brock said savagely. "Get down to the facts. Where did you see the pistol?"

"He gave it to me to keep for him," she lisped. "It was the same day the murders were commmitted. I did not have any suspicions. It was wrapped in a package. He told me not to open it. He said that it contained evidence which would convict a murderer. He said that he was afraid to keep it in his own apartment because it might be searched. He said it would be safe in my apartment because I work for UN and would not be connected to a local murder case. Last night he came for it again. He was acting so strangely that I became suspicious and opened it." She shuddered again uncontrollably. "When I saw the pistol I realized at that moment that he was the murderer."

"God in heaven!" Linda exclaimed. "It was true after all. And I never did believe it entirely." She looked stunned.

"Goddammit," Brock said. "What kind of women are you two?" Then he turned on Eva and said bitterly, "He almost killed you. He left you here for dead. You were afraid he was going to come back and finish you off. And you didn't even feel it was necessary to tell the police who the murderer was. You were just going to sit here and let him murder someone else."

"Please don't say that," she sobbed. "I wanted to tell, but I was afraid. He said he would accuse me of being a spy if I told. He said they would not find the pistol and it would be my word against his. He said all that mattered was what people wanted to believe. There are people in my country who would want to believe that I am a spy."

Linda jumped to her feet and cried, "You've got to stop him. You've got to send someone up to Jimmy's room.

Please hurry," she added as Brock made no move. "He might be uptown at this very minute laying somewhere for Jimmy."

"Sit down," Brock said roughly. "He's not uptown. I know where he is." Then to Eva, "Where's your telephone."

She gestured toward the bedroom. "Beside the bed."

The two women sat tensely across from one another, staring at his back as he walked heavily from the room. They listened in silence while he dialed, avoiding each other's eyes.

They heard him say, "Jenny? . . . Yeah? . . . No, everything's fine; let me talk to Matt. . . . Yeah? When? . . . He didn't say where he was going? . . . No, no. Did he go anywhere else in the house before he left? . . . Yeah . . . Yeah . . . No, nothing's wrong. . . . No, it's of no importance . . . No, I was just curious . . . No, don't wait up for me, I'll probably be late. . . . Yeah. Bye dear."

Linda was in the room before he'd finished talking. "You don't know where he is," she accused in a frightened voice.

"Now don't you start getting the wind up," Brock said. "He can't get far. I'll have him picked up in an hour, and I'll have someone go uptown and hold hands with your boy friend."

"For God's sake hurry!" she begged. "Jimmy's got a pistol too. He bought one today. If he finds Walker in the building he's going to try to kill him."

For an imperceptible instant, Brock stood frozen. The next instant he was dialing rapidly. "So that's it," he said softly as he waited for the connection. "So that's what scared you out of your pants. Women! And you expect the police—Hello," he said into the mouthpiece. "Sergeant Brock. Give me Lieutenant Baker. . . . Lieutenant—Brock. . . . Yeah, it broke. Better put a reader out for Walker. . . . No, for the automat murders . . . oh . . . yeah? When? . . . Bad? . . . Sure, but we didn't have it sooner. . . ."

"His gaze went involuntarily toward Linda. She clutched him by the arm. "He's been hurt!" she cried hysterically "He's been shot! He's been killed!"

"Just a minute," Brock said into the mouthpiece

He turned quickly and slapped Linda with his free hand. "Oh!" she said, and calmed down.

"Get yourself together," he said. "Your boy friend is still alive." Then he spoke into the mouthpiece again, "No, it was Johnson's girl friend; she thought something had happened to Johnson. . . . Yeah, I told her he was alive. . . . No, I'm at the apartment of Eva Modjeska in Peter Cooper —Yeah, that one. . . . Yeah. . . . Okay. . . . Send someone over to pick them up. . . . Yeah, both of them. . . . Hold them on anything; hold them as accomplices. . . . Better hurry it up. . . ."

23

There was an underground corridor connecting the basements of all the buildings in Peter Cooper Village.

Walker entered the boiler room three blocks distant from the building where his and Eva's apartments were located and entered the building by the service stairway. He stopped at Eva's back door and put his ear to the panel. He didn't hear a sound from within.

He used Eva's door key and unlocked the door silently. He pulled on the knob hard with his left hand and turned it without a sound. Holding it turned, he drew the pistol with the silencer and held it cocked in his right hand. Then he pushed the door in quickly, holding the pistol aimed straight ahead, and stepped inside. He closed the door as quickly and as silently as he had opened it.

He stood in the pitch-dark room and held his breath to listen. He didn't hear a sound.

He was in the small back laundry. He moved forward silently, his empty left hand extended in front of him. He put his ear to the kitchen door and listened again.

He didn't believe she had gone out. He doubted too if she was sleeping. It would be more like her to sit in the dark and brood, he thought.

He opened the door without a sound and groped his way silently across the kitchen. Another door led to the side of the sitting room that served as a dining room. He looked for a sign of light underneath the door but there wasn't a light in the house. That meant she had the window curtains drawn tight or there would be a dim light from the street lamps, he thought.

Again he stood with his ear to the door. He thought he heard the sound of breathing. He held his breath and didn't hear it anymore.

I hate to do this, he thought. It would be easier if I could shoot her in the dark.

He stood unmoving in the dark for several minutes, waiting for his sixth sense to warn him of any danger. But nothing came to arouse his suspicions.

He opened the door silently and groped with his left hand for the light switch. The big bright floor lamp at the end of the davenport came on before his hand touched the switch.

Brock sat in the middle of the davenport with his .38-calibre service revolver aimed at his heart.

"Drop the pistol, Matt," he said flatly.

Walker froze as though his flesh were solid stone. Slowly his fingers relaxed their grip on the pistol handle and it fell to the carpet with a thud. He smiled at Brock like a sad little boy.

"You clever bastard," he said softly.

"Sure," Brock said. "Just be careful or I'll drop you in your tracks."

"I'm wearing my service revolver too," Walker said, smiling. "Do you want that too?"

"No," Brock said, shaking his head. "You wouldn't shoot me with your service revolver."

"Don't be too sure," Walker said.

"I'tl take a chance," Brock said, and put his revolver back into its holster. "Sit down."

Walker drew up a straight-backed dining room chair and sat straddled it, facing Brock. He looked at Brock with a sad steady smile.

"Eva squealed," he said.

"Sure," Brock said. "What did you think she would do, go on keeping silent forever?"

"I knew she would squeal," Walker said. "But I didn't think she would do it so soon. I thought I'd have a chance to clean the slate before."

"Sure," Brock said. "And then silence her forever."

"That would have been the only thing to do," Walker

said. "Then no one would have ever known for sure."

"No," Brock said. "I knew before she squealed."

Walker stared at him contemplatively. "It was that story of mine," he conjectured. "I knew you didn't believe that. But without Eva you couldn't have known for sure."

"No," Brock said. "It wasn't that story. I didn't swallow your first story either—the one you handed the D.A. But when you told me that story at Lindy's I already knew."

Walker showed curiosity. "You clever bastard; how did you find out for sure?"

"I had found the prostitute—the one you slept with that night."

"You had? You knew where she was all the time?" Walker gave him a hurt, accusing look. "And you held out on me?"

"Sure. I wanted to keep her alive."

"What did she know?"

"She knew you had the gun. You threatened to shoot her with it too. Where did you get the gun?" Brock asked.

"I took it from the homicide museum," Walker said. "It's the rod Baby Face killed Jew Mike with."

"So that's where it came from."

"I thought you might have guessed that too," Walker said. After a moment he added, "I must have pitched a wingding that night. I wonder who else I threatened."

"We'll know that better later on," Brock said.

"Yeah, it'll all come out at the trial," Walker said in a soft sad voice. "Where did you find her?"

"In Bellevue hospital. You ruined her face. You broke it in with the same pistol. What happened to you that night?"

"I don't know. Just drinking too much I suppose."

"No," Brock said. "It was more than that."

"Maybe too many women," Walker said.

"No, not that either," Brock said. "Are you sick?" he asked.

Walker stared at him blankly for a moment. "You mean insane?"

"No, I mean sick physically," Brock said. "Syphilis or cancer or something like that."

Walker broke out in a sudden boyish laugh. "Not that I know of, unless I have syphilis of the brain."

"That could be," Brock said.

"What do you think they'll do with me?" Walker asked.

"It was a break for you that you beat up those two women," Brock said "That will probably get you into the nut house."

"Yeah, I guess everybody will think I'm nuts," Walker said. "Does Jenny know?"

"Not yet."

Walker gave a heartfelt sigh. "Why didn't you stop me before now, Brock?"

"I wanted to give you a chance to get rid of the gun," Brock confessed.

"After I'd killed the other one?" Walker asked.

"No, I figured you'd give up on that when you became suspicious of me," Brock said. "I kept trying to tell you that I knew without just coming out and saying it. I thought you'd know I wanted you to get rid of the gun; I thought you'd have sense enough to see that."

"I thought you were against me," Walker said. "I didn't think you'd be for me."

"I wasn't for you," Brock said. "I was for Jenny."

"You were going to let me get away with it."

"Sure," Brock said. "You've never had a wife and two children. You don't know how hard it'll be on them to have a murderer for a brother and an uncle."

"Do they have to know?" Walker asked.

"It's out of my hands now," Brock said. After a moment he asked, "Why did you kill them, Matt?"

"Brock, you won't believe it," Walker said. "Nobody will believe it. But I shot the first one by pure accident. I was waving the pistol at him and it just went off. I didn't know then it had a hair trigger on it. I was more surprised than he was. But I knew the moment it happened that no one would ever believe it. So I had to finish him."

"Sure, but what started it in the first place?" Brock asked.

"I thought they had stolen my car," Walker admitted. "I was drunk and I'd forgotten where I'd parked it. And when I saw them I just thought all of a sudden they'd been up with stealing it."

"Because they were Negroes?"

"You know how you are when you're that drunk."

"Sure," Brock said. "But what about the other one?"

"Well hell, after I'd finished the first one, I couldn't stop there," Walker said. "The other one had seen me and I had to silence him too. I wouldn't have bothered the third one if he hadn't come up the stairs and seen me too." He believed what he was saying.

"I'm sorry for you," Brock said.

"I'm sorry for you too," Walker said.

"Sure," Brock said. "It's going to be tough for the family, but we'll get over that."

"It isn't that," Walker said. "It's because you didn't take my service revolver when you had the chance. I'm faster on the draw than you are."

For a long silent moment, neither of them moved. They stared into one another's eyes as though hypnotized.

Walker sat with his arms folded across the back of the chair. Brock sat with his right hand on the davenport at his side and his left hand resting loosely on his thigh.

Finally Brock said, "Sure. But you wouldn't have any way out after that. They'd exterminate you like a mad dog."

"I know," Walker said. "But it's just that I'm started now and I can't stop."

It seemed to Brock as if it took him ten thousand years to get his hand up to his shoulder holster and get his pistol out. He saw the pistol in Walker's hand before his cleared the holster and heard the shot. He was startled to hear the second shot, the one made by his own pistol. He didn't believe it when he saw the sudden small blue hole appear directly between Walker's staring blue eyes where his bullet had entered Walker's brain. He sat unmoving in a half daze and watched Walker fall forward to the back of the chair, turning the chair over beneath him as he toppled to the floor.

He got slowly to his feet and looked behind him. He saw where the bullet from Walker's revolver had gone into the back of the davenport.

"He could have shot me five times straight running," he said softly. "Poor devil. It was his only way out."

He walked heavily across the floor and into the bedroom and began dialing the telephone.

24

"For God's sake, what were you trying to do? Make me drop dead?" Linda greeted him before she shrugged out of her fur coat and sat in the chair for visitors.

Jimmy looked up from his white hospital bed and tried sheepishly to smile.

Nine days had passed since he'd been shot and she was his first visitor. While he had hovered on the brink of death, she had been knocking on the gates of the nut house. It was very unrewarding. They both showed it.

Finally he got out through stiff lips, "I just wanted to kill the mother-raper and keep on living myself."

Linda's eyes stretched. It was meant to show disapproval.

"Wasn't nobody gonna believe me anyway," he muttered. "Til I was dead."

Linda put her hot perfumed hand over his dry mouth; it had an aphrodisiacal effect on both.

"The DA believed you—" she began.

"Bull shit!" he muttered.

"Sergeant Brock believed—"

"Linda baby, please—"

"Well shit then, I believed you."

"No you didn't!"

Her throat caught and she gulped guiltily. "Well for Chrissakes, what do you want a girl to do? Why didn't you let me help you? I could have lured him into the apartment and you wouldn't have had to take all those rape-fiend risks."

Agitation lifted him onto his elbows. Pain flickered through his lung but he ignored it. "Baby, I couldn't trust you." It sounded like a moan.

Suddenly her face felt like it had caught fire. "Well," she admitted slowly. "It don't take Malcom X to see that."

"Anyway," he said defensively. "I had it all planned out."

She passed that reply and pushed him back into his pillow. "Shut up now, you don't have to explain to me."

"But I want to explain to you. You got to know. I wanted

to kill him while he had the gun in his possession. Without giving him a chance. Like he did Luke and Fats."

She tried to show her agreement. And she understood. But her smile stopped at her teeth. There was pity behind her eyes, even shock . . . My God! she thought. He doesn't realize how obvious he'd been to Walker. He's just a baby, she thought, and very lucky to be alive. But it doesn't matter now, the only thing that matters now is to keep the terror out my eyes.

It was only then he took her look for disapproval. "What's a man gonna do?" he questioned hotly. "I couldn't keep running all my mother-raping life."

"Shush!" She leaned over and sealed his mouth with her lips. They tasted hot, wet and breathless. "You just scared the living shit out of me," she confessed, quickly adding, "But I love you for it."

His eyes, which were all that could show it, lit with hope. "Then we're still engaged?"

She looked at him indignantly. "You fool, you think I'm going to lose you now? All I been through!"